Enjoy the Journey…

Also by Sherry A. Burton

The Orphan Train Saga
Discovery (book one)
Shameless (book two)
Treachery (book three)
Guardian (book four)
Loyal (book five)

Orphan Train Extras
Ezra's Story

Jerry McNeal Series
Always Faithful
Ghostly Guidance
Rambling Spirit
Chosen Path
Port Hope
Cold Case
Wicked Winds
Spirit of Deadwood

Romance Books*
Tears of Betrayal
Love in the Bluegrass
Somewhere In My Dreams
The King of My Heart

Seems Like Yesterday
"Whispers of the Past," a short story.

Psychological Thriller
Surviving the Storm

*A note from the author: With the exception of *Seems Like Yesterday* (which has been revised to be a clean read), my romance books have SEX. A couple of them have sex more than a few times. We are not talking close the door and turn off the lights sex. We are talking glow-in-the-dark condoms (*King of My Heart*). *Surviving the Storm* is a lot darker than my other titles and may not be for all readers. While I no longer write books where the lovemaking scenes are so detailed, I am not removing them from these early books, as the readers seem to enjoy them.

Discovery

Book 1 in The Orphan Train Saga

Written by Sherry A. Burton

For more information on the author and her works, please
see www.SherryABurton.com

Follow Sherry on social media:

https://www.facebook.com/SherryABurton
author/
https://www.amazon.com/Sherry-A.-Burton/e/B005PM6QFG?ref=dbs_m_mng_rwt_auth
https://www.bookbub.com/profile/sherry-a-burton

To the children and families whose lives were greatly altered by the Placing Out Program and similar programs that followed. While the children in my series are fictional, it is my hope that by telling their stories, my Orphan Train Saga can help to keep your memories alive and preserve a somewhat forgotten piece of history. Thank you to those that told your stories, for it is through your courage that we have learned of both your hardships and victories.

Table of Contents

Chapter One

Cindy sat staring out at the cold steel structure, her hands gripping the steering wheel as if somehow anchoring herself in place. She'd given plenty of thought to just putting the car in gear and driving off, leaving the contents for others to rummage through. The only thing that held her in place was the fact that she'd spent years paying on the storage unit that housed all that remained of her grandmother's belongings. Plus, if she could get everything out by the end of the week, she wouldn't have to pay next month's rent.

While a part of her wished to pawn the chore off on someone else, deep down, she knew she should be the one who rummaged through the contents. She should be who decided what to sell, what to toss, and what to keep. That thought brought a chuckle. Keep what? The items in the unit that had no meaning to her? Tons of who-knew-what crammed into boxes and left there until some poor soul had the misfortune of holding the golden ticket? Or, in her case, the gold key. Not even real gold, she thought, glaring at the single key on the seat beside her.

"Your grandmother's belongings are yours now," her mother had said when she practically shoved the key into the palm of her hand two years earlier. "I've paid on that unit long enough. Keep the contents or sell it all; the choice is yours."

Cindy could still remember the look of relief on her mother's face, as if she was finally rid of her mother-in-law. Little wonder, since Grandma Mildred was a cold-hearted woman who rarely said a kind word to her mother, or Cindy either, for that matter. Cold as the unheated storage unit that had held all that was left of her grandmother's precious belongings for the past seven years. A storage unit that Cindy herself had paid for two of those seven. One thousand, one hundred and fifty-two dollars to be exact. Too much money spent just to have the contents sold at auction. For what? Fifty dollars? Her grandmother was a quilter, an exceptionally good one at that, hand-piecing each and every quilt. If there were any quilts in the unit, she should be able to recoup some, if not all, of the money she'd spent.

She watched as a mouse scurried through the parking lot before squeezing its body under the door of a nearby unit. *Providing rodents had not gotten to the quilts first.*

Snatching up the key, she used it to unlock the stainless-steel padlock. Lifting the door, she cringed as metal screeched against the rails, screaming to life after years of peaceful rest. Still, the noise pleased her, knowing it had probably evoked the same effect on the little grey mouse. She was surprised at how angry the thought of a field mouse chewing through the boxes to use the colorful quilts as bedding made her. It wasn't as if the stuff had any meaning to her besides monetary. Cindy scanned the storage unit for telltale signs of furry inhabitants and smiled when she didn't see any obvious sign of infestation. A pleasant surprise, given it had been at least two years since the door had been opened; much longer, knowing her mother. Probably no one had opened the door since the contents were placed inside.

Boxes were stacked neatly along the right side of the wall. Furniture painstakingly wrapped in thick blankets lined the other. A mauve wingback chair sat in the middle of the floor; the discarded blanket that had once covered it lay neatly folded just a few feet away.

So someone had been here after all; strange, since nothing else seemed amiss. Cindy stood looking at the chair, recalling its exact placement in her grandmother's house. It, along with a matching chair, an off-white couch, several decorative end tables, and an antique mahogany piano were housed in the front living room, a room Cindy had never actually seen used. A generously sized rose-colored glass lamp sat on a three-legged table in front of the large picture window. The base of the lamp was as round as a basketball and etched with roses of a lighter shade. The base narrowed then came out again with a smaller matching glass shade. The heavy dark pink curtains remained open, sheers of a lighter shade of pink used to create a thin barrier against prying eyes. The lamp was only turned on at night, its low-watt bulb offering a beacon of welcome to passersby, a hollow invitation into a room where no one was ever allowed to enter.

Cindy closed her eyes, cleared her mind, and wondered where to start. Heaving a sigh, she hefted a box. Smiling, she lowered herself onto the once forbidden chair and began ripping the tape from the cardboard. The victory with the tape was short-lived as she lifted the lid off the box, which yielded that very lamp.

"Creepy coincidence," she muttered, setting the box aside and rubbing at the goosebumps that appeared on her bare arms.

The next box was labeled "fragile." Cindy plucked it from its resting place and worked at the tape until the end released enough to allow her a grip. She ripped the length of tape from the box and tossed it aside. She pulled out something wrapped in newspaper, uncoiled the wad, and smiled when she saw the pale blue willow print on the simple china cup. A cup, one of a set, that she'd seen used nearly every time she'd visited her grandmother's home. Real china, delicate thin-lipped cups with a fan-type weave. The handles of the cup were the kind that encouraged a person to take care when sipping so not to make a mess. Not the bulky mugs that sat in Cindy's cupboards at home. She set the cup aside and opened another fold of paper to unveil a thin matching saucer. Many times she remembered sitting at the kitchen table, watching as her grandmother poured some of the contents from her coffee cup into the saucer to cool before drinking straight from the lipped plate. At the time, she found the action to be peculiar, but now the adult in her realized it was an act of a simpler time. The action of someone with manners, much more ladylike than slurping hot liquid from a mug, something she herself was guilty of doing. She re-wrapped both items, carefully placing each piece back into the box, and carried the container to her car, deciding she could use a touch of class in her life.

Returning to the unit, she lifted another box and took it to the chair to open. Lifting the edge, she had a moment's panic when she saw the faces staring back at her. Dolls! Not just any dolls; old creepy dolls. The ones that used to sit on the bed in the unused guest room, as if taunting Cindy each time she grew brave enough to venture down to the far end of the hallway. Smiling faces that seemed to say, *We are welcomed to sleep here, but you are not invited.* Cindy took a breath to calm herself. It was true, in all her childhood, she had never once slept over at her grandmother's house.

"What made you so special?" she asked, pulling out one of the dolls. Several moments passed before Cindy realized she was still holding the doll, which fortunately hadn't answered. She turned the doll in her hands, staring at it, trying to see what had drawn her grandmother to it. Maybe she just liked the way it looked on the bed, as that was where Cindy remembered seeing it each time she neared the room. It was old; rubber instead of plastic, with painted hair and features. It looked as if the head and body were a single piece with legs and arms that did not bend. The doll was in pristine shape and looked as if it had never been played with. Something obviously to be appreciated from a distance. *Then why own it?* She studied the doll a moment longer; something about her clothing bothered her. Upon further inspection, she realized the doll's gown had been handmade. The faded fabric was soft and exceptionally well made. She sat the doll on the chair and pulled out one after another, carefully inspecting each doll for a clue as to its value. Not monetarily; they were old and in pristine condition, so Cindy had little doubt collectors would clamor to bid on them when she placed them on eBay. No, she wondered at the sentiment. *Why would a woman who showed no emotion beyond polite conversation to her only granddaughter be drawn to dolls?*

As Cindy pulled the last doll out of the box, she realized she was no closer to finding the answers she sought. She played with the ringlet of dark hair, pulling it straight, then watching it spring back into place, repeating this several times. She was returning the doll to the box when it hit her: every doll had curly black hair. She sifted through the pile to be sure, a surge of satisfaction growing within. She had no clue as to what it meant, but given that her grandmother had straight brown hair before eventually succumbing to grey, there had to be a reason Grandma Mildred was drawn to dolls with curly black hair. Cindy ran a hand through her light brown hair. *Would she have liked me more if my hair was black? Or curly?* She snorted, knowing it wasn't likely.

Cindy sighed. Why was she still looking for love from a woman that obviously had none to give? She could not even remember her grandmother showing affection to her husband, Cindy's grandfather. Grandpa Howard was the best. Taking her places and telling silly jokes to make her smile. He was the complete opposite of the woman he married. Well, they must have shared something, since the marriage had produced a son.

Paul, her dad, was outgoing and likable. She closed her eyes briefly.

At least he used to be.

He hadn't seemed all that close to his mother. Sure, he called her Mother Mildred, which was odd, but he never said a bad word about the woman. She was his mother, he was her son; end of story. Now that she thought of it, he'd never really talked about his mom. The stories from his childhood involved his father and Uncle Frank. He told lots of stories about things he'd done and the friends he'd done them with. Try as she might, Cindy couldn't remember one story that included her grandmother. *Was it that she wasn't listening or could it be that she was not the only one that missed out on her grandmother's love?*

Her cell phone rang, bringing her out of her musings. Her mom's ringtone played as Cindy fished the phone from her pocket. She turned it on as she answered. "Hey, Mom. What's up?"

"I was getting ready to start dinner and realized I don't have an onion. I'm making meatloaf, and it tastes better with onion."

Sadness pulled at Cindy's heart. Her father's heart attack and subsequent death had been hard on her mother. Her parents had lived an active life until that life-altering day when their world had come crashing down. After his death, her mother had become somewhat of a recluse. While the woman was capable of driving, she hadn't left the house on her own since her husband died. In some ways, it was as if Cindy had lost both of her parents that cold November day.

Cindy looked at the pile of boxes and

blew out a sigh. She'd paid on the storage unit for two years; another month wasn't going to break her. She would call to request an extension on her way to the store.

"Sure, Mom, I'll be leaving here in a couple of minutes, and I'll run by Walmart. Do you need anything else?"

"Maybe something for dessert?" her mother said after a long pause.

"Works for me. See you in about fifteen minutes. Thirty tops, depending on the lines." Ending the call, she pushed the boxes out of the way, cringing once more as the overhead door screeched to a close. She replaced the padlock, realizing how relieved she was to take a break from memory lane.

Chapter Two

Cindy took a marker from her pocket, wrote *get rid of* on the top, and carried the box to the other side of the storage unit. She'd been sifting through boxes for several hours without finding anything that excited her. The cartons she'd sorted through thus far held clothing and personal care items that should have been either donated or thrown out long ago. Still, she was making progress and should have no problem getting everything cleared out by her new end-of-the-month deadline.

She smiled a satisfied smile and pulled another carton from the pile. The box seemed older than the rest and had something written on the side. Looking closer, Cindy instantly recognized her grandmother's handwriting from the cards she sent to her on special occasions. While Mildred hadn't said much in person, the woman always wrote a full inscription on her correspondence, and to her credit, never missed a holiday or birthday. Cindy carried the box to the chair, cocking her head to read the lettering.

O.T. 1924

"No clue," Cindy mused.

Removing the tape, she lifted the lid, peering inside. Whatever was in the box was extremely well wrapped in an enormous amount of bubble wrap.

"Huh, well, if you are that fragile, why didn't the box say so?" Cindy asked, tugging at the contents. She grinned when her endeavors were met with a popping sound, further resisting the childish urge to pop each bubble as she pulled. Removing it was a struggle, as the item was wrapped so securely, she had trouble freeing it from the cardboard. Once out, she went to work unwrapping the plastic that cloaked it. She'd removed seven layers before its shaping revealed it to be yet another doll, one Cindy herself had never seen. And not one of the chosen ones displayed on the guest bed.

"What's so special about you?" she asked when at last she'd freed the doll. "Other than the fact that you are freaking huge!"

She was too. Cindy guessed the doll to be the size of a real child, one around the age of four or five. While the doll appeared to be old, it was nowhere near as old as the delicate dress it was wearing. The once pink dress appeared pale with age and was embroidered with what looked to have been darker pink flowers. The dress's short sleeves were taken in at the arm holes, leaving her to deduct the dress had once fit a much larger child. She fanned out the fabric and discovered a note pinned to the front. The note must hold some meaning, as someone had taken the time to have it laminated. The paper inside the plastic covering was worn, aged, and handwritten with a flourish not seen in modern-day writings. She didn't have to compare it to the writing on the box to know the handwriting did not belong to her grandmother.

Mileta (Unknown)
Abandoned October 1921

"Mileta? Is that the manufacturer of the doll? And what is with the date? Why would anyone abandon a doll?" She looked over the doll once more. "You are not as old as the dress you are wearing, but together, you might do well on eBay."

She sat the doll aside, pulled out her phone, and googled the word "Mileta." The closest thing she could find was a textile mill that made shirts, handkerchief, and linens. She made a mental note to check into it further when she was near her computer.

Returning her phone to her pocket, she picked up the doll, tucking the plastic under its arms. As she began to roll the bubble wrap back in place, she heard a rattle coming from within the doll. Thinking the doll was broken, she unwrapped the plastic and carefully removed the dress for closer inspection. In the sternum area, she found what appeared to be a speaker, which verified that the doll was not old enough to be the original owner of the dress. Pleased with her earlier deduction, she ran a finger over the small circular disk.

"So you talk. Now if only you could tell me your secrets. Why did my grandmother think you were so special that she had to wrap you in a mile of bubble wrap?" When the doll said nothing, Cindy turned it over. Sure enough, the back had a square plate that was attached to the doll with tiny screws. She looked around at the contents of the storage unit then turned the doll to face her. "Don't suppose you could tell me if there are any screwdrivers in any of these boxes, could you?"

Cindy laughed and looked around to make sure no one was watching her. Not likely, given that she had yet to see another living soul in the storage lot during any of her visits. That was just one of the many advantages of living in a small farming community. While the town of Sandusky, Michigan had conveniences, such as Walmart, multiple farm stores, and a reasonable selection of restaurants, one could still drive from one end of town to the other in under ten minutes. And that was even if you were unfortunate enough to get delayed by one of the town's three traffic lights.

"The shy, quiet type, huh? Maybe that's why my grandmother liked you; you didn't give away her secrets." *That or because you have black curly hair,* Cindy thought, replacing the bonnet.

She rewrapped the doll, tucked it back into the box, and placed the carton in the "get rid of" pile before opening the next box.

The contents of this box caused a surge of excitement the second she peered into the box and saw a pillowcase. Lifting the fabric, she discovered one of her grandmother's prized quilts. She pulled the quilt from the pillowcase, hugging it as if she'd suddenly met up with a long lost friend. Though it had been in a box for at least seven years, the quilt still smelled very much of her grandmother's house. There was not really one smell, just a combination of fragrances that screamed of her grandmother. Why this should make her so happy, she hadn't a clue. But it did, and for the briefest moment, Cindy felt surrounded by her grandmother's love. She lowered the quilt for inspection, recognizing the pattern as Grandmother's Flower Garden. While not a quilter herself, Cindy had learned a great deal about quilting from watching her grandmother piece together quilts.

Most Sunday evenings when she and her parents visited her grandparents' house—the house she now called home— they would wander down the hall to the den—a converted bedroom—and find her grandparents sitting in peaceful companionship on the small couch with the volume on the television turned low. Upon entering the room, Cindy would lower herself to the floor as her parents each took one of the two remaining chairs. She would melt into the background, listening as the four adults drifted into casual conversation.

Closing her eyes, she could vividly picture her grandparents sitting on the couch working on this very quilt. In a time long before rotary cutters and quilting rulers, her grandfather had the arduous task of placing the cardboard cutout against the fabric and, using scissors, would carefully cut the fabric into tiny hexagon shapes. Her grandmother had chosen a bright yellow center for this particular quilt, then had picked fabric with which to surround the center of the flower, hand sewing each piece into hexagon circles. For this quilt, her grandmother had surrounded the yellow with a solid contrast, then encircled that with a complementary calico print. Next, she completed the hexagon ring with a border of crisp white to finish off the flower. Once she had assembled enough flowers, she pieced those together to make the quilt top. Her grandmother referred to this quilt as a summer quilt, meaning it didn't require a center batting. The top was pinned to a solid white fabric backing with safety pins, and using a large wooden hoop floor stand, Mildred would sew tiny perfect stitches around each hexagon to join the two sides together. Cindy never really saw the entire process from start to finish, as they generally only visited the house once a week. However, over the course of her childhood, she saw the entire process played out many times. Then, one Sunday evening, they would arrive to find her grandparents had begun the process anew. Even though a large stack of quilts sat in the corner of the guest room, there was always a quilt in progress.

Idle hands are the devil's workshop.

Cindy felt a chill race up her spine as if the words had been spoken out loud, reminding her it was she who was standing there when she had so much work to do. Shaking off the chill, she carefully unfolded the quilt to inspect it for damage. It appeared to be intact, but she still wanted to make sure nothing had made a meal out of the aged fabric. The cheerful colors made her smile. While the walls in her grandmother's home were muted, the same could not be said for her quilts. Whether it be shades of pinks, greens, reds, and blues, or in this case, a delightful blend of them all, each quilt always boasted vibrant colors that mingled well. She refolded it in a different direction, slid it back into the case, and set it on the chair. She lifted the next pillowcase, repeating the process until she had inspected two Double Wedding Ring quilts, a Sunbonnet Sue, A Nine Patch, and a stunning red and white Bear Paw quilt, which had been one of her grandmother's personal favorites. With the exception of a faded, threadbare patchwork quilt, each quilt looked as good as the day it was completed, giving Cindy hope she could sell them and recoup the money she'd spent on the storage unit.

Cindy tossed the tattered quilt into the trash pile and nestled the remaining quilts back into the box. She taped the box and carried it to the ever growing pile she'd deemed the "get rid of" pile, and was instantly hit with a pang of guilt. All those hours her grandmother had spent creating them, only to have them end up on a stranger's bed.

If she'd have wanted me to have one, she would have given me one. Cindy pushed the guilt aside and reached for a box marked "kitchen." The box was heavier than expected, but she managed to pull it down and drag it to her work area. Inside the box were several well-seasoned cast iron skillets. She lifted one, instantly conjuring up images of country fried ham and salty strips of perfectly cooked bacon.

Her cell phone rang, the ringtone once again letting her know it was her mother calling.

"Hey, Mom," Cindy said, placing the skillet into the small "to keep" pile.

"How's it going?"

"Slow, but it's going."

"Find anything good?"

"I found a box of quilts. I'm sure there has to be more, but I haven't found them yet. I also found an old doll."

"Your grandmother and her dolls. I never did see why she insisted on keeping those things around."

"I'm sure she had her reasons."

"Just don't bring them home."

"No worries, I put them all in the 'get rid of' pile. I just found her old cast iron skillets. I'm going to bring those home," Cindy said, placing the second skillet in the small pile.

Her mother laughed. "You don't even cook."

"No, but you do," Cindy said, reaching into the box once more. "Score!"

"What now?"

"I just found the old ice cream maker," Cindy said, setting it into the "keep" pile.

Her mother snorted a laugh.

"What's so funny?"

"You get rid of the quilts and keep the skillets and ice cream maker. What does that say about you?"

"It says I like to eat," Cindy said, frowning at her distorted reflection in the cookie sheet she'd just pulled from the box. "Huh."

"What's wrong?"

"It's weird. I just had this image of Grandma Mildred in a Christmas apron holding a pan full of something white."

"Divinity."

"What?"

"Your grandmother made divinity every year at Christmas time."

The memory came back in a rush.

"That's right. It was super sweet and nearly melted in my mouth. I remember she started making it with walnuts and cherries on top, but I didn't like that, so she always made some plain and kept them on a plate just for me. Why didn't I remember that?"

Her mother sighed. "Maybe it's easier to remember the bad stuff. Dinner will be ready soon. Should I wait or do you want me to save you some?"

Cindy placed the cookie sheet into the "keep" pile and surveyed the remaining boxes. "Let me finish with this box, and then I'll head home. See you in about twenty minutes?"

"That will give me enough time to make cornbread," her mother said, ending the call.

Cindy pulled out several other pans, and a newspaper-wrapped set of cooking utensils, which she placed in the "get rid of" pile. She lifted the box, thinking it was empty, but the weight made her look closer. Sure enough, at the bottom of the box sat a small wooden case, its coloring so close a match for the cardboard, she'd nearly missed it. The opened case instantly hit her with an aroma that jogged yet another memory. One of her grandparents standing in the kitchen polishing the silverware that now sat nestled in the velvety maroon pockets within the box. Oh, how she hated eating from those forks. Each Christmas, she sat at the table dreading that first bite, knowing the food would never taste as good as it looked. At least not in the beginning, as each early bite would be tainted by the tangy, pungent taste of the silver polish her grandparents used to shine the silverware. Cindy resisted the urge to touch one of the utensils to her tongue just to prove her point. There was no need; the smell that lingered vindicated her memory. Closing the lid, she placed the case in the discard pile. This was one decision not edged with guilt.

She transferred the items she wanted to keep to the trunk of her car then grabbed a box marked "photos" that she'd found earlier, placing that in the trunk alongside the ice cream maker. She was just about to lower the door when she remembered the doll she'd discovered earlier. She plucked the box from the pile and carried it to the backseat of her car. While she had no intention of keeping it, if she could fix the rattle, it would bring a better price. She thought about taking the items she'd slated for the trash and changed her mind. The garbage did not run until the end of the week, so she still had plenty of time. Besides, if the mouse did make its way into the unit, maybe it would be satisfied with the tattered quilt instead of the ones in pristine condition. She half considered leaving a portion of the throwaway quilt hanging out of the bottom but thought better of it. The mice had left the storage unit alone for seven years. No sense tempting fate.

Chapter Three

"I think that is the last of them," Cindy said, placing the dish in the dishwasher. "I'm so full, I can barely breathe."

"I love that you enjoy my cooking, but if you keep eating like that, you are going to end up like your father." Linda's voice was full of concern.

Cindy's father had died two years prior, a massive heart attack that no one saw coming. Devastated, Linda had moved in with her and had been living there ever since.

Cindy wanted to laugh at her mother's hypocrisy. "Coming from the woman who makes red meat for nearly every meal and just forced me to eat the last of the mashed potatoes."

"I'm your mother. I'm supposed to make sure you eat. Besides, I didn't have to push you too hard."

Cindy had been struggling with her weight most of her adult life, something she'd had better luck controlling before her mother started cooking for her. "Maybe if you didn't make so much food."

"I know, it's just that your father liked to eat. I guess I haven't figured out how to cut down the portion sizes yet." A shadow passed across Linda's drawn face. The last two years had been hard on the woman who'd not only lost a tremendous amount of weight but the spark in her eyes as well.

"I know, Mom. I miss him too," Cindy said, wrapping her arms around her. She felt the tremble of sobs overtake her mother and held her until at last they subsided, something she had done nearly every day since her father's passing. Cindy had tried to get her mother to go to grief counseling, but the woman had refused.

"I'm sorry," Linda whispered.

Cindy sighed. "It's okay, Mom; there's no reason to apologize."

"He was a good guy," Linda sniffed.

Cindy pulled the last tissue from the box and handed it to Linda, making a mental note to get some more. "Hey, I brought some things from the storage unit. Want to help me get them from the car?"

Her mother looked reluctant, and for a

moment, Cindy thought she was going to say no, but to her delight, she agreed to help. They walked to the car in silence. Cindy pushed the key fob to release the trunk and unlock the doors. "I'll get the pictures if you can bring the box from the backseat. Don't worry; it isn't heavy."

"It's light to be so big. What on earth is in it?" Linda said, hefting the box.

Cindy struggled with the hefty box of pictures. "It's one of Grandma Mildred's dolls."

Linda teetered the box on the edge of the trunk. "Oh no, you are not going to bring one of those creepy things into my house!"

Cindy bit her lip to keep from laughing. "It's my house, and since it used to be Grandma Mildred's house, I'd say the doll has more right to be here than either you or I."

Linda narrowed her eyes and turned toward the house without further comment. Cindy followed her inside and placed the box of photos on the kitchen chair. Opening the box, Cindy pulled out the first photo album.

"I don't recall ever seeing these," Cindy said, flipping through the pages.

Linda took a seat beside her. "I don't believe I have either."

"Look, there's Dad. Look how skinny he was."

"That man was skin and bones when I married him. It took me years to get some weight on him."

"Look at this one," Cindy said, keeping her mother focused. "I didn't know Dad played the French horn."

Her mother laughed a genuine laugh. "I don't know if 'playing' it is the right term. He blew a lot of air into it, which sounded more like a dying cow in a hail storm."

"Ha, now there's a visual." Cindy's face screwed up in thought. "They had that piano in the front room; I'm surprised he didn't play it. I don't believe I ever heard anyone play it."

Linda shook her head. "I don't believe I did either. Far as I know, it was just for show. It is not as if anyone ever went into the room, except maybe for Mildred. Someone had to dust the furniture."

Linda snickered. "I think your dad played the French horn just to spite your grandmother."

Cindy cast a look at her mother. "That

doesn't sound like Dad."

It was Linda's turn to laugh. "Oh, your father had a rebellious streak all right. It wasn't until after you were born that he settled down and started trying to pacify her."

Cindy studied the photos on the page. "She never did like me."

"Mildred didn't like anyone. I'm not even sure she liked herself."

"What makes you say that?" Cindy said, turning the page.

"She just always seemed miserable. I think I can count on one hand the number of times I saw that woman smile."

Cindy wasn't sure she could even count that many.

"I don't get it; Grandpa Howard doted on her. I don't think I can ever recall them raising their voices to each other. He was always helping her make her quilts and they worked together in the yard. Heck, he even helped her polish the silverware. I found it, by the way," Cindy said, flipping another page.

"Found what?"

"The silverware. I put it in the 'get rid of' pile."

"Good riddance. I never once enjoyed eating dinner over there. I cringed every time Mildred would say, 'Howard, did you bring the silverware down from the attic?'"

"See, it smelled so bad, they had to keep it in the attic," Cindy said, and both women laughed.

Linda pointed to a black and white photo of Paul, who looked to be around seven years old. He was standing next to Howard. Both were wearing suits with ties. Howard boasted a huge genuine smile; Paul's seemed a little more forced. Paul was holding a handwritten sign that said, "My Dad."

"Bring your father to school day?" Cindy mused. "Things sure have changed. Can you imagine kids wearing suits to school? We can barely get the third graders to dress up for formal events."

Linda pulled the plastic from the photo page and lifted the picture to get a better look. "I don't think they wore suits to school unless it was a special occasion. Besides, look at that face. The little guy seems a bit unsure."

Cindy took the photo from her mother. "Maybe his tie is too tight. Maybe it was because his mom was taking the picture. "You know, I never heard Dad talk about his mom that much. He shared some stories about him and his dad but not really anything about Grandma Mildred. Come to think of it, he never really spoke about his early childhood. Teenage years, sure, but that was him telling of things he did with his friends."

"I never heard him speak ill of either of his parents. It was no secret that I disliked your grandmother as much as she disliked me. He never seemed to want to talk about her, and that was fine by me. If I had nagged him about his mother's disposition, or the fact that he referred to her as 'Mother Mildred,' it might have started a fight, so we just spoke of other stuff. I guess your father just liked to live in the present."

Cindy replaced the photo, evened out the plastic film, and pointed at a photo of her grandmother standing in the kitchen in a calico print dress.

"Grandma was old school. I don't think I ever saw her wearing a pair of pants."

"That's because you mostly saw her on Sunday after she and Howard returned from church."

"And sometimes on Saturday," Cindy said, remembering the vision the cast iron skillet had conjured up. "I can remember waking up early a few times before Dad left the house and he'd tell me if I hurried and got dressed, I could go with him. I'd ask where we were going and he would say to breakfast. I remember being disappointed the first time because we drove into town and Dad drove straight here. I guess it was after they sold the farm. I felt cheated. Then, when we walked in the back door, all anger left me. The aroma of bacon filled the whole house. Just as the door slammed, Grandma Mildred would step around that corner wearing a dress much like the one in the picture with a dainty apron shielding the dress from the bacon grease. By the time we took off our shoes, she'd be pulling the biscuits out of the oven. I don't remember seeing Grandpa Howard, so I guess this would have been after he died."

Linda nodded. "Your father came over here every Saturday morning after your grandfather passed. She'd make him breakfast, and they'd drink coffee, then he'd come home."

"Did that bother you?" Cindy asked, seeing the frown that tugged at her mother's face.

"Maybe a little at the time, but now I understand," Linda replied softly.

"This is the one I've been waiting for," Cindy said, lifting the last album out of the box.

"I thought you said you hadn't seen them before," Linda questioned.

"I haven't. But…it is the last one, so it has to be the one with Dad's baby photos."

Her mother leaned forward, obviously eager to see what her late husband Paul looked like as a child, but blew out a disappointed sigh when the album didn't produce the expected photos. Instead, there were just random photos of Cindy's grandparents standing together. While they were smiling in each picture, the photos spoke volumes. Howard looked as if he'd found the woman of his dreams, and Mildred looked as if she'd rather be somewhere else. Almost as if at the last second, the photographer reminded her to smile.

"I don't get it," Cindy said, examining the photos closer. "What on earth was she so sad about?"

"Maybe she was just born hard-hearted," Linda replied.

"There was never any love lost between the two of you, was there?"

"The woman went out of her way to make my life miserable from the start. She told me not to get too close to Paul because you never know how long a marriage will last. It was as if she was waiting for us to get a divorce." Linda's lips pursed together, her eyes taking on a faraway glint. "It hurt too. I guess I was expecting to gain another mother. On my and your father's wedding day, I turned to your grandmother and asked what I was to call her now. She looked me in the eye, and in a voice as cold as that brisk September day, said, "Mrs. Moore will be fine.""

"Ouch. And you wonder why I am not in a hurry to get married."

"Not all mothers-in-law are ice queens," Linda said, rolling her eyes.

"Some of my friends would argue that point."

"So you're going to rob yourself of happiness just to avoid having an evil mother-in-law?"

Cindy shook her head. "Since when did this conversation turn into a lecture about my love life?"

"You'd first have to have a love life for us to be arguing about it."

"Low blow, Mother," Cindy groaned.

Linda rose from the chair. "I'm going to get a piece of pie. Do you want one or are you still too full?"

Cindy debated her answer before blowing out a sigh. "When have I ever said no to pie?'

Chapter Four

Cindy jumped when her mother suddenly appeared in the doorway. The screw she'd been unscrewing fell to the ground, disappearing within the brown threads of the carpet. Cindy hopped from the couch and began searching for the tiny screw.

"Jeesh, Mom, you scared the crap out of me."

Linda entered the room and bent, peering over Cindy's shoulder. "I woke up to go to the bathroom and saw the living room light on. I thought you were going to bed. There it is by your hand."

Even with direction, it took her a second to find it. "I swear you have the eyes of a hawk."

Linda straightened and plopped down on the couch next to the doll, leaving enough space so as not to risk touching it. "Aren't you a little old to be playing with dolls?"

"I'm not playing with it; I'm trying to fix it. I hear something rattling inside. It's going to be worth more if I can fix it."

"You may need to call the carpet people back in. They should have sealed that floor when they ripped up your grandmother's old pink carpet."

Linda's eyesight was great, but Cindy was suddenly unsure of her mental state. "What on earth are you talking about?"

Linda wrinkled her nose. "Don't you smell it? The second I walked into this room, all I could smell was Mildred."

Cindy nodded her understanding. "Oh, it's the doll. I guess I must have gotten used to it. I could hardly smell it. Anymore."

"Lucky you," Linda said, further wrinkling her nose.

"If you think this is bad, you should smell the storage unit. I don't even know what to call it."

"Perfume d'Mildred," Linda said with a flourish of the hand.

"Grandma Mildred did love her potpourri."

Linda sighed. "It could be worse; my grandmother's house always smelled of Jungle Gardenia."

Cindy pulled the back plate from the doll's torso and sat it on the side table next to the screws. "This doll is huge. Why don't I remember her?"

"Your grandmother kept her in the guest room; she stood in the corner where she stored her quilts. As the quilt pile grew, the doll disappeared." Linda reached around and picked up the dress. "Is this what she was wearing?"

"Yes, but it's too old to be the original dress."

"You're right. The dress I remember was bright red with white trim. The doll had a matching hat as well. It was rather pretty, considering."

Cindy slid a glance in her direction. "Considering?"

Linda snickered. "Considering I don't like dolls."

Cindy rotated the doll back and forth. "Well, never fear, I will take her back to the storage unit as soon as I can figure out what is rattling around inside."

Linda surveyed the laminated note pinned to the dress. "What is this? It looks old. Maybe that's why it's laminated, to help preserve it."

"I was thinking the same thing. I'm not sure what it means, though. I Googled it from my phone this afternoon but haven't had a chance to dig any deeper."

"If you don't need my help, I'm going back to bed. One of us has to get up early in the morning," Linda said, stifling a yawn.

Cindy bit her lip. Getting up early was of her mother's own choosing, not from necessity. Cindy, on the other hand, had the luxury of sleeping in for the next four weeks, as that was when summer break would end and she'd once again find herself in a classroom surrounded by little germ spreaders. Not that she minded—she enjoyed her job at the elementary school—but she also enjoyed having her summers free to do whatever she wished. Right now, she wished she could make her hand small enough to fit inside this beast of a doll. Closing her eyes, she gave the doll another shake and was rewarded when something hit her lap. Opening her eyes, she saw that something was an antique skeleton key with a string attached to it. She tugged at the string, but it remained anchored inside the doll. She maneuvered the doll to peek inside and was met with darkness.

She placed the doll on the couch and felt an adrenaline rush as she ran to get a flashlight. Upon returning, she shined the light inside the doll, making sure to hold the key so it wouldn't slip back inside. It took several moments of twisting this way and that way and bending her neck at awkward angles until she finally saw that the string was attached to a yellowed envelope.

"Sheesh, little missy, I was just kidding about you telling me all of my grandmother's secrets," she whispered.

Setting the doll on her lap, she slowly began pulling the string, being careful so as not to rip it loose from the paper, knowing full well doing so would mean having to dismember the doll to get it out, something she was more than willing to do at this point. She hadn't realized she'd been holding her breath until she pinched the paper between her fingers and finally pulled it from its hiding place. Setting the doll aside, she detached the string and inspected the envelope. She could not tell how long the envelope had been in the doll just by looking at it. However, the yellowing of the paper told her it had been hidden for quite some time. She took a calming breath, then, with trembling hands, peeled open the flap. She removed the paper and sat the envelope aside. Unfolding the paper, Cindy instantly recognized the writing as belonging to her grandmother.

If you are reading this, I am either dead or too ill to care. If not, then shoot me now, as you are about to discover all of my secrets. Secrets I vowed I would carry with me to the grave. Deciding you deserved to know the truth, I documented everything. Since I experienced a great feeling of relief at finally telling my story, I asked the others to do the same. I have since inherited their journals as well. If you choose to tell our stories, you must do so in an honest manner, for doing otherwise would surely be unjust.

I am choosing this next part to be cryptic solely on the off chance this doll is no longer with family. For if that is the case, our stories were never meant to be heard.

In the attic of the house I once called home, there lies a false bottom. The opening is marked by a single x, which is slightly darker than the wood that surrounds it. The opening was created by my husband Howard, delicately hidden so

as not to be found by mistake.
M.

Cindy stared at the aged message, rereading it over and over. The handwriting and signature told her the letter was penned by her grandmother. *What secrets could the woman have? And who are the others?*

She picked up the key, studying it. A skeleton key; she believed that was what they called them. Unlike the paper, the brass key was in pristine condition, ornately shaped with intertwined circles that reminded her somewhat of a king's crown. Below the crown sat two smooth bump-out ribs that smoothed into the shaft before reaching the foot of the key. The age made it look as if it should open a treasure chest.

Cindy's gaze moved up toward the attic, wondering what secrets her grandmother had left for her, for surely they were for her. Her grandmother had gifted Cindy the house in her will. The deed surprised everyone, including Cindy's father Paul, who was still alive and in presumed good health at the time.

A small piece of the puzzle slid into place. In the will, Grandma Mildred asked for her belongings to be moved to a storage unit until a time when someone could carefully go through them. The will had stipulated that a portion of the inheritance be set aside for just this purpose. Her dad had paid for the storage unit up until his death. After that, Linda took over for a brief amount of time until the depression became so intense that she stepped away from all responsibilities. Cindy had always wondered why Grandma Mildred had required her things to be put in storage and not remain in the house. Maybe this was why. If no one bothered to find out why the doll was rattling, then her secrets would remain hidden. Obviously, her grandmother was willing to let fate determine whether or not her secrets were divulged.

What secrets?

Intrigued, Cindy hurried down the hallway, turned the fan in her mother's room to high, and closed the door behind her. She retrieved a stool from the kitchen and, climbing on top, tugged at the thin rope that hung from the attic door. The stairs released from the ceiling with a screech that should have woken the dead, however, somehow failed to wake her mother.

She must have taken her sleeping pill. Cindy stepped off the stool, pushed it aside, and unfolded the bottom stair, carefully lowering it to the floor. She waited several moments to make sure she hadn't woken her mother before returning to the living room for the key and flashlight. She mounted the stairs, the stifling heat from the attic squeezing her lungs with each step. Except for a handful of boxes, some holiday decorations, and a floor lamp that had belonged to her grandmother, the attic was empty. Cindy turned on the floor lamp, but the single bulb did little to illuminate the spacious attic. Turning the flashlight to the floor, she walked the perimeter of the room. Her breath came heavy as she continued to follow the beam, narrowing the circle with each pass. She walked slowly, careful to avoid the hole the pull-down stairs had left. After several turns, she had walked the entire attic except where her personal belongings sat.

Of course.

Cindy walked back to the lamp with the intention of placing it closer to the boxes, but as she tilted the lamp, she saw the small x previously covered by the base of the lamp.

Cindy wiped the sweat from her face and cast another glance upwards. "Seriously, Grandma Mildred, you couldn't have just said look under the lamp?"

She dropped to her knees and found a two-foot seam, which had been expertly cut into the floor. There was no handle cut for the opening, only the small x that literally marked the spot. Mildred's note was correct; if not for the doll, no one would know the hidden compartment existed. She made a fruitless attempt of opening the hatch before hurrying to the garage and returning with both crowbar and flat tip screwdriver. The crowbar proved to be too thick to wedge into the seam. Thankfully, the screwdriver allowed her to pry the opening enough to get a grip on the planking, which she lifted off and placed to the side. She turned the light to the opening and found a wooden box nestled inside. It was a perfect fit, leaving just enough room for fingers to lift it from its hiding place. Slender fingers, which Cindy did not possess. Using the crowbar, Cindy carefully lifted the end of the box. She grasped the ends, easing it out so as not to scratch the wood. The box was nearly two feet across and three inches deep, expertly made and with a tiger carved into the top. It was smooth to the touch, stained a rich brown with a gloss so shiny, she did not doubt that, in better lighting, she would be able to see her reflection. It came as no surprise the box was locked. Her excitement mounted as she reached into her pocket for the key. She stifled a triumphant squeal when she inserted it into the lock and felt it give. The light from the flashlight reflected the tremble of her hands as she opened the lid. The smell of cedar invaded her nostrils as she got her first look inside at the white tissue paper with nary a wrinkle. Instantly, her mind sprang into action, visualizing stacks of money beneath the pristine wrapping.

On top of the paper was a folded note. Lifting the paper, Cindy read the note.

My dearest Cynthia, I have always held you at a distance, and for that, I will be eternally sorry. While I wanted to love you, I was afraid that by doing so I would lose you as I have lost all that I've ever held dear. I have taken great care in my writings so that you will know the real me and the truths I never told you. If you choose to continue from here, you will also hear the truths of my brothers and sisters.

Cindy blinked her confusion. *What does she mean, the real me? And what brothers and sisters? Grandma Mildred was an only child.*

Pulling back the main tissue covering, Cindy saw what looked to be stacks of books, each wrapped in bright white tissue paper and sealed with red oval stickers. Written inside each oval was a letter along with a number. She picked up the one marked M-1. Unwrapping the contents, she discovered not a book, but a notebook. *So much for the million dollars.*

Written on the cover were the words: *Mileta October 1921*

Chapter Five

It was two in the morning. Cindy was freshly showered and had a cup of hot coffee sitting in her trembling hands. She'd resisted opening the notebook after a drop of sweat had fallen onto the cover. Instead, she'd replaced the tissue paper and carried the entire box down the attic stairs and into the living room. She set her coffee aside, unwrapped the notebook, and was greeted with another handwritten note.

Whoever is reading this is about to uncover secrets I've taken with me to the grave. At least I hope that is the case, as I've worked hard at keeping the shame that is my life under wraps. While I have tried to live a good life, I am afraid that sins from my past have kept me from living a full life. I am not quite sure what sins I committed, but they must have been so great that my dear mother abandoned me when I was but a wee child.

The year was nineteen twenty-one, it

was January, and I had nearly reached my eighth year, when my mother took me to the orphanage. I still remember her face clearly and can still see the dark curls that fell loose around her shoulders. I think she was tall, but maybe that was just a child's perspective. She was thin; that I do recall. Then again, so was everyone who lived in our tenement. Maybe it was because we were always hungry.

It was raining the last time I saw my mother. I was cold and wet, and my mother told me to go inside where I would be warm. I asked her if she was coming inside and she said no, she didn't want to spoil the floors with her wet shoes. I didn't have to worry about that. I wasn't wearing any shoes. Mother was dripping wet, the rain had stripped her of her curls, and her deep black hair lay plastered against the side of her head like a hat. I asked her why she was crying. She told me it was just the rain on her face, but I could hear her sobs and knew she was lying. Before I could respond, Mother opened the door, pushed me inside, and the door closed behind me. The doors nearly reached the ceiling. A deep rich brown, they were the largest doors I had ever seen. An elephant could have walked through without issue. I have never forgotten the sound it made when it slammed shut. A solid thud that vibrated like rolling thunder. The sound has woken me from my dreams more often than I can count. Maybe that is because my mother never bothered to kiss me goodbye.

I was still staring at the door, when an older girl wearing a blue gingham dress and a crisp white apron came and asked me what I was doing. I told her my mother brought me. She shrugged and told me I must have done something very bad for my mother to have left me. I couldn't recall doing anything bad, but the girl must have been right, as I never saw my mother again.

The girl took my hand and led me down the long hall, which was empty except for a few paintings on the wall and large red crocks evenly spaced along the floor near the wall. I didn't want to leave the entrance. The building was so big, and I was afraid my momma would not be able to find me. The girl was bigger than me and looked mean, so I went with her. She took me to a room with tall windows and dark walls, where a lady wearing a black dress was sitting behind a large wooden desk. The girl told the lady she'd found me in the hall. The woman picked up a clipboard and asked me if I spoke English. I remember smiling and shaking my head yes. Not everyone in our tenement spoke English. My momma did, but not very well.

Momma and Papa and I came over the ocean on a big ship from Poland. While I remember my papa, I do not remember what his face looked like. He died before the ship reached America. They said he was sick. Two men carried him outside in the rain and threw him over the side.

Oh, how I loathe the rain.

Momma said my Ojczulek – that's the Polish word for papa – taught me how to speak English so people would like me better. I wish I could remember my papa better.

The woman asked my name. I told her my name was Mileta. She asked me what my last name was. I told her that was the only name I had. The lady didn't seem happy about that. She asked what my mother's name was. I was going to tell her it was Mamusia – which is the Polish word for momma, but then I remembered what my papa told me and I said her name was Momma. The lady smiled and wrote something on the clipboard. It was the first time the lady smiled. Papa must have been right.

My clothes were wet; I was barefoot and so cold, I was shaking. The woman must not have liked that I was dripping water on the floor because she told the girl, who she called Clara, to take me to the washroom for a bath and delouse. I wasn't sure what that meant, but from the look on the girl's face, I was sure I wasn't going to like it.

As Cindy read, the story came to life, as if she was watching it unfold.

***

Mileta followed Clara down a long hallway, admiring the large blue bow that held her hair high on top of her head. It was a fine bow. Mileta wondered how her own long brown hair would look in a bow such as that. They passed two doors before stopping in front of another. Clara opened the door and pushed her inside, closing the door with a loud bang. She was beginning to not like the doors in this building.

Mileta was standing in what she would

soon learn was the washroom, which was filled with deep washtubs. Three of the roundest women she had ever seen were in the room. Each of them wore long dark dresses covered with crisp white aprons such as Clara had on. Two of the women sat on low stools beside the large tubs, each briskly scrubbing the heads of girls not much older than she. Neither child seemed to be enjoying themselves. The third woman approached Mileta. Without saying a word, the woman took hold of her hair, twisted it close to her head, and snipped the length off with scissors. The woman examined the length of hair, then wrinkling her nose, tossed the wet locks into a large woodstove. Before Mileta could protest, the woman removed her tattered dress and tossed it into the fire along with the hair.

"You're covered with lice," the woman said when Mileta began to cry. "Now strip off your underwear."

Mileta did as she said and watched as the woman tossed them into the fire.

A scream drew her attention.

"Tis hot!" one of the girls in the tub yelled.

"Stop your wailing, or I'll pour another bucket on your head," the woman tending her said and pushed the girl's head under water. Seconds later, the head emerged. The woman plucked the girl out of the water, wrapped her in a towel, and motioned for Mileta to come. She hesitated, then found herself thrust forward by the sting of a hand on her bare backside. Not wanting another swat, she hurried to where the large woman was waiting and stood looking into the sudsy water.

"Well, go on; get in," the woman fussed.

Mileta scrambled into the tub, blinking her surprise at the warmth of the water. Still cold from the rain, the water felt so inviting. She smiled. It was the second time she'd done so since entering the building.

"What? You've never had a bath before?" The woman snorted.

Mileta shook her head. She and her mother lived in a three-room apartment on the fourth floor of a bug-infested tenement building. They shared the space with two other families, making for a total of nine people living in the tiny apartment. The water spigots on the fourth floor didn't work, so once a week, her mom carried a bucket of cold water up the stairs and, using a sponge, cleaned them both as best she could. Every other week, an extra bucket of water was brought up for washing the hair. The water was only heated enough to remove the chill. Running the stove cost money they did not have. Sometimes the water wasn't even heated. If it was cold outside, her mother would allow it to come to room temperature before using it to wash. Up until a few moments ago, she never knew such luxuries as a hot tub filled with water existed. Nor did it matter that the water had already been used multiple times. It was the first time since leaving the house earlier this morning that she'd been warm.

The feeling of contentment didn't last. The woman who sat next to the tub pulled a scrub brush from her apron and slid a bar of strong-smelling soap across the brush before, in turn, sliding the brush along Mileta's delicate skin. She tried to escape, but the woman's grip held firm. She did not let up until she had assaulted every inch of Mileta's body from scalp to toe with the coarse bristles. When she finished scrubbing, the woman poured a foul-smelling liquid into her palm, which she used to lather what was left of Mileta's hair. Using the tips of her full fingers, the woman pulled the foam through the strands of hair from root to end.

"Rinse," she ordered, then pushed Mileta's head under water.

Gasping for air, Mileta rubbed the stinging suds from her eyes. Her vision cleared just in time to watch the woman lift a bucket and douse her with the contents. The girl that had preceded her in the tub was not lying; the water was hot.

"Out!" the woman commanded, tossing the bucket aside.

Mileta clambered out of the tub without hesitation and trembled while the woman ran a rough towel over her tender pink skin.

When she finally finished, she pointed a chubby finger to the other side of the room.

"Go see Mistress Eleanora and she will get you dressed. Now!" the woman bellowed when Mileta hesitated.

Mileta hurried to the woman who'd taken her dress. Mistress Eleanora sized her up before handing her a pair of brand new underwear and a slip. To Mileta's surprise, she then handed her a blue and white gingham print dress that matched the one Clara was wearing, along with a pair of black tights. Except for the print, the dress was plain. However, to seven-year-old Mileta, used to wearing rags, it was beautiful. The lady took a ruler and measured Mileta's feet before presenting her with a pair of shiny black shoes. Once again, tears threatened. It was the first time she had ever received such treasures. She hurried to get dressed then crammed her feet into the shoes, which seemed a bit small. She did not tell the lady, as she was afraid she would take them away from her. They might hurt her feet, but they were new. Brand new, like from the store window on the busy street where people wrinkled their noses when she and her mother passed by. For the third time that day, Mileta smiled.

***

The clock on the wall chimed, drawing Cindy's attention to the fact that it was three in the morning. Closing the diary, she realized she'd been crying. *Could this child really be Grandma Mildred? If so, why had she hidden the diaries?* While she was certain the answers lay within the contents of the box, they would have to wait. The coffee hadn't helped, and Cindy could barely hold her eyes open. She replaced the notebook and locked the box, pocketing the key. She carried the box to her bedroom and was just about to turn off the light when she thought better of it. Returning to the living room, she replaced the back cover and carefully pulled the faded dress over the doll's head. She wasn't sure why her grandmother chose this particular doll to shield her secrets, but Cindy felt a sudden childish need to keep her safe. Gathering the doll in her arms, she carried it to her room.

Chapter Six

Cindy woke early after a restless night worrying about the child who'd been abandoned by her mother. Surely it was another child and not her grandmother. Still, she was concerned about the little girl in the story and anxious to see what had become of her. She walked down the hall intending to grab a cup of coffee and return to her room unnoticed, but as luck would have it, her mother was in the kitchen when she entered.

Linda laughed. "You look so pleased to see me."

"You were up late, so I thought you would be sleeping in," Cindy said, realizing her disappointment must have shown.

"Ha, when is the last time you saw me sleep in? I didn't see the doll in the living room. Did you figure out what was rattling around in there?"

"Not yet. I finally said to heck with it and went to bed." Cindy hated lying to her mother but knew if she told her about the notebooks, she would insist on reading them, and the truth of the matter was she wasn't ready to share them just yet. Obviously, if her grandmother felt strongly about not unveiling her secret, the least she could do was to take the time to figure out why.

Linda did a full-body shudder. "I can't believe you could actually sleep with that thing in your room."

"The doll isn't all that bad. Besides, I knew how much she creeped you out, so I just took her to my room."

Linda handed her a cup of coffee. "Maybe you should take her back to the storage unit when you go. Do you want a bagel?"

"Yes, please. But I'm not going today. I have an idea for a class project at school this fall. I want to do some research and jot down some notes while the idea is still fresh in my mind." Crap, another lie.

Linda sighed and placed the bagel in the toaster. "It's your money."

"Excuse me?"

"You're the one paying on the storage unit."

"Oh, that. I just paid for an additional month. I should have cleared it out a long time ago." For some reason, that comment pulled at her gut. That, or maybe she was hungry. But if she had, then she would already be privy to the information in her grandmother's notebooks.

Linda handed her a bagel and slid the cream cheese across the counter. "You are a terrible liar."

Cindy paused, knife in hand.

"You are just making excuses; you don't want to clean out that storage unit any more than I did. I don't know why Mildred didn't just get rid of the junk when she had the chance."

"I'm sure she had her reasons. But you're right; I'm not as eager to clear out the storage unit as I once was," Cindy admitted, lowering the knife into the cream cheese. "Any plans for today?"

"I downloaded a book series from a new author yesterday. It's going to be a hot one today, so I thought I would binge read. Unless you need some help on that project you're working on."

Cindy shook her head. "No, I'm good. I have a lot of notes to read through. Don't worry about lunch; if I get hungry, I'll grab a sandwich."

"Sandwiches sound good; I'll make some tuna salad before I start reading. It will be in the fridge when you get hungry."

"Mom?"

Linda turned to face her. "Yes?"

"I just want to let you know I love you. I know it hasn't been easy for you, but I really do appreciate all you do around here."

Linda's eyes grew moist. "Thank you."

Cindy wrapped her arms around her mom. "I didn't mean to make you cry."

"It's okay; they're happy tears," Linda sniffed.

***

Cindy settled into the small recliner next to her bed and opened the journal. As soon as she began reading, the story came to life…

Mileta followed behind Clara, who had come to collect her and the two other girls, both of which stood sobbing as they ran their hands through their hair. Her new shoes pinched her toes, but she didn't care.

She loved the way they clicked on the tile floor with each step. She'd never had shoes that clicked before. She followed the girls; she didn't know their names, as no one had introduced them. No one in this building seemed to care about being polite, something that her papa had always insisted on. *Papa would not approve of me being here.*

The girls appeared to be close to her age and both sported short, choppy black hair, which made them look more like boys than girls. Mileta ran a hand across her head. Gone were the long locks her mother used to braid before bed each night. She swallowed hard, realizing that she too now looked very much like a boy.

Mama's going to be mad at them for cutting my hair. Mileta looked over her shoulder, wondering when her mother would return. The procession stopped at the door, and Clara turned to address them.

"It is meal time. You are to get in line, get your tray, and find a seat at the table. There is to be no talking. If you are talking, you can't eat. If you do not eat, they will take your food away. Understand?" the girl asked, glancing at each girl in turn.

Mileta wondered who "they" were, then remembered the lady who took her dress, and nodded her head.

Clara opened the door and led them into a large, open room. The room split into two distinct sections, each side lined with rows of long wooden tables. Children of all ages sat at the tables: girls on one side, boys the other. The girls were all dressed the same as she, in gingham dresses with white aprons. The boys had black knickers that stopped at the knee, white shirts, and matching socks. Some of the children stopped to stare at the new arrivals. Others shoveled food as if they were afraid it would disappear. Mileta's stomach rumbled as she caught a whiff of freshly baked bread. The yeasty aroma nearly reduced her to tears, the smell suddenly reminding her of her hunger. She followed the other girls and waited her turn, marveling as the woman behind the counter sat a metal tray containing mush along with the end piece of bread and a metal cup half full of milk in front of her. She thanked the woman, but the woman didn't respond. Her stomach growled once more, reminding her it had been nearly two days since she'd eaten. Even then, all she'd had was a small hunk of cheese, an overly ripe apple, and three crackers. She had tried to share the crackers with her mom, but her mother kept coughing and told Mileta the dry crackers would only make her cough worse. Mileta wished her mother would have eaten some crackers, as her cough grew worse anyway.

Mileta turned and looked for the other girls, but they'd already found seats at a table without room for another. She scanned the room and saw an empty seat next to a blonde-haired girl that looked to be a few years older than she. The girl looked up, tilted her head in invitation, and gave the briefest of smiles. Slight as it might be, it was the first kind gesture she'd seen displayed since her arrival, so she hurried toward the girl. Sitting at the table, she folded her hands as Papa had taught her, and closed her eyes to say a quick prayer.

When she opened her eyes, her bread was gone.

Tears sprang to her eyes as she searched each plate looking for the missing loaf. Anger swept over her when she saw it on the plate of a girl at the far end of the table. Mileta started to get up, but the girl next to her grabbed her arm.

"Leave, and when you come back your mush will be gone too," the girl whispered. "Eat before it too is taken."

The girl who took it looked to be more than double her age. Her dark hair was pulled high atop her head and held in place with a wide blue bow. She stared at Mileta as she bit into the stolen bread.

Mileta now knew the "they" of which Clara warned. "Doesn't she know I am hungry?"

"We are all hungry. It is never enough. Anastasia is the one who took your bread, but there are many others who will steal your food. Now hurry, eat before they take your mush too."

Mileta shoveled the mush into her mouth so quickly, it was gone in mere moments. Papa would not like that she was eating like the dogs she'd seen on the city streets scrapping over a discarded bone. But Papa was not here, and she was hungry. Setting down her spoon, she picked up the cup, draining her milk in four quick gulps.

"I'm Mary," the girl next to her whispered after Mileta finished. "We are allowed to talk as long as we whisper. Remember, never speak until you are finished eating. You have seen what can happen if you do not."

"Can we not tell on them?" Mileta asked, glaring at Anastasia.

Mary shook her head. "Not if you wish to live. What is your name?"

"Mileta."

Mary's blue eyes grew wide. "Listen, Mileta, the last thing you want is to be known as a snitch. That happens, and having your bread stolen will be the least of your worries. Understand?"

Mileta didn't, but she nodded her head anyway.

An elderly woman in a black overcoat came into the room, clapped her hands, and shouted something in a language Mileta did not recognize. The boys all stood and took their trays to the door near the serving line. One by one, they placed the trays on a large rolling cart and left the room. The lady then turned to the girls' side of the room and repeated the process.

Mary pushed away from the table. "That is Mrs. Gretchen. She sounds mean, but that is because she speaks in German. She is nice as long as you do as she says."

Mileta gathered her tray. "I cannot understand her. How do I know what it is she is saying?"

"Most of us cannot. But there are some that do, so we do what the German children do," Mary said, picking up her tray and moving to the head of the room.

Mileta did as she was told and placed her tray into the large wooden bin atop the cart before following Mary from the room. "Where are we going?"

"To the play yard," Mary whispered.

Mileta noticed more of the red crocks she'd seen in the main hallway. "What is in the crocks?"

"Water."

"Why do they need so much water when they have spigots?"

"The crocks are filled with water for fighting fires. Now shush; there is to be no talking in the hallway," Mary warned.

They followed the line of girls down two long corridors and into a room lined with rows of black coats.

"We are over here," Mary said, crossing to the far side of the room. "Pick one; they don't fit anyhow."

Sure enough, the coat was at least two sizes too large. Even still, Mileta was grateful for its warmth as the outer door was pushed open, allowing the brisk, moist air to stream in. Gathering her coat against the chill, she pulled the hood over her head and followed Mary and the others outside to a large courtyard.

Once outside, the girls broke into small groups. "Over here," Mary said, leading her to the side of the building. "Press back against the wall. It will help to keep the rain from soaking you too badly."

Mileta did as she was told but didn't see where it helped much. "Why do they send us out if it is raining?"

"We go out every day no matter the weather. They tell us we need the fresh air. In truth, I think it is so they can clean the rooms without us all underfoot. They call it a play yard, but there is nothing to play with. Most of the time, we stand by the iron fence and watch the motorcars. Sometimes, if we are lucky, someone from the other side will hand us food. Where did you come from?"

"Poland. We came across the ocean on a boat."

Mary laughed. "No, today, silly. How did you come to be here today?"

"My momma brought me. I keep waiting for her to come to collect me, but she hasn't returned yet."

A look of pity crossed Mary's face. "Didn't she tell you?"

Mileta shook her head. "Tell me what?"

"She's not coming back." Mary raised her arms, moving them to include the building and courtyard. "This is the place they put children when no one wants us."

Mileta swallowed back tears. Her momma wouldn't leave her. She stomped her foot in defiance. "It's not true!"

Mary's eyes narrowed. When she spoke, her voice was as cold as the January wind. "My mother brought me here two Christmases ago. She acted as if I were getting a grand present. It was cold, and we had been kicked out of our apartment after Daddy lost his job due to the drink. She told me I would have a grand house to live in and food to eat every day. She took me to the head mistress and told her she would be back to get me just as soon as Daddy found another job. That was the last time I saw my mother. For Christmas that year, I got a new dress and this apron I wear today. And they cut my pretty hair, just like they did yours. They do that so you don't bring in any bugs."

Mileta blinked as warm tears spilled from her eyes, mingling with the cold rain that splashed upon her face.

Oh, how she hated the rain.

Chapter Seven

After recess, the children were escorted to the meeting room. Mileta couldn't figure out why they called it that, for as far as she could see, the children were not actually allowed to meet. She sat huddled in a circle of children, both girls and boys. Most sat on the floor with knees drawn to chest, trying to break the chill from yard time, as Anastasia read to them from a book. The story, *The Wonderful Wizard of Oz*, by L. Frank Baum, was about an orphan girl named Dorothy who lived with her Uncle Henry and Aunt Em. Dorothy had been carried away from where she lived on something called a cyclone. Mileta wasn't sure what a cyclone was, but she found herself wishing that one would come for her and carry her away from this place that was now her home.

Mary told Mileta it was a new book someone had sent directly from the publishing house; exciting, as they were rarely gifted such a treasure. Books were donated and generally well worn by the time they received them. *The Wonderful Wizard of Oz* was a favorite of the children, one which they begged Anastasia to read over and over since its arrival a few weeks earlier. Reading it so often had allowed Anastasia to become familiar with it and the familiarity showed in the telling.

Anastasia read as well as her papa. Better maybe, as Anastasia had a way of reading that made the story seem real. It was the first time since before her papa died that Mileta had heard anyone read. Momma couldn't read, and Mileta hadn't yet learned, though her papa had taught her some letters. Papa was always teaching her and her momma something. He was a learned man; he'd gone to school and everything. Reading was how Papa had learned about America. Mileta wasn't happy about leaving Poland, but Papa had made it clear it wasn't safe to stay there. He kept talking to her momma about something he called "religious persecution." Mileta wasn't sure what it was, but from the look on his face when he said it, she knew it was bad. He would pound his chest with his fist, and speaking in English, declare, "I am an honest German Pole. I'm going to take my family across the great sea, and we will be able to pray over the food we eat. And because it is America, there will be plenty of food."

Yes, so much food, they will take it away from you, Mileta thought, glaring at Anastasia.

The children gasped as Anastasia told of the yellow wildcat and how it was chasing a field mouse. Seconds later, Anastasia made a quick swoosh with her arm as she spoke of the Tin Woodsman chopping off the head of the cat to save the field mouse. It would be easy to like Anastasia had she not stolen her bread.

Mileta wiggled her toes, which were tingling within her new shoes. Shoes that seemed to have grown tighter since getting wet in the courtyard. She rubbed the toe of her left shoe.

"What is it?" Mary whispered.

"My beautiful new shoes. They hurt my feet." Mileta sighed.

"Are they too big?"

Mileta sook her head. "No, they pinch my toes."

"Why didn't you say something to the mistress?"

"I was afraid she would take them away."

Mary smiled. "Later, I will take you and see if we can get you some new shoes. Now listen; I love this part."

"The woman now called to them that supper was ready, so they gathered around the table, and Dorothy ate some delicious porridge and a dish of scrambled eggs and a plate of nice white bread, and enjoyed her meal," Anastasia said with a sigh that was mimicked by all who listened, Mileta included.

"Can you imagine having so much to eat and all at one time?" a little boy whispered.

"I can, but it is a very long time since," another boy replied, his words met with nods from several older children in the group.

Anastasia read quickly now, pulling the children back into the story with the fast pace of her words. She told of the visit to the Emerald City and made the smaller children laugh when she placed circles over her eyes by way of explaining the spectacles Dorothy had to wear so the green glow of the Emerald City wouldn't hurt her eyes. Their laughter stilled as Anastasia read the description of the Wizard. "In the center of the chair was an enormous head, without a body to support it or any arms or legs whatever. There was no hair upon this head, but it had eyes and a nose and mouth, and was much bigger than the head of the biggest giant."

The room was quiet now as Anastasia continued, each child doing their best to visualize the great and powerful Oz. The silence continued as the Wizard demanded they kill the witch and bring proof that she was dead, each child wishing the Wizard would grant them permission to rid the world of their own wicked witch. Mileta pictured Anastasia smiling the smirk of a smile when she took a bite of the stolen bread. She froze when Anastasia caught her eye, almost as if she'd been privy to her innermost thoughts.

One of the headmistresses stepped up, and Anastasia handed her the book. Anastasia took a quick break while the headmistress continued to read. She read with a thick German accent that pulled heavily at the story. Anastasia's break was quick, and she resumed reading, much to Mileta's delight.

Moments later, Mary elbowed her. "Get ready; here comes the scary part."

Mileta's heart quickened as Anastasia read about the winged monkeys and cheered along with the rest when at last the wicked witch was dead. She, along with the others, grew angry when the Wizard failed to keep his promise and Mileta cried along with Dorothy when his balloon took off without her. Unlike some of the children, Mileta had no trouble visualizing the hot air balloon, as she had once seen one floating about the countryside before her and her family had departed Poland.

The children all groaned as the headmistress stepped forward once more and clapped her hands.

"What is it?" Mileta asked.

"'Tis time to take our supper," Mary whispered.

Mileta couldn't believe her ears. "You mean we get to eat more than once?"

"Yes, and we will have a morning meal when we wake tomorrow. Tis all the same, and never enough, but they do feed us,"

Mary said, falling into line and motioning her to follow.

Mileta trailed behind her friend, grimacing with each step. While she wanted to love her new shoes, it was difficult when her toes ached so. She took her tin tray and limped behind as Mary led the way to an open table.

Mary was right; supper was the same mush, along with a hunk of fresh bread, only this time, Mileta opted to forgo the prayer. What was the point of saying thanks for her food if, when she finished praying, there wasn't any food for which to be thankful?

Mileta took a bite of her bread, instantly surprised at its freshness. For a moment, she wished for some honey to cover it with, then silently scolded herself for being so greedy. She wondered what her momma was having for supper and thought to save her some of her bread. Then, remembering what Mary had said about her not coming back, anger replaced the guilt. Then guilt returned the next instant, and suddenly, tears sprang to her eyes as she realized she didn't know what she was supposed to feel. She was sad her mother wasn't here but happy she had food in her belly when there were so many days when she'd had none. *I will be thankful I am here so that I have food*, she decided at last.

Out of the corner of her eye, she spied one of the older girls stealing a hunk of bread off a younger girl's tray. Mileta hurriedly shoved the last of her bread into her mouth. The girl then noticed Mileta's untouched mush and started toward her. In a panic, Mileta dipped her head, stuck out her tongue and licked the length of her mush. The girl wrinkled her nose in disgust and sought out another table.

"That was brilliant; whatever made you think of it?" Mary asked.

Mileta shrugged. "I am hungry, and I did not want her to eat my food."

"We shall tell all the girls to lick their mush." Mary giggled.

Papa would not be happy she was eating like a dog. *Then again, Papa would not have left me here.* She picked up her spoon and quickly shoveled the mush into her mouth before the girl decided to change her mind.

"You need to use the water closet,"

Mary said as soon as both girls had finished their meal.

Mileta shook her head. "No, I do not."

"Yes, you do, and I am going to show you how to get there. If anyone says anything, you tell them you do not remember where it is. Now come with me and act as if you really have to go bad."

Mileta picked up her tray and followed Mary to the front of the room where one of the mistresses stood.

"I did not call for you to clear your table," the woman said sternly.

"Oh, but Mileta has to use the water closet. Tis her first day and she does not yet know the rules. She didn't go before we came in and will surely soil herself if she is not permitted to go," Mary implored.

"Then she can go, but you stay here," the woman relented.

"Oh, but as I said, she is new and does not remember the way," Mary persisted.

The woman turned her attention to Mileta, who shook her head and shifted from foot to foot for good measure. She grimaced from the pain in her toes.

"I can see she has to go. Off with you

two but mind your manners in the hallway, or you will see the strap," the woman said with a wave of the hand.

"This way," Mary said once the door closed behind them.

"But I thought the water closet was the other way," Mileta questioned.

"We are not going to the water closet, but we must hurry," Mary said, breaking into a run.

Mileta followed her down the hall, wincing as her toes rubbed against the front of her shoes. She hesitated when Mary opened the door to the washroom. She'd already been here once today, and the experience hadn't been pleasant.

"We must hurry," Mary repeated and pulled her inside, allowing the door to close behind them. "Don't look so frightened; the mistresses are all in the kitchen helping with supper. Now quick, remove your shoes and give them to me."

"But…"

"Hurry," Mary said when she hesitated.

Mileta took off the shoes, handed them to Mary, who raced into the other room. Seconds later, Mary reemerged and thrust the shoes at her.

"Try these."

Mileta sat on the floor and stuck her foot into the shoe, only then realizing Mary had switched them for a larger pair. "They fit!" Mileta exclaimed.

"Good, now the other. Hurry!"

Mileta did as she told, then followed Mary to the door. The girls retraced their steps, except this time, they raced past the door to the dining hall. Mary slowed and turned back toward the hall. Mileta did the same, and both girls reached the doorway just as it was opened to allow the children to exit. Mary and Mileta waited for the last girl then fell in line behind them. This time, Mileta's feet did not hurt.

Chapter Eight

After the evening meal, the children gathered in the common room, an open space that allowed each child room to mingle and enjoy the various activity stations. The children broke into smaller groups. Some of the girls played with dolls; little boys lay prone along the floor shooting marbles to each other. Some of the older children read books and others sat at tables, while a woman Mileta hadn't seen before wrote letters on a large blackboard. The woman was tall and thin, and wore a crisp white button-up blouse tucked into a long black skirt. The woman's curly brown hair bounced around her shoulders with each turn of the head, but what captured Mileta's attention most was that she smiled as she spoke. For a moment, she was reminded of her mother in much happier times. Times before they'd arrived in this frightening land that had promised such hope. The woman saw her staring and winked at her before turning to draw a new letter onto the blackboard. When she finished, she traced a slender finger over the curved shape and sounded out the letter, making a hissing sound like a snake. The children at the tables watched her with great interest before bending over individual slate boards, copying the letters onto their tablets with chalk.

"Over here," Mary's voice called to her.

Mileta tore her gaze from the classroom and joined Mary and several other children milling about on the other side of the room. Each child held a wooden stick with a curved box on the end. In the center of the box were two holes. Mary slipped a card into the box, placed it to her face, and smiled.

"Here. It is called a stereoscope; take a look," Mary said, handing it over.

Mileta looked through the holes, and her breath caught. The image looked as if it were standing right in front of her. "It is an elephant!"

The small group giggled at her enthusiasm. Mileta blushed and handed the device back to Mary.

"Tis no reason to be upset." Mary took the stereoscope and changed out the card. "It was like that for all of us the first time. But then you haven't officially met our little group, have you? Where are my manners?"

Mileta turned to the small group of children. With the exception of hair and eye color and varied height, the children were hard to tell apart. Each girl wore the same blue and white gingham dress covered with crisp white aprons like the one she'd been given after her bath. The only thing that separated them from her was each girl had long hair, which was held in place by a large blue bow. The boys were no easier to tell apart, each wearing the same knickers and matching shirts, sporting identical short haircuts that looked as if the children were paper dolls, each cut from the same pattern. Then again, even paper dolls came with more than one set of clothes.

Mary pointed to each child in turn. "This is Henrietta; she has been here two years. Ruth is three. She arrived here as a baby. Esther sold flowers on the street before they brought her here."

The little blonde jutted her chin in the

air. "Yes, and I made six pennies a day. Eight on Sundays, so I had enough to get by."

Mary turned to another girl and smiled. "Emma does not talk much. She prefers to listen to everyone else."

Mary pointed to a girl with milky white skin and eyes that looked to be almost violet. "That is Iris; her mom was killed in a big fire when she was three."

"My father is still alive. He will take me out of here someday," the girl said, cutting her off.

"This is Dorthia," Mary said, turning to a brown-eyed girl who was older and more developed than the others. "She is friendly."

This evoked a snort from one of the boys and Mary turned to him. "This is Percival. Everyone calls him Slim. That is Geo; everyone calls him Shorty, although I am not sure why," she said, pointing to the tallest boy in their group.

"That is Levi; he is a newsie."

Mileta nodded. She'd seen the newsies on the corner selling papers.

Mary pointed to a boy with dark features. "Gideon makes us all laugh."

The children, Mileta included, laughed when Gideon dropped to the floor, wrapped his legs around his arms, and hand-waddled the length of the room.

"Cecil is the quiet type and the exact opposite of Gideon," Mary said, nodding to the smallest member of the group.

Mileta watched as the boy's face turned a brilliant shade of pink.

Mary smiled at a boy with scorching red hair. "Last but not least is Paddy. He's Irish. And this," Mary said, taking hold of Mileta's hand, "is Mileta. She is going to be part of our gang. She is a smart one. Did any of you see what she did at the supper table?"

"I did." Paddy smiled a near-toothless grin. "She showed ole Anastasia who was boss."

"What did she do?" Ruth asked.

"She saw her coming for her mush, and she bent over and licked her food just like a dog," Paddy replied, mimicking her actions.

Mileta felt her face grow hot. She wasn't used to so much attention, especially for doing something for which her papa would have scolded her.

Mary handed Mileta the stereoscope and turned to the small group. "Anastasia didn't say a word, just wrinkled her nose and left our table alone. We shall all do it from now on."

The group nodded their agreement.

Piano music filled the air, and all the children turned toward the sound. The music surprised her, as she hadn't noticed the piano until now. Mileta cringed as the player plucked at the keys, the broken song echoing against the walls in an out-of-tune jumble. She turned, surprised to see it was Anastasia attempting to play a tune. As she struggled over the piano keys, the girl didn't look so menacing. Maybe that was why Mileta felt compelled to push through the crowd that was now circling the girl and watch as Anastasia's fingers plucked aimlessly at the keyboard.

Taking a deep breath, Mileta approached the bench where Anastasia was sitting. There was a collective gasp when she brazenly took a seat beside her. Anastasia stopped playing and gaped as Mileta motioned toward the keys.

"Please? May I try?" Mileta asked softly.

She released her breath when the girl nodded her assent. Mileta closed her eyes as her fingers danced along the keyboard. As she played, she visualized her mother sitting at the piano playing the same song, "Three Waltzes," by Mary Szymanowska. She knew this tune as well as she knew any song by the composer, as she was her mother's favorite. In Poland, her mother's job had been to teach the piano, something she was starting to do on a limited basis before becoming sick with a racking cough. Mileta had not been able to go with her mother to these jobs, but in their country, her mother gave lessons in their home. Her mother had been so pleased when, at the age of three, Mileta had climbed onto the bench and played the first few notes of this very song. Her mother told her she had an ear for music and began teaching Mileta along with her other students. By age four, Mileta could play the entire song. When she finished her tune, she realized the room had grown quiet, and Anastasia wept silently beside her. Even the mistresses were gathered around the piano, eyes glistening as they stared at her in awe. The woman with the brown curls stood near, smiling and nodding her approval. Her bouncing curls reminded her so much of her mother, Mileta had to look away.

"How did you learn to play so well?" Anastasia asked on a sob.

"My mother taught me. She taught many."

"Will you teach me to play as you do?"

Mileta studied her for a moment. While she had never actually taught anyone before, she had watched her mother many times. Maybe if she agreed to teach Anastasia how to play, then the girl would stop stealing food from her and her friends. She sought Mary out of the crowd. "I will, but in return, we will need something from you."

Anastasia glanced to where Mileta was looking. She saw Mary, then wiped her eyes and nodded in understanding.

The headmistress clapped her hands, and all the children groaned. The boys bade goodbye then walked to the other side of the room, forming a line.

"Where are they going?" Mileta asked as they left.

"Upstairs to their sleeping quarters. They go first, and we will follow shortly. The boys are on the third floor. We are on the second. They take the boys up first and lock the doors so the boys do not sneak down the stairs to our rooms."

This idea seemed strange to Mileta, who'd shared a room with her mother and father in Poland and with nine strangers, both boys and girls, here in America. "Why are they not permitted in our rooms?"

"Sometimes boys do things to girls," Mary said, wrinkling her nose.

"What kind of things?" Mileta pressed.

"Terrible things," Mary said with a glance to Dorthia.

"Not so terrible, sometimes," Dorthia replied.

There was a loud clap of the hands.

"Tis time to line up," Mary said, taking Mileta by the hand and leading her toward the door. "This is the only time we are allowed to be together with the boys. We are even separated by a wall in the play yard. Best you take care around the ones you do not know."

On the second floor, Mileta experienced her first standup shower. It was like standing in the rain, only the water was warm and one did not wear clothes.

She gave a thought to her mother, wishing she could tell her about bathing while standing. With the exception of water closets and the shower rooms, the second floor was open to the sleeping quarters. Rows of single metal beds with crisp white sheets took up the entire room. Mary waved her over when she came into the room.

"Hurry, sit on this bed before one of the mistresses selects another for you," Mary said when she neared. "Tis freshly vacated. Flora went to live with a lady who lives on the east side just this morning. Did you like the water shower?"

Mileta sat her shoes on the floor and placed her day clothes and apron on top of the shoes. "I did. But why make me bathe in the soaking tub when I first arrived if they have showers in which to stand?"

"Tis the bugs. They have to rid you of the wee varmints before we all start scratching. You can always tell the new girls by the hair and the pink skin."

Mary brushed out her long blonde hair. Then, taking three sections, she twisted it into a long braid. She looked up and saw Mileta watching her. "Do not worry; your hair will return fast enough. When it does, it will not itch.”

The lights blinked, sending all the girls rushing to their beds. A minute later, the room went dark. Girls started speaking in low, hushed tones. Mileta pulled the covers up to her chin and felt a tear slide down her cheek. She tried to silence her sobs to no avail.

“What is it?” Mary whispered in the dark.

“I was excited when you said I would have my very own bed. But the truth is, I have never slept in a bed alone before.”

***

There was a rap on Cindy’s door, pulling her out of the story.

Cindy sighed. “Yes?”

The door opened a fraction, and Linda stuck in her head. “I know you said you didn’t want lunch, but it’s after two. Can I fix you a sandwich?”

Cindy checked the notebook and realized she was on the final page. “Sure, Mom. I’ll be out in just a minute.”

When the door shut, she read the last

page of the first notebook.

That first night was the hardest. I was so lonely, I cried and cried until Mary took pity on me and climbed into bed with me. She was a good friend, that one; she possessed an old soul and became the mother to our little group. Even the older children looked to her for advice. I don't know why other than she just had a way of taking charge and nurturing people. With the exception of classroom time, which was Monday through Friday six hours a day, the adults left us alone, preferring to let the older children tend to us younger kids. While they always hovered near, they never stepped in unless a child became unruly and then an adult would intervene with a strap in hand. Most times, that took care of the problem. In the years I was at the asylum, I taught many children to play the piano. Some took to it better than others, but none better than Anastasia. The girl was like a sponge, and as Momma would say, she had an ear for music. She was also older and therefore bigger than most of the children in the orphanage, so after that first day, I was able to pray before eating, and we never had to worry about having food taken from our table again. Other tables were not so lucky. I would not truly call her a friend. I had something she wanted, and so she looked out for me. She and Dorthia, although I never knew why Dorthia took such an interest in me.

The days all blended to become weeks. Weeks became months. Months became years. In that time, I never heard another word from my momma. The orphanage was my home for three and a half years until some of us, my little group included, were picked to ride the Orphan Train one mid-October day in the year nineteen twenty-four.

Cindy closed the notebook and pulled it to her chest with trembling hands. Could this little girl, this Mileta, really be her grandmother? She pictured the old piano that once sat in the front room and was now sitting amongst her grandmother's belongings in the storage unit. It was old and seemed to be in pristine condition, yet she couldn't remember ever hearing her grandmother play. If she was as good as the child in the journal, why not show the world her talent? *Better yet, why not teach her granddaughter how to play?* Her dad had not been interested, but Cindy would have jumped at the chance to learn. She would have jumped at the chance to do anything with the woman in whose home she now lived. She found Mileta's story fascinating and yet until now had never heard of that name. For some reason, that made her angry. Snatching up the notebook, she headed to the kitchen. It was time to let her mother in on what she'd found.

Chapter Nine

Cindy entered the kitchen to find her mom pouring a glass of milk. Linda placed the glass on the table. "Have a seat. I've got you a sandwich already made. Do you want chips?"

"Yes, please." Cindy sat and placed the notebook on the chair beside her. "You don't have to wait on me, you know."

Linda sat the plate in front of her. "Habit. I waited on your father for fifty-three years. Besides, it makes me feel useful."

Cindy plucked a chip into her mouth, savoring its salty crispness. "How is the book you are reading?"

Linda pursed her lips. "I've read better in the tabloid section at the checkout lines. I deleted the whole series before I even got to the third chapter. You look tired. Are you sure the project is worth it?"

Cindy took a bite of her tuna sandwich and considered her words while she chewed. "I'm not researching a project, not one for school anyway."

"Oh?"

"No, I'm reading something that was given to me by a friend." Okay, still not the truth, but Cindy had a new reason for keeping the facts from her mother. She wanted Linda to read the journal with an open mind, and the sad truth was, when it came to Mildred, her mother was anything but open-minded.

Linda frowned. "And you felt you couldn't tell me this?"

"I know how much you enjoy reading. I knew you would want to read it and I wanted to have a go at it first to see if it was worth sharing."

"Well, you're telling me about it now, so that means one of two things. Either it was as bad as the series I started, and you are tossing the whole thing, or it is some juicy stuff, and you are ready to share with your dear old mother."

"Actually, I think it is something you would really enjoy. I don't want to spoil it for you, so I'm not going to tell you what it's about."

The lines near Linda's eyes creased as a smile replaced the frown. "Well, it has to be better than that garbage I just tried to read. So count me in."

Cindy handed Linda the journal, praying she did not recognize her mother-in-law's handwriting. She watched her mom read the first page, sighing when she closed the cover.

"This sounds ominous. I can't wait to get started. Are you sure your friend won't mind if I read it?"

Cindy shook her head. "It's okay. The person who wrote this knows how close we are; I'm pretty sure she knew I would let you read it."

Linda stood and pushed in her chair. "There isn't much to it; it shouldn't take me very long."

"Well, if you like it, there is more. Take your time. I'm just starting the second part, and you can't have it until I am finished reading." Rising from the table, Cindy placed her plate in the dishwasher before following her mom down the hallway, each going into their separate rooms.

Cindy reached into the box and pulled out the next notebook. Unwrapping the tissue, she sat in the recliner, opened up the cover, and was pleased to see the story pick up where it left off.

***

It was a cold, drizzly October day in nineteen hundred and twenty-four when Mileta and a group of children were led out through the iron gates of the place they called home. Mileta heard a noise and looked over her shoulder to see a mingled look of fear and excitement on Ruth's face. It was the first time since Ruth's arrival as an infant that she'd stepped foot outside the main gate. It was that way for most. Though some of the older children were allowed out for additional schooling or jobs, they were required to return at the end of each day. As for Mileta, it was the first time she'd left the asylum grounds since her mother had brought her there just over three years prior. As she followed the line of children out the front gate and down the sidewalk, she craned her neck, hoping that somehow her mother had learned what was taking place and had found a way to come and reclaim her. It wasn't to be. The weather was dreadful, and the streets in front of the home proved mostly deserted.

There were fifty-three children from that asylum chosen to ride what they called the orphan trains that day, including the thirteen friends Mileta had made on the day she arrived. Way too many to place in a motorcar, so someone brought around a large Ford dairy truck, and they all climbed inside the back. The milk urns had been removed for the trip, but spoils of earlier deliveries remained puddled on the wooden floor of the truck bed.

Each orphan carried a suitcase that held a fresh new set of clothes, a gift from a church that took pity on them and wanted to see they got a fresh new start. Each case had the recipient's name—a good thing, as the driver, seeing there wasn't room inside, hefted each bag onto the roof of the truck. It made a terrible bang inside and reduced some of the younger children to tears. While the ride should have been exciting, as most had never ridden in a motor coach, it was, in fact, miserable, as the inside of the cargo section of the truck smelled like sour milk. The children had to stand, as there was not enough room for them all to sit. As they huddled together for warmth, the headmistress stood holding on to a leather strap affixed to the ceiling. As the truck bounced along its way, Mileta recalled the events that had led up to this day.

She, along with the others, were pulled from their daily studies and ushered into the dining hall, where they received a rare treat. Each child enjoyed a glass of cold milk and two sweet cakes that melted in their mouths. Such delicacies were normally only given at their Christmas meal, and even then, they had to rush to eat them so they did not get stolen. This day, the headmistress had stood over them while they ate so there was no fear of anyone taking their food. When they finished, she told them that a train would soon be leaving the city, and as luck would have it, there was room for each of them to ride.

In a rare show of excitement, she smiled and waved her arms, telling the small group that the trains wanted to send some lucky children out west, and their home, along with a few others, had been chosen to relocate children. The headmistress spoke of their plight as if it were the best news any of them could hope for. She told of homes in the country where farmers grew so much food, they would feast at every meal. Of fields so vast, you could run for days and never see another soul. Of small towns where everyone knew each other's names. She sounded like a preacher giving a Sunday sermon. The more she spoke, the more animated she became. For the next three weeks, the children had received special schooling on manners that were supposed to help them get chosen over less polite children with whom they might be traveling.

Mileta trembled. She wasn't sure if it was because the headmistress' words echoed her father's when he spoke of the riches that awaited them in the new country, or if simply chilled from the rain and the damp confines of the truck. Maybe both.

She pulled her overcoat tight to her chest as the truck swayed back and forth, making its way to the train station. The stench inside the truck combined with the movement made her stomach churn.

One of the children, a boy Mileta recognized but whose name she did not know, turned white and lost his breakfast. It soiled his clothes and caused a greater stench than the soured milk. He was pulled from the group by the headmistress as soon as the motor truck reached Grand Central Terminal. She made a great point of saying he would be returning to the asylum with her and telling the rest of them they too would join him if they were to soil their clothing or act out in any way. None of the remaining children wished to return, so they made sure to stay on their best behavior. Most of them hadn't seen, much less been inside, a building as grand as the train station, with its massive ceilings, grand archways, and marble so polished one could easily see their reflection. It is easy to behave when your senses are overloaded with such sights.

Still, a few of the older boys got threatened with the strap for talking too loud. Paddy, who had just turned eleven, was cuffed upside the head for whistling to see if the sound would produce an echo in the great hall. He smiled at Mileta and winked, his way of telling her the risk was worth it.

The children followed two matrons down a long, wide hallway with shops on either side. One of the shops boasted a sign that offered freshly baked lemon pies. They walked through several immense archways and into the largest room Mileta had ever seen. The massive windows were also arched and would have let in streams of sunlight if only it hadn't been raining. Wet shoes squeaked on the marble floors as the children followed in single file, stopping when they reached a wide staircase. Soon their little procession was joined by three additional groups of children of all ages, including infants, until their small group of fifty-two had nearly quadrupled in size. A low murmur spread through the cluster as children began speaking in hushed tones. A few of the children met up with friends they'd made on the streets, and in one instance, three brothers that had been separated for two years found themselves suddenly reunited.

Mileta's group of friends stood close together while some of the other children huddled on the floor next to the stairs. The train station was a bustle of activity as families hurried past on their way to and from the trains. Hordes of people chatted as they hurried to their destination. Several children ran through the grand lobby laughing while an older child raced ahead, enticing them with a red ribbon tied to a stick.

Mileta stared at them, waiting for someone to scold or discipline them for being so rambunctious, yet no one seemed to notice their exploits. Three inquisitive children wandered over to where the orphans waited. The children stopped to stare, only to have their mothers pull them away, whispering in hushed tones. For the first time since leaving the asylum, Mileta yearned for the safety of the metal gates. At least in the home, Mileta felt a small sense of belonging.

"They think their children will catch something from us," Mary whispered over Mileta's shoulder.

Mileta sighed. "I know."

Mary nodded toward the newly reunited brothers. "I fear their joy won't last."

Mileta looked to where the boys were gleefully chatting away, each telling what had transpired since they'd last seen the other. "How do you mean?"

"People will be hard pressed to take in

three scrawny waifs, do you not think? Look how big they are. Surely they would eat everything the farmers grow."

Mileta shivered as a tear slid down Mary's cheek.

"What troubles you, Mary?"

Mary, normally the one to hold everyone together, began to sob. "Tis not only the brothers who will have their hearts torn away. I cannot imagine my life without you or the others," she said, looking at their little group.

The others had been listening, but it was Ruth that spoke up. "What do you mean without us? Are we not all going away on the same train?"

"Didn't you hear what the headmistress said? We are all going to be adopted," Slim chided.

"Yes, she said all of us," Ruth agreed.

"But not by the same family," Slim said, shaking his head.

Ruth grew pale, and Dorthia moved beside her. "Don't you get sick. Remember what happened to the boy on the truck."

"Yes, we all need to be calm," Mary said, wiping her eyes. "The last thing we need to do is give them a reason to send us back."

Iris' eyes grew wide. " I'm not going back to that old place."

"Not now that Anastasia's going to be one of the matrons," Paddy agreed. "Although I have to admit, she's not been so bad since Mileta showed up."

Mary smiled. "That is because Mileta gave her a purpose. Anastasia plays the piano almost as beautifully as Mileta does. We should all be so lucky to find someone who would make us feel good about ourselves."

Mileta felt herself blush at the compliment.

"I can't believe we won't be staying together," Henrietta sobbed. "You are all the only family I've ever known. How will I know what has happened to each of you?"

The small group grew quiet, each child contemplating that question. It was Paddy who finally spoke up. "When I grow up, I shall put an advert in the paper and find you."

Mary's face grew hopeful. "But what paper, and how will we know tis you?"

"I will put it in every paper, in every city. It will be a grand advert that says we rode the train and I am looking for my brothers and sisters. I shall sign it with my name. When you see that, you will know it is I," Paddy said, looking directly at Mileta.

Gideon smiled. It was no secret Paddy was smitten with her. "And then we can meet one day. We shall all have lemon pie and talk of our lives."

"Do you even like lemon pie?" Shorty asked.

Gideon thought about this for a second. "I don't know, I've never tried it."

And with that, the small group erupted in laughter.

"Silence!" a portly matron from one of the other asylums said with a clap of the hands. "Have you children forgotten what you were told about being disruptive?"

"No, ma'am," Levi said, speaking for his friends. "We are sorry, ma'am. We just have so much joy in our hearts this day. Thank you for choosing us to go out into the world and find ourselves grand new homes."

"Hmp," the woman said, eyeing him closely. "You are a slick one, aren't you, son? I best be keeping a close eye on the likes of you. Now it is time to board the train; you will each follow and remain silent. It is not too late to return you to your asylums, where you will remain until you reach an age to be legally released."

That last statement was enough to ensure silence while walking to and boarding the train. Mileta followed in line behind the other children, suitcase in hand. One by one, she watched her friends climb the steps to board the car. Mary handed her suitcase to the baggage attendant, then stepped up to board. Mileta switched her suitcase to the other hand and started to follow. A train attendant took hold of her arm.

"This car is full; you will have to move to the next," he said, pointing at the next car in line.

Mileta froze. Over a hundred children, including all of her friends, had already boarded the car in front of her.

"Oh, please won't you let her on," Mary pleaded from the doorway.

"No room," the man said and closed the door in Mary's face.

Mileta fought back the tears as she turned and walked to the next car. She glanced at the windows as she passed. It seemed as if each window held a familiar face: Gideon, Cecil, Geo in one; Slim, Henrietta, Emma, and Esther in another. Two additional steps and she saw Levi, Dorthia, and Iris. The last window nearly broke her heart; Ruth bent over with her face in her hands. Mileta didn't have to see her eyes to know the girl was sobbing. Hovering over Ruth with a look of panic she'd not seen before was Paddy, impossible to miss with his brilliant red hair. He placed a hand on the window as if reaching for her. She smiled, and he returned the smile with trembling lips.

"Come on then, on with you," an agent that had arrived with one of the other groups fussed. "When you get on board, move to the front and take the first empty seat."

Mileta sniffed and moved to the next cabin. She gave her suitcase to the attendant and boarded the train, moving to the front of the train as instructed. The first empty seat was three rows back. A sour-faced woman sat next to the window. She looked to be as round as she was tall and wore a long coat covered with silver fur. The ends of the sleeves and collar were darker and fuller than the rest of the coat, which shimmered when she moved. A thin man in a dark suit and overcoat sat in the middle. He was engrossed in the newspaper and didn't bother to look up as Mileta took the empty seat beside him. Mileta could hear whispers as children took up seats behind her. Someone kicked the seat of the sour-faced woman, who stood and glared her displeasure.

"I'm sorry, ma'am," came a small voice from behind.

"See it does not happen again, or I'll have you moved to the baggage compartment," the woman replied gruffly. "We should be in a cabin car, Stewart, not in the back of the train with the likes of these ruffians."

The man lowered his newspaper. "It was your idea to head home early. If we had waited until tomorrow, they could have added another car."

The woman brushed at the fur on her coat. "I got what I came for; there was no need to stay any longer."

"Unless you wish to reconsider, we will just have to make do with the commoners," he said and winked at Mileta.

The woman turned her attention to Mileta. "I trust we will not have a problem with you."

"No, ma'am," Mileta replied.

"She will be fine, dear."

"Street urchins," the woman mumbled under her breath. "Probably crawling with lice."

The man peered at Mileta. "Do you have any bugs?"

Mileta swallowed. "Not in over three years."

"There. You see, dear, nothing to worry about. You probably don't even live on the street now, do you."

"No, sir, I have never lived on the street. I came from the asylum."

"And where would you be going on this fine day?"

Mileta looked out the window to see if the rain had stopped, something impossible to determine since the terminal was enclosed. "We are going west to find a home."

"Ah, yes, the orphans. I was just this moment reading an article about you."

Mileta blinked her surprise. "About me?"

The man laughed. "Well, not you exactly. The article said the trains would be taking a large group of orphans out of the city today. Said they are going to find you good homes where you can grow up to be good, upstanding citizens. It said you will get a nice home and can help with the family chores to help you earn your keep."

His comment seemed to pique the interest of the woman sitting beside him. "Let me see that article."

The man handed her the paper and pointed to the article. As she read, he turned to Mileta, "Now we've gone and done it; by the end of the trip, she'll have me convinced to bring you home with us. Now wouldn't that be just awful?"

Mileta felt her stomach flip. She wasn't sure what she'd been expecting by way of parents, but this couple was not it. While the man seemed pleasant enough, the woman sitting beside him frightened her to no end.

Chapter Ten

As the morning wore on, the rain ebbed and the skies cleared. Mileta's seatmates had bombarded her with questions about her family and how she had come to be an orphan. She told them she was not a true orphan, as her mother was still alive. If they were surprised that her mother had abandoned her, they did not show it. She remained closed-lipped about any other details concerning her mother; even though it had been over three years, the pain of her leaving her at the asylum was still too great. She spoke of how they had come to be in America, and how her father had not lived to see what he had called a great new land. She didn't bother to tell them that, at the mature age of eleven, she had yet to see what was so great about it. She was afraid they might scold her if she appeared ungrateful.

Even though her destiny remained uncertain, Mileta felt a surge of excitement each time the train whistle blew. Inside the car was not heated; the air was as cool as it was loud. Still, with each passing mile, Mileta grew a bit more hopeful.

The man who shared her row of seats introduced him and his wife as Mr. and Mrs. Shively, and after whispering to his wife, excused himself to stretch his legs. Within seconds of his leaving, Mrs. Shively fell asleep with her head against the window. How the woman could sleep when there was so much to see, Mileta did not know.

Mileta, on the other hand, didn't want to miss a thing. She sat forward in her seat and craned her neck, trying to take in as much of the passing countryside as possible. She could not remember ever seeing so much open space that went on and on without as much as a house or building to mar the landscape. And forest after forest of trees, some of them as tall as buildings. Mileta wished her father and mother could see this, a thought that brought with it a familiar wave of sadness.

The children that accompanied her murmured with excited chatter as one child after another called out something he or she had seen. A horse. A pasture full of cows. An animal most had never seen, later determined to be a deer, caused quite the buzz.

A pumpkin farm created so much excitement the agent traveling with them had to remind the children to lower their voices. Pointless, really, as the noise generated by the train was much greater than the commotion caused by the children. Mileta decided Mrs. Shively must have seen everything in her lifetime, for surely that was the only reason the woman could sleep so soundly.

Mileta felt someone kick her seat and looked up just in time to see the boy sitting behind her brush past. There was a loud noise as the door to the train car opened and the boy disappeared into the other car. The door closed behind him, dampening the rush of air as it slid shut. It was the third time he'd wandered from their car, supposedly making his way to the privy, which was located in the car ahead of them. Mileta herself had gone once, a nearly terrifying experience since the privy was nothing more than a closet with a hole cut in the bottom floor of the train. She thought of the few houses along the train's path and wondered if persons living near the tracks ever saw what the train left in its wake.

The connecting door opened once more, and Mr. Shively returned to his seat, using caution as not to wake his wife. "I have good news," he said in hushed tones.

Mileta raised her eyes in question.

"I spoke to one of your chaperones in the next car. I told her Mrs. Shively and I are interested in adopting you. She was hesitant at first, but I offered her a donation to her asylum. She was extremely receptive and has agreed to allow you to come and live with Mrs. Shively and me. You would like that, wouldn't you?"

Mileta looked past Mr. Shively to the woman seated next to him, mouth hanging open as she slept, allowing a trickle of drool to dribble down her chin. "I...I guess so."

Mr. Shively noticed her hesitation and slid a glance toward his wife.

"Yes, well, never you mind about her; she will not trouble you much. I'll see to that as long as you and I get along." He placed his hand upon Mileta's thigh and smiled.

Mileta swallowed. Before she could react, the door to the forward train car opened and the boy that had exited moments earlier stepped through.

An older boy, he had come in with one of the later groups that had joined them in the train station. His hair, mussed from the wind between the train cars, swept forward over his deeply tanned face. He brushed the locks aside; his thick eyebrows narrowed as his gaze drifted to the hand on Mileta's thigh. His nostrils flared as his eyes narrowed. The boy took a step forward, and Mr. Shively hastily removed his hand.

The door to the front of the cabin opened, and a train agent stepped through. The agent placed a hand on the boy's shoulder, and the boy turned toward him, hand fisted.

"Easy there, lad, I didn't mean to startle you," the agent said, releasing the boy. "Have a seat there now; I have an announcement to make."

The boy glared at Mr. Shively, then returned to his seat without a word.

The agent inhaled his breath and bellowed for all to hear. "I just came through to tell you, folks; we will be stopping in Syracuse shortly for a water stop. We have to replace the water so the engines can make steam. They are also going to replace a hose that seems to be having an issue, so it will be a slightly longer stop than before. We will be idle for approximately twenty-two minutes for those of you who would like to stretch your legs. No need to worry about the extra time, as we should be able to give her a little kick and make it to our next stop right on time."

The agent moved past where Mileta was sitting before adding, "Remember, only twenty-two minutes, so back to the train as soon as you hear the first whistle."

The moment the agent moved to the next car, the buzz of the children increased.

Mrs. Shively opened her eyes and rolled her neck. "What on earth is all the commotion about?"

"Nothing to fret about, my dear. The train is making a stop to refill the water for steam. It seems as though we will be stopped a bit longer than expected, so the children are excited to explore."

Mrs. Shively sat up, wiped the drool from her chin with the back of her hand, and fluffed the fur on her sleeves. "Well, I should hope they have a mercantile nearby. I would like to find a proper privy. Do chat with the train agent and see that we get off the train first. I shan't wish to have to wait for the urchins to finish before I have my turn."

"I'm sure they will give the paying customers consideration," Mr. Shively assured her. "Now, remember that matter we discussed before you fell asleep?"

Mrs. Shively's eyes grew bright as she slid a glance to Mileta. "I most certainly do."

"Well, I spoke with the guardian in charge of Mileta here, and she has agreed to let the girl come home with us. There will be a few papers to sign, but that is just a formality."

The woman's mouth curved upwards. "And she will be ours to do with as we please?"

Her husband nodded.

The woman's eyes twinkled. "The paper said we need not adopt her. We must merely agree to provide the basic necessities for her and she, in turn, must work off our kindness. I've always wanted a servant girl. Who knows, if this one works out, maybe we shall send word for more. Just think of the possibilities, Stewart."

The man's smile increased. "Oh, I am, my dear."

Mrs. Shively frowned. "I would be willing to take on more girls if only we didn't have to have them all underfoot."

"We could convert one of the outbuildings into sleeping quarters," Mr. Shively offered after a moment's consideration. "And don't you worry about a thing, my dear, I would take it upon myself to go out and check on them from time to time."

As the couple conspired, Mileta's heart sank. This wasn't at all what the headmistress had promised. She had promised them new mothers and fathers who would love them and take care of them. These people were already speaking about her as if she were not even there. They didn't want a daughter; they wanted a servant girl, and not just any servant girl. They had chosen her. While she knew she was supposed to be happy about being the first one chosen, she was dreading going home with these people and further dreading the life they promised. The train whistle sounded the impending stop. As the train slowed, growing unease replaced Mileta's excitement. She did not like this couple, nor did she feel pleased she would be going home with them. The woman looked at her oddly, and the man, while he seemed nice enough, there was something about him that worried her. Maybe it was the way the boy had glared at him when he saw him touching her leg. *Why had he touched her there anyway?* Mary had warned her that boys would do things to girls they should not do. *Did this include grown men as well?* The only grown man she'd ever had dealings with was her father, and he had never touched her there. *Was Mary talking about them touching her leg?* Mileta didn't know, but she planned on asking her when they stopped at the water station.

As the train pulled into a station, Mrs. Shively pointed out the window. "Oh, look, Stewart, there is a mercantile. It is small, but I should be able to find us something to eat."

"We shall be having supper in the dining car soon," Mr. Shively reminded her.

Mrs. Shively shrugged off his comment. "Well, I am hungry now, so I will see what I can find to hold us until then."

The train eased to a halt, and the children all sprang from their seats, Mileta included.

"Not so fast, children," the agent said with a clap of the hands. "We will not be heading into the mercantile."

Her words sent groans of disappointment throughout the car.

Another clap silenced the children. "Now, now, none of that. We will gather on the lawn with the children from the other car, where we will all enjoy bread and honey."

Mileta's tension eased. Not only would she be able to speak with Mary, but it had been years since she'd tasted honey. Her mouth watered at the thought of the golden sweetness. She stood and started toward the back of the car. Before she could follow the others, Mr. Shively placed a hand upon her shoulder.

"This way, Mileta. You belong to us now. Let's go see what kind of goodies the mercantile has to offer," he said, leading her in the opposite direction.

Mileta's eyes filled with tears as she followed the Shivelys toward the front of the train. She stepped through the center connection and turned to look behind. Standing in the passageway at the rear of the train stood the boy with the dark hooded eyes. There was something in the way he looked in her direction, a mixture of anger and something else she'd never seen before that sent chills through her. Their eyes met, and the boy stepped forward as if willing her to break free. As if sensing her indecision, the hand that held her increased its hold, pulling her forward to the prison that was to be her new life.

Chapter Eleven

As soon as they stepped off the train, Mr. Shively excused himself to smoke a cigar.

Upon entering the store, Mileta learned "mercantile" was just a fancy term for a country store. The store was small, the shelves fully stocked with sacks of flour, beans, coffee, and other items one would expect. There were baskets of fresh bread, boiled eggs, and a barrel-shaped jar of large dill pickles that made Mileta's mouth water. She had not seen a pickle in years. She saw a wooden bin overflowing with large red apples and sighed. The counter to her right held several rows of jars, each stocked full of colorful candy. Mileta longed to taste something sweet, but she had no money and dared not ask for such trivial indulgences. Instead, she waited without speaking while Mrs. Shively purchased three boiled eggs, a small loaf of bread, and two hunks of cheese. As the merchant wrapped the eggs, Mileta wandered to a table with rows of colorful fabric.

"Mind your manners, girl," Mrs. Shively said as Mileta reached to touch one.

"They are on sale," the merchant said, eyeing Mileta's appearance.

"The girl will be getting a proper uniform when we get back to Chicago," Mrs. Shively said and placed a dime on the counter.

The merchant picked up the coin and put it in the till. "Oh?"

"Heavens, yes, I could not have her running around the house in those rags she is wearing, could I? Lord have mercy, what would the neighbors think."

"Indeed. I take it the girl's not your daughter, then?"

Mrs. Shively pulled herself taller, which was difficult to do at her height. "Hmph, I dare say not. She is one of those orphans out of New York City. You should have seen them running the streets begging for food and stealing money. You go there, you better watch your pockets or they will be picked clean."

Several women were milling around

the fabric table and listening to the conversation at hand. Looking down their noses, they clutched their purses and moved away from Mileta.

"You dare say," the merchant said, eyeing Mileta.

Mrs. Shively nodded. "I do, and those urchins are free for the taking. I tell you, I am simply doing my basic duty and helping the poor child out."

The merchant nodded his head. "Well, she best be thanking her lucky stars a woman of your obvious stature has taken pity on her."

"Yes indeed," Mrs. Shively replied, looking pleased.

The door opened, and Mr. Shively stuck his head in and looked around. He had his pocket watch in his hand and held it out for them to see. "Ready, Sonia? They will be sounding the whistle momentarily."

Mrs. Shively picked up her purchase and bade the shop owner farewell. "Coming out now, Stewart."

Mileta dragged her feet as she followed. The colorful sights and inviting smells inside the store did little to ease her dire mood. It didn't help that the adults spoke about her as if she were not even there. And to be so hateful. Sure, there were kids that would do the things she said and more. However, she was not one of them. As they exited the store, she could see the other children sitting on the grass, smiling and enjoying their lunch. A few boys wrestled amongst freshly fallen leaves.

Mrs. Shively shook her head. "Heathens; just look at the way they are wallowing around on the ground like hogs."

Mr. Shively gave Mileta a nudge. "Come along now, girl, no dawdling. You are not a part of that group anymore."

She saw her friends huddled together. The boy that sat behind her was with them. The group all turned to stare, but none called out to her. What he said was true; her friends had already replaced her. Her mood darkened as she followed her new guardians to the train.

"Here, girl," the woman said once they were seated. She handed Mileta a hardboiled egg, then pulled a cloth from her pocket and handed it to Mileta. "Place the napkin on your lap and use it for the eggshells."

Mrs. Shively handed her husband an egg, half of the bread, and one of the two hunks of cheese. She placed the rest of the bread, the second hunk of cheese, and the last egg in her own lap.

Mileta had not eaten a fresh egg since she'd left Poland. She knew she should be thrilled to have something so extravagant. Instead, her sour mood deepened as she took her time peeling the shell.

The train whistle blared its impending departure. Within seconds, the car was alive with excited voices as everyone made their way back to their seats.

"Do be careful there," Mr. Shively reprimanded over his shoulder when someone bumped into the back of his chair.

Mileta smiled, fairly certain she knew who that someone was. Her smile waned as she remembered it was he who had taken her spot among her friends.

"Heathens, all of them," Mrs. Shively uttered once more.

The whistle sounded its second warning.

"All aboard," a man's voice called from somewhere outside the train.

Mileta looked towards the window and

gasped, surprised to see a man at their level cleaning the pane.

Mr. Shively looked at the window. "It is done anytime the train stops for any length of time. The glass gets filthy with the smoke and oil off the engine."

"Stewart, leave the girl alone so she can eat her egg. I want the cabin agent to collect the eggshells before the girl makes a mess. It wouldn't do to have those shells underfoot now, would it?"

I am not a baby, and my name is not "girl." She was about to open her mouth to say just that when she had a better idea. She peeled the last of her egg, plopped the entire thing into her mouth, and proceeded to chew.

"Mmm, this is so good. I have not had eggs in so long." As she spoke, large bits of egg dropped onto the front of her coat and settled into her lap. Pretending to clean up the mess, she lifted the napkin, sending shells and egg parts flying.

Mr. Shively pushed back in his seat in an attempt to avoid being pelted with egg remnants. While he managed to avoid the mess, his wife was not as fortunate. Pieces of chewed egg landed on her coat and mingled with the fur.

Mrs. Shively jumped from her seat, her crimson face a strong contrast to the silver fur on the coat. "Why you wicked little street urchin! Look what you've done to my new coat. I traveled all the way to New York just to purchase it from Russeks on 5th Avenue. Do you have any idea how much this cost me?"

Mr. Shively stood and made a vain attempt of removing the egg from the fur.

Mileta was suddenly regretting her actions. She'd never purchased a coat before. In truth, she'd never purchased anything. Of course, she had no clue how much the coat cost, but Mrs. Shively seemed so angry, and she had asked Mileta a question. Obviously, she expected an answer. She remembered what Esther had said about selling flowers. She'd earned six pennies a day, eight on Sunday. Since it wasn't Sunday, the coat probably didn't cost as much, but then again, it was a coat and not a flower, and Mrs. Shively did seem pretty upset, so Mileta decided to go with a higher number. "Nine pennies?"

Apparently, that was not the correct answer, as Mrs. Shively began to tremble and Mr. Shively stared at her, mouth agape. Laughter erupted from the seat behind them.

"There, there, dear, we will get it cleaned as soon as we get home. Let's all calm down now. It appears we are making a scene."

Mr. Shively glared over the seat, and the laughter stopped.

Mrs. Shively collected herself and sat once more. She looked at Mileta, eyes narrowed, then turned her glare to her husband. "If this acquisition is going to take place, I will expect you to teach this girl some manners."

He looked at Mileta and smiled. "Don't worry, Sonia, I plan on teaching Mileta everything she needs to know."

The headmistress said the children would be sent to school, so maybe living with them wouldn't be so bad, especially if they were planning on teaching her things. As the train continued on its way, Mileta wondered if she'd been wrong about the couple.

As the day progressed, children started making their way to the forward privy. More than once, Mileta recognized one of the children, but thus far, no one from her group had ventured forward.

Then suddenly, Mary was standing next to her seat.

"Oh, Mileta," Mary said in an excited tone that could be heard but would not merit a warning from the agent in the back of the train car. "I just heard you are to be adopted. We are all so very happy for you. Tis must be your new family."

Mileta nodded her head.

"Oh, and what a nice-looking family and they appear to be so well-to-do. I must say you are a lucky one. And they not caring about your affliction. We should all be so lucky," Mary said sweetly.

Mrs. Shively leaned forward. "And just what affliction would that be, girl?"

Mileta blinked her confusion. She had absolutely no clue what Mary was talking about.

"Oh, my. I'm dreadfully sorry, Mileta. I should have simply wished you your happiness and been on my way. It is just that I thought you had told them that you soil your bed each night. Since this family appeared not to care, it gave the rest of us hope that we too could go to a nice home."

Mileta was mortified. She hadn't wet herself since she'd been a wee baby. Why Mary would spread such lies was beyond her. She opened her mouth to call Mary a liar when her friend stopped her.

"Oh, don't be mad at me, Mileta. I'm sure your new family will not mind. You hide it so well, and the stench is not all that bad. Why, we never hardly notice it anymore." She leaned in and sniffed. "There, see, I can barely smell you today. Then again, it might be because you had a rain bath and dressed in clean clothes this morning."

Mileta could not believe her ears, and here she thought Mary was her friend. Never had Mary spoken so unkindly of her. If she didn't stop, the Shivelys would not wish to…wait, was this what Mary was doing, trying to keep them from taking Mileta home with them? But how did she know? It was then she remembered seeing the boy standing near her friends, all of them staring as she passed by. Mileta slid a side glance at Mary, who gave the slightest of nods.

Mileta smiled, then stuck her finger in her nose. She rooted around for a second, removed it to study the digit, and then wiped the finger on the hem of her dress.

Mary raised her hand to her scalp and scratched her head, then made a show of scratching her arms and legs for good measure. "Oh, Mileta, how did you get so lucky to find a home when you do such silly things?"

Mrs. Shively sucked in her breath. "Get out of here! Both of you are nothing but filthy, lice-infested heathens! I will not have you, any of you, in my home! I would rather pay five cents a day to have my house cleaned by a housemaid than to deal with the likes of you! Be gone!"

"Come now, Mileta, don't be mad at me. I thought you had told them of your affliction," Mary said, grabbing Mileta's hand and all but pulling her from her seat.

As they passed the seat behind them, the boy winked at Mileta. Mileta smiled her gratitude.

***

Cindy placed a hand to her chest and realized her heart was racing. She set down the notebook and took a breath. It was only when she stretched her fingers that she realized she must have been gripping the notebook. How could people be so cruel, and how fortunate her grandmother didn't get adopted by that horrible couple. She picked up an ink pen and jotted the couple's names onto a notepad. One of the teachers had a brother that was into genealogy. She was going to see if he could dig up anything on this couple for no other reason than to see if they ever ended up adopting any children.

There was a light rap on her door.

"Come in," Cindy said, lowering the pen.

"I just finished."

"And, did you like it?"

"Like it? I loved it. Your friend is a great storyteller." Linda handed her the notebook and looked at the one Cindy had just finished. "Are you almost done?"

Cindy considered telling her mother who wrote the story but decided to wait and let her find out for herself. She handed her mother the second notebook. "I just finished. I think I am going to start on the next one, unless you need anything."

Linda laughed and clutched the journal to her chest. "The only thing I need is to get my hands on this.”

Linda was halfway out the door when Cindy stopped her.

“Mom.”

“Yes?”

“This one gets a bit intense, but keep reading. Things work out.”

“Don’t you say another word. I want to find out what happens to this sweet little girl,” Linda said and left the room.

A frown creased Cindy’s brow as she unwrapped the third notebook. “So do I, Mom. So do I.”

Chapter Twelve

Mileta sat next to Mary, and the two talked until well into the night. After darkness took hold and the others drifted off to sleep, Mary had told Mileta things that made her skin crawl. Things that boys and men did that weren't always nice. When Mileta asked Mary how she knew such things, Mary had grown silent.

As the sun lifted, the children ate a morning meal of cheese and crackers, finishing shortly before the train pulled into Detroit. The children were quickly ushered to a large empty room in Michigan's Central Station to change out of their travel gear and into the new outfit each brought for the occasion. The boys and girls had been sectioned off by sheets with the agents inspecting their appearance and the older children helping the younger ones dress. As each child finished, they were allowed to gather in the open space on the other side of the room.

Upon opening her suitcase, Mileta marveled at the new pale pink dress with flowers embroidered around the sleeves and hem. A paper was attached to the fabric at the waist with a large safety pin. A frown flitted across her face as she read the note, a few short words that in essence stated she was free to be adopted. She pulled the dress over her head and marveled at the color. She hadn't worn anything this nice since leaving her home in Poland. As she ran a brush through the length of her hair, she wondered what her papa would have thought of her current predicament. He had been excited when he learned they gave away free land. Would he have been as excited to learn they gave away children as well? His child? She didn't think so.

While she loved the new dress, the sleeves were short and the fabric much too flimsy for the coolness of the room. She considered the overcoat she'd worn on the train. While it would add warmth, it was filthy from the long train ride. Deciding against the risk of spoiling her new dress, she crammed the coat into the suitcase with the travel clothes she'd just removed.

She pulled her long hair back and placed the matching pink bonnet on her head to keep it in place.

Shivering, Mileta looked around the room, astonished at all the lovely colors. It was the first time since arriving at the asylum the children were not all dressed the same. The boys had on dark suits and knicker pants that stopped at the knee. Long black socks and black shoes completed the outfit. The girls each wore a bright new dress and matching bonnet. Mary wore a light blue dress that matched the color of her eyes. Mileta waved to get her attention, and Mary hurried to where she was standing.

Ruth joined them a few seconds later. She was wearing a long-sleeved burgundy dress with matching bonnet. She pulled at the paper pinned to her dress and frowned. "Why do we have papers on our beautiful dresses?"

Mary smiled and straightened Ruth's bonnet. "We all have them. They tell our story."

Ruth pointed to Mary's note. "What does it say?"

"It says, Mary Faulkner. Relinquished

December 25th, 1919. Date of birth, January 8th, 1914.”

Ruth's eyebrows scrunched together. “What does 'relinquished' mean?”

Mary leveled her chin. “It means my mother did not want me anymore.”

“And mine? What does it say?”

Mary smiled. “It says you are very special. That you arrived as a baby and that you need a wonderful home, as you never knew your mother.”

Ruth looked at Mileta. “Does it truly say all of that?”

Mileta met Mary's eyes. Obviously, the older girl didn't have the heart to tell the child that the note simply read *Mother died in childbirth, father unknown. Date of birth, March 6th, 1918.*

Ruth nodded her head. “What does Mileta's say?”

Mary looked at the note on Mileta's dress. “It says Mileta (Unknown). Abandoned October, 1921.”

Ruth's face screwed up. “What does it mean?”

Mileta traced the words with her fingers. “It means I only have one name and the only thing they know about me is my mother did not want me."

Ruth thought about that for a moment. "Don't worry, Mileta; you will get new parents who will love you. We all will."

Mary nudged Mileta's arm. "Here come the others."

The others being the rest of their little group, plus the boy who'd sat behind her in the first train car. While she hadn't spoken with him, Mileta now knew his name—Tobias—and that he was the one who'd approached Mary and helped to form the plan of keeping her from going home with the Shivelys. As the kids approached, they all chatted and compared the notes on their clothing. Tobias was the only one of their group not wearing a note. She studied him, wondering if he had dared to take it off. Somehow she thought him the type who would rebel.

Tobias noticed her staring and winked.

Mileta ran her hands along her bare arms to combat the chill.

Tobias moved closer to her. He had a couple of years on her and was at least a head taller. He regarded her and shook his head. "That is the poorest excuse of a dress I ever saw."

Mileta looked down at her new pink dress, surprised at his words. Sure it was probably best suited for summer, but it was pretty. "You don't like my dress?"

Paddy took a step forward. "Don't you listen to him, Mileta. There is nothing wrong with your dress."

Tobias waved him off. "There is nothing wrong with the dress. The girl wears it just fine, except for the fact she is freezing to death. Damn do-gooders. If they weren't going to give her a proper dress, the least they could do is to give her a coat."

Paddy eased his stance. "You don't have a coat, Mileta?"

She smiled at him. "I do, but it is an old one and filthy from the train. This dress is so pretty, I didn't want to soil it."

Tobias shook his head. "Don't be daft, girl. You end up catching a cold, and they are going to send you back to the asylum. The people out there don't mind taking in a healthy kid, but you let on that you are sick, and they will wash their hands of you real quick."

The younger kids hung on to Tobias' words, listening and taking mental notes.

Ruth looked like a girl who'd just found the boy she would marry, round eyes blinking, hanging on every word. "Boy, Tobias, how did you get so smart?"

Tobias laughed. "You don't get to be fourteen years old without learning a thing or two. Besides, this is not my first train ride."

There was a collective gasp amongst the group.

"You've ridden the train before?" Slim asked.

Tobias nodded.

"And you never got adopted?" Emma and Geo asked at the same time.

"Sure I have, but like I told you, do something they don't like, and they will send you back."

"What did you do?" Esther asked.

Shorty pointed at Tobias' jacket. "Why don't you have a note?"

"Yes, you don't have a note," Gideon agreed.

Mary stepped closer to Tobias and addressed the small group. "Please stop. There is no need to gang up on the boy. He helped one of us, and suddenly, you are treating him like some kind of criminal."

"Well, he was sent back twice," Cecil reminded her.

Mileta moved to his other side. "Probably through no fault of his own. And Mary is right. If he hadn't helped, I would be on my way to Chicago with that dreadful couple."

The conversation stopped when Dorthia joined the group, a toddler resting on her left hip.

Mary was the first to break the silence. "There you are. I was getting worried about you. Who do you have there?"

"Since I am older, the agents made me help with the little ones. This is Louie; he is not yet a year. Miss Agana told me I am to take care of him until one of us finds a home."

Louie stuck his thumb into his mouth and leaned into Dorthia's shoulder, watching them.

"Who is Miss Agana?" Mileta asked.

"She is an agent from one of the other groups. She's rather brisk… Oh gracious, here she comes now. She is the tall one that looks like the wind could blow her over."

The agents moved to the center of the room, clapping their hands to gain attention. The agents stopped, each extending a finger to their lips to shush the children. The room went silent in an instant, the group eager to hear what was coming next.

"For those that do not know me, I am Miss Agana. Today is the day you have all been waiting for. Just outside those doors," she said with an exaggerated sweep of the hands, "is a horde of people willing to offer the majority of you a home. An agent from my very establishment traveled this way just a few short weeks ago, spreading the word that you children would soon be on your way."

She held out a sheet of paper. Irrelevant, as the majority of children in attendance could not read. "The agent posted notices such as this asking families to open their homes to give a child such as yourself a fresh new start. He told everyone that would listen about you and asked them to spread the word to their neighbors and family. When he finished, he then went to the churches and spoke with pastors, priests, and clergymen. Together they prayed for each of you to find a good, honorable home that will take you in, teach you a trade, and make sure you all become fine, upstanding citizens in the community. And their prayers were answered. People came forward asking about the children that would soon come. So the heads of the churches and communities were asked to see to the good moral standing of the families who wish to adopt you."

"Yeah, and those who weren't considered fine and upstanding could just bribe their way," Tobias said with a nod toward Mileta.

"Not everyone will be adopted today." Miss Agana glared at Tobias then continued her speech. "Maybe some won't get adopted at all."

"But what if we don't get adopted today?" Ruth asked.

"Those children who are not adopted today will continue on to other stops. If at the end of our journey there are any children left," she paused once more, eyeing Tobias pointedly, "you will go back to New York and return to your home."

"At least I will have gotten another free train ride." Tobias laughed.

"Tobias!" Mileta said, grabbing his arm. "Are you trying to get sent back?"

"It's just a matter of time," he said wistfully.

Miss Agana turned to one of the other agents and pointed a slender finger at Tobias. "Which group is he with?"

The matron agent leaned forward and whispered something in Miss Agana's ear. Miss Agana leveled her eyes in their direction. "Yes, well, take him away. I will deal with the likes of him later."

Mileta stepped forward, blocking his way. "Please, he does not mean the things he says. He is scared. We all are, only he is too proud to show it. Please give him another chance. I am sure he is sorry for what he said. Tell them, Tobias."

Tobias studied her for a good minute before letting his shoulders fall. Looking past Mileta to Miss Agana, he took off his hat and lowered his eyes. "Yes, ma'am, I am sorry."

The tall woman sized him up. "I'm not sure if you are truly sorry or if you are merely playing the part, but I will allow you to stay. Boys like you are usually picked rather quickly as long as you can keep your disrespectful mouth closed. As for the rest of you children, do not let this boy influence you. If you want to find a good home, mind your mouth and remember your manners. In a few short moments, we will all move into the main station area. When we do, I expect you, all of you, to be on your best behavior. Remember to smile and be pleasant. And, if you have a special talent, you might want to mention that when the families are looking you over."

The doors swung open and the children funneled through the opening, all vying to see what was awaiting them on the other side. In the process, Mileta lost sight of those she knew best, the small group of children who in the last three years had become her family.

Chapter Thirteen

Mileta stared at the crowd of people that stood gaping at the throng of children. She'd seen a circus once before leaving her country. She and her parents had arrived early and approached the cages, staring and pointing at the inhabitants. This was much like that day, only now she was the one on display. She and at least a hundred others.

The children were fidgeting as Miss Agana spoke to the crowd, giving a similar speech as was delivered to the children only a few moments earlier. As she spoke, prospective adopters craned their necks to get a better look at the children.

Miss Agana wore a black suit coat that stopped at the waist of her long black skirt, the length of her blonde hair pinned to the back of her head in a tight bun. Round black spectacles sat near the bridge of her nose, lending to a no-nonsense look. Pushing back her spectacles, she raised her voice to be heard above the murmurs. "You do not need to adopt the child you choose. You merely have to provide for your charges in sickness and in health."

"I don't aim to take in no sickly child," a man shouted from the crowd.

As if on cue, one of the children sneezed, and Miss Agana's face went ashen.

"No, of course not. Nor would we expect you to. The child just took in too much smoke and dirt from the train. We only brought the best with us on this trip. I assure you these children are in prime health. Why, you will never see a better batch of children as we've brought this day. Now, as I was saying, we do not require you to adopt the child. However, if you do, they will get full rights as any child born to your own blood. The rules state that whether you adopt or merely take them in and agree to be their legal guardian, you are required to give them a place to sleep, make sure they are properly fed, and send them to school full time."

The murmur amongst the crowd grew.

"Full time? Then who's going to work in my fields while they are at school? How can I afford to feed my family, much less take in another man's cast-off if I have to send them off to school full time?" another man shouted.

As voices rose, several of the younger children began to sob.

Miss Agana raised her arms and patted the air to silence the crowd. "You don't harvest year-round, do you? The children can go to school after the crops are harvested. Once the boys reach sixteen, they no longer need to go to school. They can stay at home. However, you must pay the boys for their labor. "

Mileta noticed no equal offer extended toward the girls. Then again, it wouldn't, as girls mostly did household chores like cooking, cleaning, washing, and ironing, not like the real work boys were expected to do.

A man stepped forward, pushing aside those in his way, including a child who lost her balance and fell to the floor. Ignoring the child, he spoke. "What if the boy is lazy and doesn't want to work? I have enough mouths to feed to be burdened with another."

"If for any reason things do not work

out, return the child to us." Miss Agana leveled her eyes at him. "Someone from our establishment will visit once a year to check on how things are going and to ensure the wellbeing of the child placed. In the meantime, if you need to send the child back to us before our visit, post us a letter or send a telegraph, and we will make arrangements to remove the child from your home, at no cost to you."

The man returned to his place, seemingly appeased.

"Now, if there aren't any more questions or concerns, I think it is time to make the introductions. We will have you each come up and interview the child that has caught your eye. Remember, there are plenty of children to choose from, so ask questions and take your time. Get to know the child; we have all evening to find the child that is right for you and your family."

The words were no sooner out of her mouth when the congregation swarmed to the area where the children were standing, hovering over the youngsters, looking them over as one would choose a slab of meat in a butcher shop.

An old woman with stringy hair

approached Mileta, smiling at her through broken teeth. She reached a gnarled finger out, tapping Mileta in the middle of the chest. "How long does it take you to thread a needle?"

Mileta shook her head. "I don't know; I've never tried."

"You are worthless to me, then," the woman said, limping off in a huff.

A broad-shouldered man with a thick mustache stepped forward and peered at her over his spectacles. "What's your name? Where did you come from?"

"Mileta. I just got off the train."

"Are you Italian? Can you cook?"

"I am from Poland, and I do not know anything about cooking."

"Pity, I own an Italian restaurant here in the city and am in need of a cook. I've got no use for you, then," the man quipped, leaving without a further word.

A heavyset woman approached, eyeing her critically. Without a word, she grabbed Mileta's arm, twirling her around. She stopped and pulled a purple velvet dress from the cloth sack she was carrying.

"It is beautiful," Mileta said and reached to touch soft fabric.

"My daughter died last year. I have six dresses and no one to wear them. If the dress fits, you can come home with me." She held the dress up to Mileta's shoulders, inspecting the fit. Sighing, she lowered the dress, carefully folding it and tucking it back inside the sack, then walked away.

A young dark-haired woman heavy with child stepped forward next. She had a small boy hoisted on her hip, and her dress clung tight to her protruding stomach, making it obvious a baby would soon take the toddler's place in her arms. Two additional children not much bigger than the one she was holding gripped the hem of her dress. The children were covered in grime, their heads twisting toward the crowd of potential adopters, round eyes showing their bewilderment.

Mileta was fairly sure her face mimicked that of the children standing before her.

The woman's face was one of desperation. "What do you know about babies?"

Mileta shrugged. "They cry."

The woman's eyes turned upwards.

"Yes, and do you know how to quiet them?"

"Tell them a story?"

The woman shook her head. "Not when they are first born. Never mind, you won't do."

As the woman left, the children silently toddled behind.

Mileta sighed, grateful she would not be joining that family. The relief was short-lived as an older couple took her place. The man's face was creased with wrinkles, his dark eyes peering out through thick, round spectacles. The woman he was with sidled up beside him, her aged frame so crooked, she had to lift her head to look Mileta in the eye.

"Show me your teeth," the man said, then stuck a dirty finger in Mileta's mouth.

"Now, Ferris, you know you can't check the children like you do your horses," the woman fussed when Mileta gagged.

"Don't you go telling me how to check the girl. She's not going to be a bit of good to us if her teeth get festered. The Johnsons had one of these kids go ailing on them, and they were in a world of hurt. They were all attached to the child and had to shell out good money to get the girl's teeth pulled so she didn't die on them."

"Well, I don't think this girl is going to die. Are you, girl?" the woman asked.

Mileta shrugged her shoulders. "I don't think so."

The old man took two fingers and pried open her right eye. "How is your eyesight?"

Mileta pulled her head back in disgust. "I can see that your fingers are filthy."

Undeterred, the man repeated the process with her left eye. As he did, something slid beneath her eyelid, causing the eye to water.

"There now, you see, this one has weak eyes." Without another word, they both turned to make their way to the next child.

The next couple who approached were younger by half and appeared to be clean. Both were trim but not malnourished. They were well-dressed, the man in a dark suit and, while Mileta couldn't see the lady's dress, her coat was clean and stylish.

The man looked at his wife and nodded toward the note on Mileta's dress.

"It is close," he said softly.

"It is," she agreed. "Can it be changed?"

He smiled lovingly at the woman. "They said we could do whatever we wish."

"Do you have manners?" the woman asked Mileta.

"Yes, ma'am."

"Do you know how to cook or sew?"

"No, ma'am." The questions had been asked of her numerous times, however, unlike before, her answers did not seem to disappoint the people standing before her.

The woman smiled at her. "I could teach you. Would you be willing to learn?"

"Yes, ma'am, I would like that very much."

"Your name is Mileta?" she asked but pronounced it Mi-lee-ta.

Mileta shook her head. "It's Mile-ta."

"How old are you?" The woman's voice caught as she asked.

"Eleven, ma'am."

The woman looked up at her husband. When she lowered her eyes, they were moist.

"My name is Helen Daniels, and this is my husband, John. I'll tell you right now, we are not rich, but we have enough. We were blessed with a child of our own, but she died when she was but three days old. If she had lived, she would have been your age. The lord never saw fit to give us any more. I would like to have a daughter I could teach to quilt the way my grandmother taught me. If you are willing to learn these things and use proper manners, then we will take you home with us. Is that agreeable?"

Mileta thought about the couple she'd met on the train. They too had mentioned cleaning and cooking; somehow, this seemed different. This woman appeared nice and said she would teach her how to do these things. Then when people asked if she knew how to cook and sew, she could say yes. While she couldn't explain it, something told her the couple standing in front of her needed her as much as she needed them. Taking a deep breath, she nodded and picked up her suitcase.

Mileta followed behind as the couple made their way to the signing office. A small office with a single desk was opened and being used to document the placing out, the official term for the process, since not every child would find themselves lucky enough to be officially adopted. An elderly man sitting behind the desk stood and extended his hand as they approached.

"John, nice to see you here. I was hoping you and the missus would be able to make it. Wish you'd had better weather for the drive."

"Ah, a bit of sleet was all. Gave Helen and me a chance to try out some of those quilts she'd been making. This is Mr. Webber, dear. He is the gentleman who advised we should make the drive down here today," he said, releasing the man's hand.

"Then I must thank you, sir," Helen said, resting her hands on Mileta's shoulders.

"I see you found yourself a nice orphan girl," the man said with a nod toward Mileta. "She going to keep that name?"

John shook his head. "No, Helen and I prefer Mildred."

Webber jotted something down on the paper and pushed it across the desk. "Mildred it is. You have to sign these forms. Just a formality, I assure you, as I will attest for your character myself."

John signed the paper and slid it back

across the desk, and just like that, Mileta – now to be called Mildred – was released to go home with her new family.

***

Cindy's hands were shaking when she closed the notebook. It was true; Grandma Mildred had really written the journals. Why hadn't she ever mentioned any of this to Cindy? Had her dad known? If so, he didn't mention it either. What was wrong with these people? Why all the secrets? She opened her bedroom door, tiptoed across the hall to her mother's room, and placed the journal on the floor outside her bedroom door. Returning to her room, she unwrapped the next journal, anxious to learn more about the people she thought she knew.

Chapter Fourteen

It was late in the afternoon by the time the newly formed family exited the train station. Much to Mileta's chagrin, Helen had coaxed her into wearing her tattered coat out of the station. As they cleared the building, the wind intensified, making Mileta grateful for the warmth it provided. The rain that had greeted the train when it came out of the Michigan Central Railway Tunnel had stopped. However, from the looks of the skies, it was a brief reprieve.

She followed behind the Danielses as they crossed the muddy street and stopped at a motorcar. The motorcar looked to be new and would have been shiny black if not encased in mud. There were two extra tires tied to the left door, making it impossible to enter from that side. Not that anyone would want to, as the tires were dripping with brown ooze. John raised the front panel and turned the hand crank, and the motor sputtered several times before settling into a loud rumble.

He lowered the panel, wiping his hands on a rag. Climbing in on the right, he slid across the seat to his place behind the wheel. Helen climbed in beside him and motioned for Mileta to join them. Once inside, Helen wrapped her with a colorful patchwork quilt and handed another to John. While John tucked the quilt around his legs, Helen did the same with a quilt of her own.

Mileta was astonished by all the vibrant colors and wondered if Helen had made it and further wondered if she herself would ever be able to make something so beautiful. She was just about to express this thought when movement caught her eye. She watched in awe as the wand in the center of the window cleared the remnants of rain from the windshield.

Mileta pulled her arm from under the quilt and pointed toward the windshield, smiling. "It's moving the water from the glass."

"Of course; that is its job," John replied. "Haven't you ever been in a motor car before, Mildred?"

It took Mileta a moment to realize he

was speaking to her. Before she could answer, Helen interjected.

"Mildred, answer your father."

Mileta lost her smile. First, they'd changed her name, and now she was supposed to call the man she'd only just met her father. It was all so confusing. "No."

"No, what, Mildred?" Helen asked.

"No, I've never been in a motor car," Mildred answered.

"Remember our manners, Mildred. No, sir, I have never been in a motor car," Helen corrected.

"No, sir, I've never been in a motor car," Mileta repeated. Once she started speaking, she couldn't stop herself. "I rode in a machine in New York. But just to the train station. And we were all smooshed in the back, and there were not any windows. It smelled terribly bad of spoiled milk and made one of the boys get sick. The headmistress got mad and took him back to the asylum. She was not pleased. She said if anyone else got sick, she would take us back as well."

"Ha, well, I dare say I would get sick too if I were crammed into a truck smelling of rotten milk," John agreed. "Helen, how about one of those egg salad sandwiches while we are waiting for the motor to warm?"

Helen lifted a small basket from the floorboard and opened a cloth to show three sandwiches with yellow showing between the slices of bread. She handed one to John and another to Mileta, who stared at it in wonder.

"Do not tell me you have never had a sandwich before," John said then took a bite.

"Not for a very long time," Mileta said, sniffing the contents. "We only had mush at the asylum."

"Mildred, manners please, and do not play with your food," Helen scolded softly. "Did they not feed you anything else?"

"Oh, yes. We had bread as long as we ate it before the bigger kids stole it. Unless Anastasia was there, then the other kids did not dare bother our table. She was mean at first, but then she was nice to me. I told her she had to be nice to my friends too, so she was. " She took a bite and marveled at the tangy flavor. "It is good."

Helen sighed. "Mildred, proper ladies do not speak with food in our mouths. We chew, swallow, and then speak. Understand?"

"Yes, ma'am," Mileta said and took another bite. She finished chewing and looked up at Helen. "Ma'am, will you teach me how to make food this good?"

Helen's mouth trembled. "Yes, I will. But will you do something for me?"

Mileta had food in her mouth, so she merely nodded.

"Will you call me Mother?"

Mileta considered this for a moment. *Could she really call this woman Mother when she already had one?* What if her birth mother didn't approve? Well, if she cared, she wouldn't have taken her to the asylum in the first place, much less leave her there without so much as an explanation. Her mother may have left her there, but this lady took her out. Sure, she wanted her to say and do things a certain way, but she wasn't mean about it. Nor had she raised her voice when correcting her. She looked at Helen and smiled. "Yes, ma'am."

John reached for Helen's hand and brought it to his mouth for a kiss. "The motor is warm. How about we take our daughter home?"

His comment took Mileta by surprise. Was she really their daughter now?

"Make sure you keep your blanket pulled up, Mildred; we would not want you to catch a cold," John said as he turned onto Michigan Avenue.

Mileta instantly thought about what Tobias had said about being sent back. Would they really send her back after just referring to her as their daughter? Not taking any chances, she pulled the quilt closer.

Helen looked at her and shook her head. "It just doesn't make sense, John; they can invent devices to sweep the rain off the window, so you would think they could find a way to keep the inside of this machine warm."

His hand drifted from the steering wheel and touched the quilt at Helen's knee. "Just be patient, love. I assure you there are things in the works that will astound you."

"John, not in front of Mildred," Helen admonished. She waited for him to remove his hand then turned her attention to Mildred. "John works at the Ford Rouge

Plant. He is part of the design team. He has some great ideas, not that I understand everything he tells me."

He leaned in close and lowered his voice. "I will let you in on a secret, Mildred. If all goes as planned, next year, we will be building airplanes that soar through the heavens. Can you imagine that? Mr. Ford is reaching for the sky and taking us with him."

"John, maybe you shouldn't say such things." Helen turned to Mildred. "Your father likes to share the ideas he and his team are working on. But you must remember, Mildred, just because you hear something does not mean you should run and tell all your friends. Proper young ladies do not gossip. Understand?"

"Yes, ma'am." Not that it mattered; she didn't have any friends. Not anymore.

"These are exciting times we live in, Mildred; you remember that." John veered to avoid another puddle of mud. Not an easy task, given Michigan Avenue was one long, sludgy mess. "Someday they will put a coating over all this dirt so people won't have to drive in the mud. And when they do, no more holes in the road; just smooth lanes."

Helen laughed. "Oh, John, you are such a dreamer. That is what I love about you. You have visions of beautifying the world. Your high hopes will undoubtedly win you anything your heart desires."

He turned his head to look at Helen then cast a glance at Mileta. "I have a beautiful wife, and now we have an equally beautiful daughter. What more could a man ask for?"

Mileta felt her eyes moisten. If not for his American accent, she could close her eyes and picture her birth mother and father sitting next to her having the very same conversation. She swallowed to keep the tears at bay. The last thing she wanted was for her new mother and father to think she had weak eyes and return her on the very first day.

John's smile grew wide. "Mildred, I just know you are going to love it here. Detroit is an amazing city. Do you know we have a concrete avenue? It is a road as smooth as the walls of a building, and it is not too far from here. It is called Woodward Avenue and was the first concrete avenue in the country. Detroit also had the first four-way stoplight in the whole world! And next month, our great city is having a massive parade. People will be coming from near and far to see it. It is called America's Thanksgiving Parade. There will be floats, clowns, horses, and at the end, do you know who's going to be there?"

Mileta shrugged, then seeing the look on Helen's face, added, "No, Father."

John's face lit up. "Why, ole Kris Kringle himself."

Mileta crinkled her nose. "Who?"

"Kris Kringle. You know, Saint Nicholas."

John was so excited, Mileta thought about pretending to know who he was talking about. Instead, she simply stared.

John slammed on the brakes, stopping the motor car in the center of the street, and turned his body toward her. "Now, Mildred, are you telling me you don't know who Santa Claus is?"

Santa Claus? Why didn't he just say so? Although she wasn't sure what he was so happy about. Everyone knew Santa Claus didn't bother visiting orphans.

"Oh." She tried not to let her lack of enthusiasm show.

"Oh? Is that all you have for the jolly old man that brings good little boys and girls presents?" John asked, staring.

Mileta jumped when a loud *aaoogha* sounded behind them. John stuck out his left hand and waved the other machine around. Unfazed, he waited for her answer, but Mileta wasn't sure what he wanted her to say.

Finally, it was Helen who broke the silence. "Mileta, have you never gotten a present from Santa Claus?"

"No…Mother."

Tears sprang to Helen's eyes, and suddenly, Mileta wished she had lied about not getting presents. "It is okay, Mother; the headmistress always made sure we had a present on Christmas day."

"She did?" Helen asked, wiping her eyes with a hanky.

"Oh, yes. We each received an apple or an orange on Christmas morning. It was a great surprise, as we never knew it was Christmas morning until the baskets arrived in the dining hall."

John didn't respond, but Helen retrieved her hanky and once more blotted tears from her eyes. "Mildred, that just might be the saddest thing I have ever heard."

Mileta shook her head. "Oh no, there is nothing to be sad about. The headmistress stayed while we ate our fruit, so no one took them away!"

"There now, love, see; everything turned out just fine." John's words were reassuring, although his voice sounded rather shaky. When he turned toward Mileta, she noticed his eyes were glistening with tears. "There is no reason for any of us to get all worked up over what happened in the past. Mildred is here, and she belongs to us now. I will do everything within my power to see she is safe in our home."

Chapter Fifteen

Home ended up being a lovely white two-story house on East Fort Street. The house had a small front porch with three steps that led up to the front door. Burgundy, orange, and red leaves littered the yard, crunching beneath their feet as they walked.

Mileta stopped and looked at the house, which was mostly square except for the peaked roof. "Which floor do you rent?"

"We don't rent. The house is ours." John extended his arm. "And the whole yard is yours to run in."

Mileta thought about this for a moment. "Why should I need to run? What shall be chasing me?"

"Nothing will be chasing you. You can run and play."

"Well, who should I play with?"

"You can play with yourself. And your toys," Helen offered.

Mileta's heart sank. *They think I'm a*

baby. What will happen when they find out I am too old to play? John and Helen were still looking at her expectantly, so she plastered on a fake smile.

The strategy worked as they each turned and walked toward the front of the house. John climbed the short steps, held the door for Helen, and waited for Mileta to follow. She was halfway up the steps, when she caught sight of something moving in a nearby tree. A small grey furry creature scurried down the base of the tree, ran a short distance, hopped onto another tree, stopping midway up, tail flicking.

"It's a hoppy thing! A hoppy thing!" Mileta repeated.

Helen had already disappeared inside the house with Mileta's suitcase, so John turned to see what had captured her attention. Laughing, he descended the porch stairs and looked at her quizzically. "Why, Mildred, are you telling me there are no squirrels in New York?"

"Not so close. They never came near the asylum," she said, watching the animal.

"What about when you left the asylum?"

"I did not see much that day. It was

raining."

"What about the other times?"

She stared at him, trying to figure out what he meant.

"You went outside, did you not?"

"Yes, but there were so many of us, and it was the only time we got to talk and make noise, so a lot of the younger children did. Make noise. Mostly the older children stood by the fence, hoping a passerby would give us something to eat."

John knelt beside her. "Did you not get enough to eat at the asylum?"

"Oh yes, Father. They fed us mush and bread three times a day. It is just sometimes the passersby would bring us something different. One time, a lady in a blue dress stopped by. She asked each of us our names and how old we were. The lady would ask us a question and plop a peanut into our mouths. She did this for three days, and we were all eager to oblige her questions. I remember laughing, thinking we all looked like baby birds waiting for our momma to drop food into our wee beaks. Then one day, she handed a peanut to a little boy. I do not recall what his name was, but I remember being scared because he grabbed his neck and fell to the ground. All the kids started screaming and yelling for the mistresses, who hurried out. They shooed us away and carried him inside. We never saw him again, and the nice lady never came back. I guess she did not like all that screaming."

"Mildred, you have had an interesting life. I am afraid you may find our home rather dull by comparison. On the other hand, you will not have to spend your free time begging for food. I can readily say, Helen, your mother," John corrected, "is an accomplished cook and will see that you learn all she knows. Would you like to go inside to see your new home?"

Mileta nodded, and John stood and offered her his hand. She took it and instantly recalled walking hand in hand with her father as they walked up the gangway of the cargo ship. It was to be the last time she held her father's hand. She tried to extinguish the memory, but it was too late; a tear slid down her cheek. She reached with her free hand and brushed it aside.

"Are you not happy, Mildred?" John asked, seeing her distress.

"Yes, Father, I am," she said, brushing

at yet another tear.

"Then why are you crying?"

Mileta wanted to make up a story, but she couldn't bring herself to lie to him. "I remembered the last time I held my father's hand. It was on the ship when we were coming to America."

"What happened to your father, Mildred?"

"My mother said I should not talk about it. She said it made her too sad."

John's expression softened. "Sometimes it helps to talk about the things that make us sad. Your mother is not here, so I think it is okay if you wish to tell me about it."

"He took ill on the ship and died. The workers came down to where we were staying and took him away. I wasn't supposed to follow, but I did. They took him up the ladder and carried him to the side of the ship. The captain took one look at him and agreed he was dead. He then said he was returning to his bed and told another man to get his name and make a note in the log book. The two men searched his pockets; thankfully, Momma had already collected his papers and what little money he had. The men grumbled, then tossed him into the ocean like he was a bundle of garbage and walked away. It was raining, but I did not care. I went over to the rail, and I said a little prayer into the darkness. Then I ran back to my mother. I never told her I watched the men. Nor did I tell her what they did to my father." With that, the floodgates opened.

John knelt beside her once more and gathered her in his arms until she stopped crying. As her tears subsided, he handed her a white handkerchief to dry her eyes. Mostly composed, Mileta followed him into the house, her chest still heaving.

"What happened?" Helen asked the moment they entered the house.

"Mildred saw a squirrel," John said, removing his coat.

"Oh." Helen appeared to want to say more but instead reached for John's coat and placed it on a hook behind the door.

Mileta followed John's lead and removed her dirty coat.

Helen took it from her, moved to place it on the hook, then reconsidered and hung it on the glass doorknob instead. "What is it, Mildred?"

"Those door handles are so lovely." Mileta's gaze moved to the rest of the room. The walls were brightly colored with raised orange leaves, as if someone had brought the fallen foliage in from the yard. There were chairs in a softer shade of the same color scheme and a long bench-type chair that looked like it could fit all three of them at the same time. "It's all so lovely, but how did you get the leaves to stick to the wall?"

"Why, thank you, Mildred. But they are not really leaves. It is called wallpaper. I just had it put up. This pattern is called Floral on Auburn."

Mileta ran her hand across the wall, enjoying the velvety texture. "It feels soft and fuzzy."

"If you like this, I am sure you are going to love your room." Helen picked up Mileta's suitcase and motioned her to follow. They walked up a flight of stairs. Helen opened the door to the left of the stairway and flipped a switch, illuminating the room with a soft glow. Pale pink paper with darker pink fuzzy roses lined the walls. A small bed to the right of the window was draped with a white quilt covered with pink flowers, and a doll with a long white flowing dress lay in the center of the bed. The single window had pink and white curtains that matched the quilt and stopped just below the windowsill. A tall weave-back chair sat next to a brown wooden dresser, which perfectly matched the color of the bed frame.

Mileta stared at the room open-mouthed. *Surely this was all a dream.*

"Close your mouth, Mildred. Proper young ladies do not gape. You are going to swallow a bug." While the words were firm, the tone was not. "I hope you like the color of your new room."

Mileta closed her mouth and stepped inside. She walked to the wall, rubbing her hand against the fuzzy texture. "Everything is so lovely."

Helen placed the suitcase on the chair and opened it. As she peered inside at the dirty travel clothes, she wrinkled her nose and closed the case once more. "I think we will have to visit Kresge's Department Store to get you something decent to wear."

"There is no need. I already have a new dress, and it matches my room."

"It is a fine dress, but it will do nothing to keep you warm. Besides, proper young ladies need more than one dress. We shall go to the store in the morning after our household chores are completed, of course. Your father will have the Ford, so we will have to take the streetcar."

Mileta's heart sank. She had only just arrived and had already become a bother.

Helen motioned toward the doll. "I bought her last week when I learned the train would be coming. I hope you like her."

Mileta felt another stab in the heart. It would only be a matter of time before they realized she was too big to play with dolls. "She is lovely."

"You have had a long few days. I will draw you a bath, and you can soak in the tub." Helen left the room, leaving the door open.

Mileta reached up and removed the bow from her hair and let her fingers glide through the length of her locks. She felt her lips quiver, took a deep breath, and went in search of Helen.

The washroom was two doors down the hall. Light blue tile ran through the room with a line of black separating the room midway across the wall. Helen sat on the edge of a large bathtub, her fingers floating under the water as it flowed from the spigot. She looked up when Mileta entered.

"The water is a little touchy. You have to keep a close eye on it, or it will get too hot and burn you. You can use the pink towel on the holder; it should be easy for you to remember, as it matches your room."

Mileta nodded. It was the best she could do under the circumstances.

"There is soap in the dish. Make sure to wash your hair. Take your time and get clean. You can wear the same clothes for now. I am going to start supper. John will want to eat soon." Helen turned the knobs to stop the water, then wiped her fingers with one of the other towels. She returned the towel to the hook, smoothing the creases.

The second Helen left the room, Mileta sank into the tub and burst into tears, all hopes she had of staying dashed.

***

"Mildred, you have barely touched your supper. Is it not to your liking?" John asked.

Mileta looked at the plate in front of her. A scoop of mashed potatoes smothered in brown gravy, glazed carrots, and a thin slice of perfectly cooked roast beef sat mostly untouched. She had not had such offerings since she'd left her home in Poland. That was the issue. If she were going back to the asylum, she'd rather not get used to such delicacies. "Oh, yes, sir, this is much to my liking."

"Eat up, then. You will not get food like this tomorrow," John encouraged.

Mileta felt the tears coming but could do nothing to stop them. As they spilled from her eyes, she sprang from her chair and raced to the room at the top of the stairs. She had her suitcase in her hand moments later when John and Helen entered the room.

Mileta pushed her chin out and swallowed hard. "I am ready to go back now."

Helen waited in the doorway as John approached and sat on the edge of the bed. "What is this all about, Mildred? I thought you like it here."

Mileta swallowed once more. "I do, but since you are going to send me back, I would much prefer to return today."

John exchanged glances with Helen, who shrugged her confusion.

John addressed her once more. "What makes you think we are going to send you back?"

"Clearly, you were hoping to get a baby."

"Why would you say that?" John asked.

Mileta nodded toward the doll.

John let out a breath. "It is just a doll, Mildred. All little girls like to play with dolls."

Mileta stared at him.

"Have you never played with dolls, Mildred?" This time, it was Helen who spoke.

"Not that I can remember." Mileta was surprised to see tears pool in Helen's eyes. "Why does that make you sad, when you want me to go away?"

Helen dropped to her knees. "Mildred, what have I done to make you think I don't want you?"

"You called him John instead of my father."

"What?"

"When you picked me, you said you

would teach me to cook. Then after you found I am a burden, you said you were going to cook supper by yourself, and you said John would want to eat."

Helen smiled through her tears. "Oh, Mildred, this was all a misunderstanding. I called him John because that is what I am used to calling him. And I did not ask you to help me cook because I thought you would be too tired."

"Then why did you not cut my hair?" Mildred asked through fresh tears.

Helen's eyebrows knit together. "Why would I cut your beautiful hair?"

"Because that is what people do when you are going to stay. When my mother took me to the asylum that day, they made me take a bath. Before the bath, the woman cut my hair. Mary told me they always do that when you are going to stay."

Helen wiped at her tears. "Mildred, I need to be honest with you. Remember I told you about the baby we had that died?"

Mileta nodded her head.

"Well, her name was Mildred. She would have been the same age as you. I like to think she would have even looked like you. That is why we picked you and gave you her name. We want you to stay with us and have the life our little girl never got to have. We want to give you the love we never got to give to her. Will you allow us to do that, Mileta?"

Mileta considered her words for a moment then shook her head. "On one condition."

Helen looked at her expectantly.

"Will you call me Mildred again?"

***

Cindy was just about to read the last line when her mother interrupted.

"Just a moment, Mom," she said, brushing away her tears. Glancing back at the page, she read the last line of the notebook. *That was the last time I can remember ever thinking of myself as Mileta.*

"Why in the heck didn't you tell me Mileta was your grandmother?" Linda asked the second Cindy opened the door.

Cindy shrugged. "I guess I wanted you to enjoy the story, not just judge its authenticity."

"Do you really think that's what it is;

just a story?"

"Sadly, no. I think it's real. I think Mileta was indeed Grandma Mildred."

Linda's shoulders slumped. "I cannot believe how children were treated back then. We have stronger vetting policies for people adopting dogs from the shelter than they used for those children. And changing her name like that without even asking her. No wonder the woman was so cold."

"I know, right?"

"What about all the other children? What happened to them?" Linda paced back and forth as she spoke. "I'm worried about that little one, what was her name?"

"The baby or Ruth?"

Linda let out a sigh. "Ruth. But, now that you mention it, I am worried about that baby too."

"I know, Mom. Just remember they're not babies anymore. Whatever happened is already done, so don't get yourself too worked up."

"Too late. I need to find out what happens to your grandmother. Is her new family nice to her? Does she ever see her real mother again? Between you and me, I think the woman was sick. Remember the cough? Mileta, Mildred, whatever her name is, never hinted that her real mother didn't love her, so I think the woman must have been desperate."

Cindy nodded her agreement. "Sadly, that is what I think too. I am not sure what kind of records they kept back then, especially with people being able to change a child's name with the stroke of a pen. What do you say we do some more reading and see if we can find any answers?"

Linda took the next notebook and held it to her chest as if it were gold. "You know, if the woman would have bothered to tell us about this when she was alive, we would already have the answers to our questions."

Cindy had to admit she had been thinking the same thing. "I'm sure she had her reasons for keeping this to herself. Just be grateful she kept journals, or we would never have known."

Linda started for her room and paused, looking at the notebook she held.

"What is it, Mom?"

"I guess I'm just wondering how I would have turned out if I had lived in her shoes. I just thought the woman to be cold;

now it appears she just needed someone to have been nice to her."

"Mom, you were as cordial to her as she to you. I never heard you raise your voice or say anything mean."

Linda pondered that for a moment. "I guess we never fully know what is going on in a person's mind, do we, Cindy?"

Cindy looked into her mom's eyes and saw sadness she'd seen all too often since her father died. "No, Mom, I guess we never do."

Chapter Sixteen

November 27th, 1924

Helen placed the turkey in the oven, took off her apron, and folded it neatly. "Mildred, are you nearly finished? Your father will not wish to be late for the parade."

"Yes, Mother. I just have to finish forming the rolls," Mildred said, pinching off a piece of dough and rolling it into a ball.

Helen smiled. "I believe this is going to be the best Thanksgiving ever."

Mildred shook her head in agreement. "It will be my first real Thanksgiving. At least the first one I can remember. Will the turkey be finished in time?"

"Yes, of course." Helen frowned. "I just hope it doesn't become too dry without anyone here to baste it."

Mildred matched her expression. "If you tell me how to baste it, I can stay here and do it. I've never seen a parade before; missing it will not be too terrible."

Helen shook her head. "You shall do no such thing. If anyone is going to stay home, it will be me."

"What is all this staying home nonsense?" John asked, coming into the room.

"Mother is afraid the turkey will be dry if no one is here to baste it," Mildred said, balling the last roll and placing it inside the tin with the rest.

"Nonsense. Mr. Hudson did not plan this event so that people would stay home. This is Detroit. We are trendsetters. This is the biggest event of the season, and we will all be witness to it. The turkey will taste marvelous, dry or not. Now hurry so we can catch the streetcar and get there early enough to get a good spot on Second Avenue. I hear that is the best place to see Santa Claus."

Mildred laughed.

"Tisk tisk, scoff if you must, but he will be there. A little bird told me so."

Mildred chuckled once more. "Birds don't talk."

John walked over and gave Mildred a kiss on top of her head. "My poor sweet Millie, if only you had come to us before they stole your innocence away. Of course birds talk. I have witnessed this myself on several occasions."

"You have?"

"Truly."

Mildred searched his face and determined him to be telling the truth. "One day I hope to see one of these talking birds."

"That you shall. However, today I am afraid you will have to settle for Mother Goose."

"Who?" Mildred asked.

"Maybe more innocent than last I thought. Come along, ladies; we have a streetcar to catch."

***

Mildred understood the need to take the streetcar once she saw the crowd that lined Vernor Highway. Hordes of bystanders gathered, all vying for the best place to stand to see the coming parade. While she could not yet see it, music from the bands could be heard in the distance.

"Have you ever in your life seen so many people?" Helen's voice was a mixture of excitement and fear. "There must be thousands of people here."

"I'd venture to say hundreds of thousands," John said, leading them through the crowd and stopping at a less crowded spot near a light post.

"Yes, I have," Mildred replied once they'd stopped.

"Yes, you have what?" Helen asked.

"Seen this many people. When my mother and I first arrived in America, there were people everywhere. It was so crowded, we had to walk slowly, and I had to hold my mother's skirt tail to keep from getting lost. Everyone seemed to speak at once, and there were so many languages, I didn't know what most of them were saying. We didn't have much money. My father used most of what we had for safe passage. My mother didn't speak much English, and she was crying because we had nowhere to go and no man to care for us. A gentleman approached my mother and told her he knew of a place where we could stay as long as we were nice to him. She told him that she would be nice but told me I didn't have to be. I remember wondering if my father would approve of her telling the man I didn't have to be nice to him."

Anger flashed across John's face, making Mildred wonder if he was mad she was talking about her other parents. She relaxed when he smiled and took hold of her hand.

He smiled down at her. "Mildred, I think your father would have approved very much."

As the parade grew closer, Mildred felt her excitement intensify. Bands led the parade, and men wearing matching outfits with large white collars marched and played instruments as the crowd cheered.

Mildred was astonished to see a man twice as tall as her father walking down the street. She tugged on her mother's coat and pointed. "Oh my word, how did he get to be so tall?"

Helen's surprise matched her own. "I imagine he used some form of magic."

"Stilts," John corrected. "Look there; see how his legs don't bend? He has some kind of device he is standing on. I would think the poor chap would have a devil of a time should he take a spill. Think I should trip him and see how he fares?"

Mildred felt her eyes grow wide. "Oh no, Father, that would be oh so cruel."

Helen smiled and snuggled closer to John. "Do not fret, Mildred; your father is far too much of a gentleman to do such a thing."

The words had no sooner left her mouth when a boy dashed out of the crowd, rushed into the street, and sent the poor man toppling to the ground. His assailant stood hands on hips, roaring with laughter. The boy's back was to her, but that didn't stop Mildred from recognizing him. It was Tobias, the boy who had saved her from the couple on the train. She was just about to call out to him when two police officers rushed in from the opposite side of the street, eager to get their hands on the disruptive lad. One of the officers blew a whistle, his mistake, as it gave Tobias warning to flee their approach. The boy turned away from the officers and fled in her direction. As he neared the sidewalk where she was standing, Mildred could see the recognition in his eyes. He slowed, his face showing his regret. Just behind him, one of the officers lunged for him. The man was not fast enough. Tobias winked and disappeared into the cover of the crowd. Both officers followed, only to return empty-handed moments later.

"I don't know what this city is coming to," Helen exclaimed.

"Now, dear, you know as well as I that things are bound to happen when you have a crowd this size. It was nothing more than a childish prank," John assured her. "Oh, look. Here comes Mother Goose."

Mildred turned to see where he was looking. Sure enough, a team of horses approached pulling a large wagon with an enormous white goose that spilled over the sides, making it look as if the wayward bird was indeed flying. Seeing the bird, Mildred sighed. "Oh, Father, I should have known you were jesting."

John moved closer. "What troubles you, Mildred?"

"You were wrong. The bird, she does not speak."

"She is but paper mache. But don't you fret. I promise you talking birds do exist. You will find this to be true one day. Today, I wish for you to discover another of life's wonders." A wide smile brightened John's face as he pulled a coin from his pocket and handed it to her. He hoisted her up and pointed. "See the man in the red and white striped coat pushing the cart?"

She peered over the crowd to where he was pointing. "Yes, Father."

"Run over to him and give him this coin."

"Whatever for, Father?"

"He has something in his cart that will change your life forever."

Helen looked to see where John was pointing and sighed. "John, you are going to ruin Mildred's dinner."

"Nonsense. What is Thanksgiving but a day to be gluttonous? Now off with you, Mildred, and hurry back. You don't want to miss too much of the parade."

Gripping the coin tightly, Mildred made her way through the onlookers to the man with the striped jacket. He held out his hand as she approached. Taking the coin, he placed it in his apron and handed her a box. She opened the box and peered inside at the white fluff. She sniffed the box, smelling nothing.

The man's face lit up. "Ah, I can see you have not tried this before."

She shook her head.

He motioned toward the box. "Go on, give it a taste."

She stuck her hand into the box, removed a section of the white fluff, and placed it into her mouth. To her amazement, the fluff dissolved into sweet sandy textured crystals the likes of which she'd never tasted. Mildred took another sniff. How could something that was devoid of smell prove to taste so delightful? "What is it?" she asked, reaching for another piece.

Seeing her reaction, the man beamed. "Some call it fairy floss; we call it cotton candy. It's good, is it not?"

"Oh yes, quite," she agreed, licking the sticky substance from her fingers. Hearing another band, she turned. "Thank you. I must go. I do not wish to miss anything."

Mildred walked several feet then paused, trying to gather her bearings. She was sure she was heading in the right direction. Well, almost sure. She was about to take another step when a boy stepped in front of her, blocking her way.

The boy was a good head taller than her and dressed in rags. "Gimme the box, rich girl."

"I shall do no such thing," Mildred said, pulling her treasure close.

The boy took a step forward and made a grab for the box. Mildred felt herself jerked to the side and looked to find Tobias standing in front of her, hands fisted, challenging the boy. His cap did little to shield the cold, as was apparent from the red ears that stuck out slightly from the side of his head. Though his clothes looked a bit large, they were at least clean and free from holes. He wasn't wearing a coat, but then again, neither was the boy standing in front of them.

"Leave the girl alone, Mac." Tobias' voice was low and threatening.

The taller boy sized Tobias up. "And if I don't?"

"You saw what I did to Butch."

Mildred wasn't sure who Butch was or what Tobias did to him, but apparently, the boy did. Stepping back, he shrugged his shoulders. "What's she to you anyhow? You sweet on a baby?"

Tobias raised his fist a bit higher and squared his shoulders, causing the boy to take another step back.

"She is none of your concern. Just let it be known this girl is under my protection. Anyone messes with her…" Tobias opened his right hand and extended his index finger slowly, sliding it across his throat. "Get the message?"

"Loud and clear, Mouse. Loud and clear," the boy said, slinking away.

"You okay there, kid?" Tobias asked once he was gone.

"I'm not a kid. Or a baby," Mildred said, pulling herself taller.

Tobias chuckled. "Says the girl with the candy."

She reached into the box and pulled out a tuft of white. "Have you ever tasted this?"

He took it from her and brought it to his nose. "It doesn't smell like much."

"Just try it," Mildred encouraged.

He shoved the entire piece into his mouth. Instantly, a look of wondrous disbelief crossed over his face. "Ha. It's gone."

"It's marvelous, is it not?"

"Not bad, kid…Mileta," he corrected.

Mildred shook her head. "They, my new parents, call me Mildred."

Anger flashed over his face. "Damn do-gooders. How bad is it? I can get you out if you'd like."

His venom surprised her. "Oh, no. It is not like that. My mother and father are very nice. They treat me extremely well. My father gave me a dime for this cotton candy."

"You paid a whole dime for stuff that disappears before you can even chew it?" he scoffed.

Mildred glared at Tobias. "I did, and I would do it again, thank you very much. You liked it too. Why all the fuss?"

He shook his head. "You really are a baby. You get plucked up by a rich family who tosses money at you, and you see nothing wrong with them changing your name. What kind of name is Mildred anyway?"

"It is my name, and I like it," she responded coldly. She wanted to add that it was the name of their daughter that died but thought better of it, knowing he would not be impressed.

"It doesn't fit you."

"My father sometimes calls me Millie," she offered then wondered why she felt it so important to try to appease him.

"Millie. That's not bad, kind of a mixture of your old and new name."

Mildred looked at his clothes once more. "What about you?"

He pulled himself taller. "What about me?"

"How are you getting along with your new parents?"

His face turned crimson. He leaned over and spat on the sidewalk. "Parents? Not for boys like me. The man who took me threatened to send me back the next day. I waited until he went to sleep and I took off. Dang do-gooders. Who needs them anyway?"

Mildred was instantly concerned for Tobias' safety. "You took off? Where do you live? How do you eat?"

"These streets don't have nothing on The Five Points," he said, referring to the streets of New York. "A man knows where to look, he gets by all right. I've made a few friends, so I manage well enough. As a matter of fact, it's time for me to move on. Places to go, people to see; speaking of which, you had better get back before you are missed."

Tobias was right; she had already been gone longer than she should. She watched him slip into the crowd and turned, trying to get her bearings. She had only taken a couple of steps when Tobias joined her once again.

"You are heading the wrong way," he said, taking her hand. He turned her in the opposite direction and led her a short distance. "There," he said, pointing.

Mildred smiled her gratitude and handed him the box of cotton candy.

"What's this for?" he asked, taking the box.

"It's Thanksgiving. My mother and father said we are supposed to give thanks for our blessings. I just wanted you to have something to be thankful for."

"Millie, I know you are being taken care of; that is enough for me." A sly smile slid across his face.

"What?"

"I'll see you around, kid." He took a bit of cotton candy, thrust the box into her hands, and then he was gone.

Mildred was still wondering how Tobias had found her as she made her way through the crowd and returned to where her parents were anxiously awaiting her return.

Chapter Seventeen

October 24th, 1926

They were seated in the Venetian Room in one of Detroit's most prestigious hotels. Located on the corner of State Street and Washington Boulevard, the Book Cadillac Hotel catered to Detroit's elite providing fine dining and state-of-the-art rooms, which included private baths. The Italian Renaissance style was apparent in the expansive ceilings, massive arch windows, crystal chandeliers, and second-story balconies that overlooked the room where they were sitting. At the time it was built in nineteen twenty-four, the hotel was the largest in the world, boasting thirty-three floors and over one thousand guestrooms. Mildred breathed deeply, inhaling the smells that wafted through the room, beef being the most prevalent. She studied the menu, practically drooling over the options.

"See anything you like, Millie?" John

asked

"Only everything on the menu. But tonight, I think I would like steak," Mildred replied and licked her lips.

Helen sighed. "Mildred, please sit up straight and do try to remember your manners."

Mildred adjusted her position. "I'm sorry, Mother. I am just so terribly excited."

Helen's expression softened under the brim of her new hat, her violet eyes widening as she took in the sights of the room.

Waiters dressed in black pants, white shirts, and black bowties topped with short white jackets flittered around the room servicing patrons all decked out in their Sunday finest. Mildred and her mother were dressed for the occasion, both wearing new modern dresses, which had been purchased at Hudson's only yesterday. Mildred was wearing a mint green dress with darker green flowers. The dress pleated at the waist and stopped just below the knee. Her mother's dress was a bit more daring, gold with matching beads and fringe, showing just enough of Helen's slender legs to keep the waiter frequently returning to ensure she had a sufficient amount of water in her goblet. Both Mildred's and her mother's hair were freshly cut with edgy bangs. Helen had painstakingly sculpted a single curl, which peeked from underneath the hat and lay against the side of each of their faces. The hats perfectly matched their dresses, a feat that took several hours to attain during yesterday's shopping trip. At the time, Mildred had questioned the effort, but now, looking at the way others in the room were dressed, she was grateful for her mother's insistence. Well into her thirteenth year, wearing a pair of high boots with a significant heel, not only did Mildred fit in with the adults in the room, she looked as if she belonged.

John lifted his water goblet, extending it to Helen and Mildred in turn. "To be surrounded by the loveliest ladies in the room. I daresay I am the luckiest man in the world this evening. Here's to an evening we shall not readily forget."

Blushing, Helen picked up her glass and took a sip. She frowned, then extended the water goblet toward her husband. "And to the most handsome man in the room."

John leaned in and placed a kiss on his wife's lips. "Are you happy, darling?"

Helen beamed. "Ecstatic."

The waiter returned, breaking the moment. Tall and thin, he brushed around the table taking orders and collecting menus. He paused at Helen's chair. "Would the lady care for more water?"

John's face turned serious. "It is the lady's birthday, and she would like a glass of something with a bit more bite."

The waiter closed his eyes and smiled, as if remembering simpler times. "You find a way to stop Prohibition, and I will join you."

John motioned him closer. "If you happen to find something in the basement, see that it makes its way to our table."

The waiter straightened, adjusted his jacket, and glared at John. "I assure you this establishment adheres to the letter of the law."

"This establishment, yes, but I am well aware that things go on in this town that the law does not keep track of." John opened his suit coat, and the waiter's eyes grew wide.

"Now, sir, there is no reason for

violence." The waiter's voice trembled.

John withdrew his wallet, lifted two bills from the leather, and tucked them under his water goblet. "I assure you my methods are far more, shall we say, civilized."

The waiter eyeballed the bills. "So it would seem."

John tapped the bills. "We wouldn't expect you to break any laws. One for you, and one for whoever can bring us some…tea."

The waiter cast a nervous glance around the room. "I'll see if we have any stronger…tea brewing."

Never having seen this side of her dad, Mildred watched the scene carefully. It was not her mother's birthday, and furthermore, it was not at all like her father to lie. She turned her attention to her mother, who seemed to be as surprised as she.

"What was that about?" Helen asked as soon as the waiter was out of earshot. "You know Detroit has been dry for years."

John chuckled. "I have it on good authority that our good city is not as dry as you think. Now tell me, dear, would you not like a little nip to bring out the flavor of your steak?"

Helen lowered her voice. "Well, it is my birthday."

Mildred thought about calling her mother on the lie but decided against it. The last thing she wanted was for them to regret bringing her along, especially when they still had the Garrick Theater ahead of them. It would be her first trip to a theater, and she looked forward to seeing the illusionist everyone was talking about. Her father had surprised her and her mother with the tickets, assuring them Harry Houdini's performance would be one they would never forget. She took in the bustle of the room until the waiter returned with their dinner.

The man moved around the table, placing white plates rimmed in blue and gold in front of them so that the hotel's gold crest faced the guest. Each plate was piled high with potatoes, fresh carrots, and large perfectly cooked steaks. The waiter lifted a tall glass of iced tea from the tray and sat it in front of Mildred. "Here you are, my dear. I took the liberty of adding raspberries and found you a long spoon should you decide to fish them out."

The waiter straightened, his eyes shifting to the bill still resting under her father's water goblet. "I am sorry to say that your tea has been delayed. I had to send out for more...ice. It shall be here momentarily, and I am sure it will be well worth the wait. Will you be needing anything else until then?"

John glanced around the table. "No, I believe we have everything else we need."

Mildred took a bite of her steak and moaned her delight, then proceeded to eat most of the steak before stopping to sample either the potatoes or carrots. Even though Helen was an incredible cook, never in her life had she had anything that tasted so good. She was just about to say that very thing when piano music sifted through the air, stopping her mid-bite. While she had heard piano music since leaving the asylum, this was the first time the song that played was one she knew. Knew very well, in fact, as her birth mother had taught her the song, "Für Elise," which the person currently playing was butchering. She looked around, realizing she was the only one who had observed the error. Either people didn't notice or they were so involved in their meals and conversations, they didn't care.

"Is something wrong with your dinner, Millie?"

Mildred hurried to swallow the food in her mouth. "No, Father, the food is divine."

"Glad to hear. At two dollars, I would hate for you to be disappointed."

Mildred smiled and took another bite of steak. As she chewed, she fought the urge to find the piano player, pull him off the stool, and show him how the song should be played. She placed her hands in her lap, her fingers drumming out the tune as it was meant to be. The player hit the wrong keys once more, and she closed her eyes, the notes screeching against her senses. It was not often that she missed her natural mother, but this was one of those times. She would have had the courage to confront the player and show him the beauty of the melody.

"Your tea, sir."

It was only three simple words, but she knew who'd spoken them as clearly as she knew the piano player was butchering the tune. She opened her eyes, and sure enough, he was there.

Tobias. Wearing an apron over a pinstripe suit, his hair was cut much shorter than the last time she had seen him. His shoes were polished to a high gloss, making him look rather respectable. She could see the recognition in his eyes as they took her in, from the hat on her head to the boots on her feet. Before she could say his name, he shook his head in warning.

Her father took a sip of the tea and removed the bill from beneath the goblet. "I must say that was a very good year for tea."

Tobias took the bill. "If you find yourself in need of a refill, just let your waiter know. He knows where to find me."

He was going to leave without as much as a word of acknowledgment. Hoping to delay his departure, Mildred removed the long spoon and thrust the glass in his direction. "I would like some more tea, if you please."

Tobias turned his attention to her. "I will ask the waiter to bring you some fresh from the kitchen."

She eyed the pitcher in his hand. "And what is wrong with the tea you have?"

"I'm afraid this tea is rather strong. It would not blend very well with the berries in your glass."

Mildred lowered the spoon into the glass, fished out the berries, and shoved them into her mouth, swallowing them whole. Lowering the spoon, she offered him the glass once more.

Tobias studied her for a moment before looking to John for direction. To her surprise, John nodded his approval. Tobias placed his fingers against the spoon, then proceeded to fill the glass. When finished, he removed the spoon and handed her the glass. "Try not to spit it out. It would be a shame to waste any."

Mildred lifted the glass, sniffed the contents, then took a taste. The second it hit her throat, it began to burn. As much as she wished to spit it out, she would not give him the pleasure. Instead, she drank the contents and handed him the glass once more.

"That will be enough, young man," John said, dismissing him.

Tobias nodded and walked away without another word.

"They are over there," John said,

pointing.

"What?" Mildred whispered through the burn in her throat.

"The facilities; you look a bit green," he said solemnly.

Mildred leapt from her chair without comment, hurrying across the room to the women's lounge. She expected to get sick. She also expected Helen to follow her into the room and tell her she had acted out of line. Neither of which happened. After composing herself, she exited the lounge and was pleased to see Tobias leaning against the far wall. She narrowed her eyes at him and started for her seat. She had taken but three steps when he grabbed her by the arm and spun her around.

"You will be so kind as to remove your hand."

He laughed.

"What is so funny?"

"Oh, Mileta, if I didn't know any better, I would say you were born to this crowd. Playing hard to get when your face says otherwise. Look at how you are dressed, all prim and proper."

Mildred struggled to get out of his grip. "If you are going to make fun of me, I have nothing more to say to you."

He released his hold, then straightened the hat on her head. "Don't go getting your feathers ruffled; I'm glad you found a nice home. You clean up well, kid. You remind me of someone."

Her heart skipped a beat. All of her friends at school told her she looked like the silent film actress Clara Bow. Could it be Tobias saw the resemblance as well? "I could say the same about you… that you clean up nice."

He laughed once more. "The suit? Na, it is just a loaner to get me into this establishment."

Mildred jutted her jaw and narrowed her eyes. "I'm not a kid."

He brushed his hand down her arm. "No, that you are not. You've filled out pretty nice there, Mileta."

The piano music grew louder. The player had changed the tune, but the playing was just as poor. She closed her eyes briefly and felt the room spin. "I am not Mileta. I left that name behind when I left everything else I know. My friends, my piano. Oh, what I would give to play again. That player should be ashamed of himself butchering the keys like that," she said heatedly.

His brow creased, his nostrils flared slightly. "Want me to cut off his fingers for you?"

Something in the way he said it made her think he might not be kidding. "No, of course not. I just wish someone would give him lessons."

"Why don't you play? Your family is loaded. Can't they buy you a piano?"

"They do not know I play. We do not talk about my past. Mother said it is better that I leave that life behind me. She said the girls in my school would not be nice to me if they knew my background. We invented a story of how we had just moved here." The piano player missed another key, causing her to cringe. "I have to go; my parents will be worried about me."

Tobias pulled her close, pressed his lips to hers, then, just as quickly, he released her and was gone.

Mildred made her way back to her table on wobbly heels. She could still feel the warmth of Tobias' lips on hers. She thought back to the things Mary had told her and how awful she had made them sound. Then she remembered what Dorthia had said, *not so terrible, sometimes*. While Mildred trusted Mary, she wondered if she had gotten this one wrong. One thing was for sure, Tobias' kiss had not felt wrong in the least.

"I'm sorry, Mother and Father," she said, once seated.

Helen remained silent as John dabbed his mouth with his napkin then addressed Mildred. "We could have told you no, but then you would have always wondered. Better to see for yourself than to have you seek what we forbid. It is an acquired taste, and I pray you never acquire it."

"I think I will stick with raspberry tea," Mildred replied, lifting the glass that had made its way to the table in her absence.

***

Cindy jumped when her mother came into the room. She'd waited all day to hear what she had to say about the latest notebook. "Well?"

Linda handed her the notebook. "I don't know where to start. She was thirteen and her father allowed her to drink. Do you realize that woman witnessed Houdini's final show and never once thought to mention it? And what do you think about this Tobias kid? I think he is sweet on her. Wouldn't surprise me if she marries the boy."

Cindy had to admit she'd been thinking the same thing. "Except we both know she married Grandpa Howard."

"Well, she is at least going to sleep with the boy."

"Mom! This is Grandma Mildred we are talking about. Prim and proper, remember?"

"She flirted with the boy right in front of her parents," Linda reminded her.

"Right! I can't believe she acted that blatant. Especially in front of her mother."

"I am dying to find out how the story ends. How many more of those notebooks do you have?"

"It ends with her marrying Grandpa Howard. I have several more."

"Exactly. Do you think there would be that many notebooks if Mildred were only discussing her life with Howard? You saw them together. Not exactly a steamy relationship. How much can there be for her to write about? You sleepy?"

Cindy stifled a yawn. "Not in the least."

"Me either. I'll make coffee."

"Good idea. I'll grab some more notebooks."

Chapter Eighteen

July 4^{th,} 1929

"Come in," Mildred responded to the knock on her bedroom door.

The door opened, and Helen stepped into the room. "Are you sure you don't want to come with us to Point Pelee? The weather is supposed to be most agreeable."

Mildred sighed. Her parents had been trying to get her to change her mind since telling them she would not be joining them on the holiday day trip across the bridge to Canada. She was hand piecing a quilt that she intended to sell to earn money to purchase a special anniversary present for her mother and father. "I just can't. This quilt is taking forever to finish."

"If you come with us, I will help you with the quilt," Helen offered.

Tempting as it sounded, she shook her head no. The fact that her parents paid for the fabric was bad enough. Getting further help from her mother would be no different than asking for the money in the first place. She had been relying on her parents' money from the day she first arrived. This was her chance to use her own money to buy them something special to show how much she appreciated everything they had done for her. "You and Father go and have fun. But you must promise to tell me all about it when you return."

"I promise." Helen frowned. "Maybe we should just stay home. I've been on edge all morning."

Mildred paused her sewing. "Nonsense. You and Father have been looking forward to this. You are just upset about yesterday's St. Aubin Street Massacre."

Helen rubbed at her arms. "You are probably right. I simply cannot believe something like that happened so close to our home. Five miles; it might as well have been five houses down. To kill a whole family, what kind of animal does that?"

"Now, Mother, you must not let this ruin your holiday. The paper said they arrested someone of interest."

"True, but I would feel so much better if you were to join us."

Mildred smiled. "And I would feel so much better if I could finish this quilt. I promise to lock the doors."

"Locking the doors; I never thought I would see the day when we have to lock the doors in this neighborhood. What is happening to Detroit?"

John's voice drifted up the stairs. "Helen? Are you ready? We will have to leave soon to avoid the holiday rush."

"I'll be right down." Helen smiled. "He's just anxious to go because I told him I have a new bathing suit and I even plan on getting in the water. Last time I did that, your father had to dive in to save me."

Mildred pictured her parents frolicking in the water and blushed. "Then you would not wish to have me along to spoil your fun."

Helen gave her a peck on the cheek. "There is a roast in the icebox if you get hungry."

"And bread in the breadbox," Mildred finished.

Helen sighed and moved to the door. "We will be home in time to collect you to go see the fireworks. I love you, my daughter."

"I love you too, Mother."

And with that, Helen was gone.

Mildred waited until she heard the door shut before making her way downstairs. Moving through the house, she double-checked the doors and lowered the windows, only relaxing after making sure everything was secure. It was not like her mother to be overly dramatic, and by being so, she had managed to get under Mildred's skin. Shaking off her unease, Mildred returned to her room and her quilting.

***

It was nearly two before she made her way back downstairs. She carved off a slice of beef and placed it between two slices of bread. She considered sitting at the table then, realizing how stuffy the first floor of the house was with the windows shut, changed her mind. Taking her sandwich, she opened the front door and studied the street, looking for anything out of the ordinary. Not seeing any cause for alarm, she sat on the top stoop and ate her lunch. The sun was hot, but the slight breeze helped. Closing her eyes, she leaned back, stretching out her legs. She felt the hem of her dress touch her upper thigh. She pulled it higher, fanning it a bit to cool her legs.

"You keep that up, and you are going to give the neighbors the wrong impression."

Mildred jumped, pulling at her dress to cover herself. Much to her surprise, Tobias was leaning against the tree staring at her. It frightened her that he had gotten so close without her knowing. What if it had been someone with ill intentions? Even more frightening to think about, what if Tobias was the one with ill intentions? She hadn't seen him since the evening at the hotel when he had offered to cut off the piano player's fingers. Since he had disappeared so quickly, she had never gotten to ask him if he was serious.

She worked to keep the fear out of her voice. "What are you doing here?"

He feigned hurt. "What? You're not happy to see me?"

"Not when you sneak up on me. How did you know where I live?"

A smile played at his lips. "Doll, I know everything about you."

Now he was just being fresh. "That is impossible."

"You just turned sweet sixteen. I am the only boy you have ever kissed. And you wish I would kiss you again," he said with a waggle of his dark eyebrows.

She narrowed her eyes.

"I will have you know I've kissed lots of boys." It was a lie, but his arrogance was maddening.

"You're cute when you lie." He pushed off from the tree.

She stood and reached for the door. "I am not lying. And you stop right there or I will scream for my father."

He chuckled. "You had better scream loud enough for him to hear you in Canada."

Panic ebbed at the pit of her stomach. "How did you know they were not at home?"

"I told you, doll; I know everything about you. Relax," he said, leaning back against the tree. "I just came by to check on you. There is a crazy man on the loose or haven't you heard?"

She relaxed slightly. "The paper said the police had arrested a suspect."

Another chuckle. "There's not enough evidence to hold the guy. Not that it matters. They put the bracelets on him to still the fears of the public."

"He had a bloody knife," she said, repeating what she had read in the newspaper.

"No matter. I'm telling you, the coppers will set him free."

"Because you know everything."

"Because I know enough," he corrected.

"If you know where I live, why have I not seen you before now?" she asked.

His smile faded. "I have my reasons."

"Which are?"

He took off his hat and spun it on his fingers. "Maybe I was waiting for you to grow up."

"And now that I have?"

His face turned serious and he stilled the hat. "I plan on courting you."

There was something in the way he said it that warned her not to laugh. She had found herself smitten with him from the moment he saved her from the Shivelys all those years ago on the train. After the day at the parade, she found herself looking for him whenever she was in public. Then, after he had kissed her at the Cadillac Hotel, she had memorized the way his lips felt on hers, even though they had only lingered for a moment. Still, she had not expected this. Not after all this time. "Courting me?"

He returned the hat to his head. "Will that be a problem?"

She lowered her eyes. "I would like that very much."

"Very well, I will speak with your father when he returns this afternoon."

Her heart sank. "My father will not allow it."

He glared at her. "And why not?"

"He wishes for me to marry an educated man. He has a friend who has a son. He has been speaking very highly of Robert of late. His family is supposed to come by this weekend for dinner."

Tobias puffed his chest. "How do you know I am not an educated man?"

"Robert is going to college."

"Do you like this Robert?"

She wrinkled her nose. "He sounds

like a bore.”

Tobias’ face remained surprisingly calm. “I will speak with your father this evening. He will agree to allow me to court you.”

“You seem so sure of yourself. Do you even have a job?”

“I have enough scratch to take care of the both of us.”

“You did not answer my question.”

“Listen, doll, where my dough comes from is my business.”

Mildred shrugged. “My father will expect more of an answer than that.”

“Let me worry about your father. I have dealt with tougher nuts than him.”

“Promise me you will not hurt him.”

Tobias’ eyes grew wide. “What would make you think I would hurt anyone?”

“Obviously, you do not remember our last conversation.”

He smiled. “Actually, I remember it rather well.”

“Then you remember offering to cut a man’s hands off just because he could not play the piano.”

“Just his fingers,” he corrected. “His playing was causing you grief. I merely wished to alleviate your pain."

"By inflicting pain on him?"

"By doing whatever necessary to make you smile."

"Why?"

"Why what?"

"Why do you care about me? Even before I met you, you were protecting me. That time on the train…" She shivered against an unseen chill.

"It doesn't matter."

"It does to me."

He kicked at the dirt with the toe of his shoe. "Back then, it was different."

"Different how?"

"You were a little kid who was about to go to a very bad place. I was not going to allow that to happen."

"I'm not a little kid anymore."

"Don't I know it." He leaned against the tree once more.

She patted the concrete stoop. "Would you like to sit beside me?"

"That's not such a good idea."

"Why not?"

"As you just said, you are not a kid anymore. I don't trust myself not to soil your reputation."

She laughed. "You think I could not resist you?"

"I think should I wish to have my way with you that you wouldn't have a choice." He shoved off the tree. "I will return in a few hours to speak with your father. Not to worry, I have a way of getting what I want."

She watched him walk down the street a ways, slide into a burgundy Model A convertible, and start the engine. Maybe he wasn't lying about the money. She observed him driving off before she finally returned to the house. A small part of her wished she had asked him to join her. A larger part was glad she had not, for she had no doubt he could indeed be extremely persuasive. She busied herself with her sewing. However, as the day wore on, she was finding it difficult staying on task. Instead, she found herself wondering what it would be like to be courted by Tobias. Not for the first time, she wished she could speak to Mary then simultaneously wished she could speak to Dorthia, who she was certain would have more positive things to say on the matter. She couldn't talk to her friends at school as that would mean she would have to tell them how she'd come to meet Tobias in the first place. While she'd made friends, she'd never allowed them to get too close to her. And never had she mentioned the trains, not after seeing how the people in the mercantile had acted when Mrs. Shively told them she had come from New York on the trains. The last thing she wanted was for her friends to think less of her.

Sudden loneliness washed over her, as if just thinking of her friends could make her current life disappear. Setting the quilt aside, she moved to her closet to look over her wardrobe. She selected a cheerful blue cotton print dress to bring out the blue in her eyes. After changing into the dress, she wandered around the house, opening the windows, all thoughts of the dangers that lay outside forgotten. She wondered how long her father would make them court before allowing them to marry. The sound of the Ford rumbling to a halt pulled her from her musings. She hurried to the window, expecting to see her mother and father in the driveway, only to be disappointed. There was a firm knock on the door, and she hurried to answer it, thinking they must have parked on the street. Opening the door, she stared in the face of two slender men wearing dark-colored suits. Detectives. The thought crossed her mind even before they confirmed her suspicions. No one else would be dressed that way on such a dreadfully hot afternoon. Instantly, she wondered if their visit had something to do with the murders they had read about in the paper. If what Tobias had said was true, they would still be investigating. It did not occur to her to wonder if they were looking for a murderer, why they would be knocking on her door.

The taller of the two men opened his coat and produced a badge. "Detective Stokes and Johnston, Detroit P.D. Are you the daughter of John and Helen Daniels?"

Unease crept into the pit of her stomach. "I am."

"May we come in? It is important," he added when she hesitated.

Her unease intensified.

Mildred moved aside, allowing them access, and watched as they moved through the living room, sizing up the space.

"Please sit down," she said, waving a

hand toward the sofa, and took a seat on the loveseat after they were both seated.

"Young lady, there is no easy way to tell you this, so I will just come out and say it. Your parents are dead. There was a water incident at Point Pelee. According to witnesses, your dad ignored the signs, which denoted a strong current. Your mother rushed in to try and save him, and they both drowned. We were fortunate enough to have recovered both bodies."

Mildred burst into sobs, and the detective who had delivered the news moved to sit beside her. He placed a hand on her shoulder as she continued to cry. The front door opened and Tobias walked into the room as if he had done so hundreds of times before. The detective who was consoling Mildred stood and Tobias eased into the spot he vacated and draped a protective arm around her.

Mildred was in a fog, trying to make sense of what was happening. The fog lifted as she was yanked from her grief the second Tobias opened his mouth.

"What seems to be the problem here, officers, and could someone please tell me why my wife is crying?"

Chapter Nineteen

"Are you so shameless that you would prey on my grief?" Mildred screeched the second the detectives left.

Tobias moved to the front window and peeked past the curtain. "Shhhh, keep your voice down. The bulls will hear you."

She wanted to scream but did as he said and lowered her voice. "The bulls are police detectives. Why did you lie to them? Do you not think they will find out?"

He glanced out the window once more. "They might if they decide to follow up. By then, we'll be married, and they will not be in a position to do anything about it."

Mildred was trying desperately to remain calm. "Did you not hear what they just said? My mother and father have died. How could you possibly court me now? It would not be proper."

Tobias moved away from the window but still kept his voice lowered. "Mileta, please calm down."

"Stop calling me Mileta; my name is Mildred."

"I'm sorry, doll. I thought that maybe since your parents no longer had a hold over you that you might want to use your real name."

She whirled on him. "Mildred is my real name. My parents gave it to me."

His expression softened. "Did they formally adopt you, Mildred?"

"They did. We went to court and everything."

"That's a good thing. Less likely they will send you back on the trains," he said softly.

The meaning of his words hit her hard. Her parents were dead. With no way to contact her birth mother, she would now be officially labeled an orphan. Fresh tears sprang from her eyes. "Oh, Tobias, I cannot go to another asylum. Not after all of this," she said, looking around the room.

"Don't you worry about that. I wouldn't dream of letting anyone take you away from me again."

"But how can we stop them?" she asked through her sobs.

"We will get married." The casualness

of his statement surprised her.

She looked into his eyes, trying to gauge his sincerity. "I…I don't know."

"It's the only way, doll. If you stay here, the bulls will find out, and when they do, they will take you to an asylum. I don't know if it would be here or somewhere else. Either way, you will be locked up. And at your age, if you are lucky enough to find a home again, it could be with someone like those uppity folks on the train. That man had his sights on you, and he was up to no good. We need to go soon." He moved closer and captured a tear with his thumb. "You trust me, don't you?"

"Yes." At least, she wanted to.

"Millie… is it okay if I call you that?"

She nodded.

"I know you are hurting inside. But we have to get hitched right away. You are right; the bulls will find out. When they do, it could mean a lot of trouble. But if you have a manacle on your hand, there won't be anything they can do about it."

"A manacle?"

"A wedding ring. Something big and sparkly." He smiled. "A beautiful girl like you needs a large piece of ice to show she is taken."

She felt her face turn red with his compliment. "Oh, Tobias, you don't need to spend all of your money on me. I don't need anything expensive."

"Don't you worry your pretty little head. I'm going to take care of you just fine. Now you go on upstairs and pack."

"Pack? Where are we going?" It was all so overwhelming.

"I'm taking you to my place. They can't send you away if they can't find you."

Marrying him was one thing, but leaving her home terrified her. "But... I thought you said it would be okay if we get married."

"It will. All the same, I think you and I should lay low for a while. Now do as I said and go pack. I am going to go pick up a larger machine. My Tin Lizzy looks good, but she doesn't have room for all your stuff. I'll be back in a shake, so be ready."

He gave her a nudge toward the stairs.

"Millie."

She turned toward him. "Yes?"

"Go through your folks' room. Take anything of value. Cash. Jewelry. Anything you want to remember them by. The stuff belongs to you now. If you don't take it, someone else will. They are gone. They're not going to miss it," he added when she hesitated. "Also, when you pack your bags, pack as if you are never coming back."

Mildred turned when she reached the top of the stairs, but Tobias was already gone. He was good at disappearing, only this time, she had no doubt he would return. When she got to her bedroom, she paused, staring and hoping to ingrain it into her memory. She loved her room. Helen had offered to redo it many times over the years since Mildred first arrived. But she had always refused. It was the same lovely pink as when she'd first arrived five years ago. She loved it just as much now as she did then. One thing was for sure; someday, she would have another room in this very color.

Her legs felt weak as she moved through her bedroom gathering her things, placing them in neat piles on the bed. She pulled all the clothes from her closet. Surely she would need these. Even though it would not be needed for its original intention, she gathered the quilt she'd been working on, folded it neatly, and placed it and her sewing kit beside her growing pile. As she turned, she saw the doll her mother bought her lying in her usual spot on the bed. She'd never played with it. However, she had shared many secrets with it. She looked over her shoulder to make sure no one was watching and added it to the things she was taking.

Opening her keepsake box, she debated over the ticket she'd saved from Harry Houdini's performance. She remembered the day as if it were yesterday. It was a day of firsts for her. She had worn her first pair of heels. Gotten her first kiss from Tobias. It had been her first trip to the theater to see a live performance. She'd been distracted by Tobias' kiss for most of the performance. If she'd have known it was to be Houdini's final performance, she would have paid better attention. As it was, when her friends had asked if she could tell he was ill, all she could say was he seemed fine to her.

Tobias' words echoed in her head. *Pack as if you are never coming back*. She tossed the ticket onto the bed with the rest of her belongings and continued going through her things.

Was this really happening? Had her world truly capsized so quickly? She thought back to the last conversation with her mother. Helen had been worried about leaving her alone. Had she somehow known she would not be returning to care for her? Was that the ill feeling she could not shake? And what if she would have relented and gone with them, would she too now be dead? At least she would not be alone for the second time in her life.

Not alone. Tobias wanted to marry her. He had asked if she trusted him. While he was somewhat evasive in answering her questions, he had protected her on more than one occasion. Whatever Tobias was, she felt certain he would not let anything bad happen to her. She placed the items she was holding on her bed, and taking a deep breath, moved to her parents' room.

The second she entered, tears began anew. Her parents might be dead, but the room was alive with memories of them. Everywhere she looked, everything she touched, every breath she took reminded her of her mother and father. She picked up a photo of the three of them taken the day of her adoption. She traced her parents' images with her finger, her tears spilling onto the beveled glass. She tried to console herself with the knowledge they were not her birth mother and father, but it did not work. While not related by blood, John and Helen had taken her in, wrapped their arms around her, and breathed life into her shattered soul.

Grief threatened to suffocate her, but fear overrode the desire to curl into a ball, cry herself to sleep, and pray when she woke this would all turn out to be just a terrible nightmare.

She placed the photo on the bed and moved to the dresser, opening drawers and sifting through the contents. It pained her to invade their privacy. She had to keep reminding herself that her parents were dead just so she didn't feel as if she was stealing from them. Only that knowledge kept her moving forward, claiming everything of value. She lifted a nightgown and froze. Under the gown was the pink dress she had worn the day her parents selected her. It had been washed and pressed and was now snuggled amongst her mother's most intimate things. She pressed it to her cheek, wondering why her mother had never mentioned keeping it. She thought about returning it to the drawer but decided against it. If her mother had found it worth saving, then she too would take it with her, if only to remember the woman who had chosen her when another had given her away.

She pulled the empty travel trunk from the closet and began filling it with items she'd scavenged. She put her mother's jewelry into a small silk sack along with a wad of bills she had found in her father's sock drawer. She didn't find much to take that belonged to her father. He wasn't the sort to collect things.

She took the cap off his cologne, closed her eyes, and breathed in the sent. She could almost hear his laughter and watch the way the skin near his eyes crinkled when he told her of his own childhood, saying, "Millie, let me tell you about the good old days."

Almost.

She screwed the cap onto the bottle and lowered it back to the dresser. As her fingers left the glass, the memory faded. She plucked the bottle from the dresser and placed it with the rest of the items she would be taking with her. She found the pocket watch her father wore on special occasions, the one that no longer worked. Her mother had been on him to get a new one, but John had resisted, promising her he would take it in to have it fixed. He never did.

The watch belonged to his father and his grandfather before that. Mildred always envied the fact that both Helen and John had grown up with their birth parents. She liked to listen to stories of when her parents were young. They both had such fond memories of their parents, all of which were long dead. A pity, as she would have liked to have known her grandparents. If she had known the rest of their family, maybe that was where she would be running to now, and not to a boy she hardly knew.

Mildred heard an automobile outside and hurried to the window. She held her breath until she saw Tobias exit a shiny black truck with bright red wheels. He looked up, saw her, patted the rounded fender of the truck, and smiled. While the cab of the truck looked small, they would have no trouble fitting the travel trunk into the back of the bed. If nothing else, Tobias was true to his word.

Chapter Twenty

It was nearly dark when Tobias stopped the truck at an apartment building on Detroit's lower east side. The street lights did little to hide the trash that littered the street. Tobias got out, slid two fingers into his mouth, and whistled.

Five boys who looked to be between ten and twelve leaped from a nearby stoop and rushed in their direction. Barefoot, filthy, and bone thin, they arrived, eager to do his bidding.

Tobias looked them over, pointed to two, and nodded toward the truck. "Think you boys can haul that trunk to the third floor?"

Both boys nodded, the taller of the two adding, "For enough dough, we'll haul the whole truck."

"The travel trunk will be enough for now," Tobias replied and dismissed the three smallest boys.

At seeing the disappointment on the

remaining boys' faces, Mildred reached into her coin purse.

Tobias stopped her. "Never give them money unless they earn it."

"Oh, you are right, I would not wish to hurt their pride."

Tobias frowned. "Pride don't have nothing to do with it. You give them scratch, and they will be begging at your heels like a stray pup. Eyes just as sad as one too. It's important for the lads to learn that or they will be living on the street all their lives."

Mildred noticed Tobias' sudden use of street lingo. "You sound as if you are speaking from experience."

He shrugged off the comment. "Just don't want you to be giving handouts is all."

Mildred watched as the two boys tried to finagle the heavy trunk from the truck bed, grunting and groaning with each push and pull.

"Can we at least allow others to help?" she asked softly.

Tobias sighed and beckoned the other boys back. "Fine, a nickel to each of you, after you get the trunk inside."

"Ten cents," Mildred countered and

laughed as the boys raced to give their friends a hand.

"Fifty cents just to carry a trunk up the stairs? Ha, you've got a lot to learn," Tobias said, shaking his head.

"It is heavy, and why must they use the stairs?"

"Have you smelled them?"

"No."

"Good. We are going to keep it that way. Up the stairs, number three-o-seven, and don't take all day."

"We won't, Mouse," one of the boys said. Another boy gave him a stern look and nudged him in the ribs. The boy who'd spoken turned beet red and turned his attention back to the heavy trunk.

It was the second time she'd heard someone refer to Tobias as Mouse. From the look on his face, he was not pleased she had heard his street name, not that having one mattered to her. Having a street name wasn't such a big deal; a lot of her friends had them. Her mind instantly went to Shorty, Slim, and Paddy. She smiled, even though thinking of her friends made her sad. She'd often wondered where her little group had ended up, Tobias being the only one she'd seen since leaving the train station. And even though he came over on the train, she did not count him as one of her trusted group, Mary's Gang, as they had called themselves. Mary was not the oldest, but she took on the part of big sister and surrogate mother to them all. Mary was the problem solver and peacekeeper of the group. In some ways, losing touch with her group of friends was like losing her family all over again. Tears welled in her eyes as she remembered the reason she was here. Brushing them aside, she followed Tobias into the building. They took the elevator and arrived well ahead of the boys. Tobias opened the door to the apartment and motioned her in.

The unit was sparsely decorated but seemed to be clean. The windows were open and devoid of curtains. Two simple chairs and a side table sat in the middle of the room. The bedroom had a tall dresser and a small bed, which looked hastily made. There was a bathroom in the unit. It was small, but at least it was private. One thing that surprised her was there didn't seem to be any personal belongings in the apartment, nothing that said anyone lived there.

"This is where you live?" she asked, turning to Tobias.

"It is where *we* live," he corrected.

"Where are your belongings?"

He shrugged. "In the closet."

She walked to the closet and opened the door. On the shelf were a couple of blankets and a thin grey-striped pillow. Hanging on the wooden bar were three button-down shirts, the suit he'd worn earlier, and a pair of grey trousers. "This is everything you own?"

He shrugged. "I'm a man with simple needs."

She thought about all the items she'd packed into the travel trunk and wondered if he would find her choices extravagant. As if thinking about the trunk made it appear, the door to the apartment burst open. Perspiring heavily, the boys pushed their way in, carrying their heavy load.

"Where do you want this, Mou…Mr. Lisowski?" one of the boys asked.

"Take it into the bedroom and put it on the floor beside the bed," Tobias replied.

Mildred watched in unspoken horror as the boys lugged everything she owned into Tobias' bedroom. While she'd agreed to come away with him, and he'd spoken of marriage, she had yet to fully realize the implications. She would be expected to share a bed with Tobias.

The boys emerged from the room smiling, obviously relieved to be rid of their heavy burden. Tobias paid them each separately, each child wrapping grubby fingers around the treasured coin. "You boys did a fine job and got rewarded for your hard work. I want you each to remember that. If you are willing to work, you will always have money in your pocket."

One of the younger boys flipped the coin, caught it, and shoved it into his pocket. "That's rich! We know how you earn your dough and working has nothing to do with it."

Another boy slapped the boy on the back of the head, and they all ran from the apartment.

"Ingrates!" Tobias yelled and slammed the door behind them. "It's getting late. You've had a long day. You must be ready for bed."

Once again, her thoughts drifted back

to Mary and the conversation they'd had about the awful things boys would do to girls in bed. Clutching her coin purse, she raced through the open door and hurried down the hallway. The elevator doors were closed, so she opted for the stairs instead. She'd gotten down two full flights when Tobias caught up with her, grabbing her arm and pinning her to the wall.

"What is the matter with you, girl? Are ya daft?" He was breathing hard, his breath heavy on her face.

"I…I cannot do this." Her heart was pounding, and she felt as if it would explode in her chest.

His voice grew tender, but he kept the weight of his body on hers. "We talked about this, Millie. We must get married; you agreed it is the only way to keep you from being sent back."

Her voice shook when she spoke. "I would like you to take me home. I prefer to take my chances there."

Tobias pulled back but kept his hands resting on both sides of the wall to prevent her from escaping. She blinked, wondering at the thoughts behind his dark eyes.

His expression didn't change. "Then

why did you agree to come with me?"

"I was not thinking straight. I didn't realize that we would be sleeping together."

His face remained stoic. "What did you think it would mean to get married?"

"I did not consider it. I just thought it would keep me from being sent back to the home. But this, us, you and I..." She struggled to find the right words. "There is only one bedroom. Mary told me bad things would happen in there."

"Is that what this was about?" he finally asked.

Afraid to speak, she simply nodded.

"I may not be the smartest of men, but I know the world you've grown up in. At least since coming to Detroit. I see it in the way you carry yourself. The way you dress and even in the way you speak. I would never take you against your will and never before we are properly married."

"There is only one bedroom," she repeated.

"And you will sleep there by yourself until we are married tomorrow," he said softly.

"Tomorrow?"

"The sooner, the better. If it wasn't so

late, and a holiday, we would have been married today."

Mildred felt the tension ease. She nodded her acceptance. She followed as Tobias led the way back up the stairway and hesitated as he went into the bedroom ahead of her. She heard a drawer slide open then close again. Seconds later, Tobias reemerged from the room. He walked to where she was standing and handed her a hanky. She unfolded the cloth and pulled out a long silver spoon. Turning it over, she read the inscription on the end of the handle. Book Cadillac. The spoon she'd used the last time she saw him. "You kept the spoon from my tea glass."

"I did."

"But why?"

"Because I love you."

His confession surprised her. "That was three years ago, Tobias. We haven't seen each other since."

"You haven't seen me," he corrected.

"What do you mean?"

"I told you I know everything about you. I know the route you take to school when it is in session, who your friends are, and where you go."

She blinked her surprise. "You have been following me?"

"Me or someone I trust when I am not there to watch you myself."

"Why?"

"To keep you safe...I love you," he repeated. "I have always known it on some level. But that day I gave you your first kiss, I knew I wanted to be the one to give you your second, third, and all the kisses after that."

"Then why did you not come to see me before this?"

He laughed. "Because your father would have never allowed us to be together. I saw the way he looked at me when he realized you were interested in me."

"Interested in you? I have no idea what you are talking about."

Tobias laughed. "The day you insisted I fill your glass. Your game was not lost on either of us."

Mildred remembered and blushed.

"Your father saw me for what I was at the time. A nobody with nothing to offer you." Tobias continued. "I knew if I had any chance with you, I would have to make something of myself. Show him I could buy you the things you deserve. I kept this silver spoon because it reminded me of you. It kept me focused on what I had to do to be with you. I'm giving it to you now so that you will see my intentions. I am not here to hurt you; I am here to protect you. The same way I treasured this spoon all these years, I will treasure you."

"I don't know what to say."

"Say you will give me a chance to make you happy. And that maybe someday you will come to love me as well. Will you stay with me, Millie? Will you go to the courthouse with me tomorrow and become my wife?"

Mildred wasn't sure if either set of parents would approve of her answer, not that it mattered. Tobias was here, and they were not. Clearly, she needed someone to look out for her. "Yes, I will marry you."

At her words, Tobias visibly relaxed. He moved to the bedroom and gathered the bedding from the top shelf of the closet. "Good. Now to bed with you; you've had a rough day."

Mildred watched as he spread the blankets on the floor of the living room. She felt guilty to be taking the only bed but not guilty enough to ask him to share it with her. Without another word, she closed the bedroom door.

Chapter Twenty-One

July 5th, 1929

Mildred woke in the same position as when she first lay down. She rolled over, stretched, and tried unsuccessfully to gauge the time. Her stomach growled, reminding her she hadn't had anything to eat since the roast beef sandwich the previous afternoon. A sudden sadness hit her as she remembered the events that led her to be here. Tobias said they were to be married today. Shouldn't she be happy on her wedding day? Wedding day? She was sixteen. While admittedly she had dreamed of marrying Tobias on many occasions, her dreams had her doing so in a church surrounded by friends and with her parents' blessings. Neither of her fathers was alive to walk her down the aisle, so how could she get married?

An image of her and Tobias standing in front of a judge suddenly came to her, adding to her distress. The judge would look upon her as if she were unclean, as if she'd been soiled and had to marry Tobias to protect her reputation. Nothing could be further from the truth. While she had told Tobias she had kissed many boys, the truth was he was the only boy she'd kissed. In reality, he had been the one doing the kissing. She'd just stood there in shock while he'd stolen the kiss. Just like he swooped in and stole her from her house last night while she was grieving.

Anger suddenly replaced her grief. She was angry at Tobias. At John and Helen for dying. At the train for bringing her to a place where she would feel safe, only to have her heart broken yet again. She was angry at her birth mother for abandoning her and her birth father for not only not making it to America but from uprooting them from their home in Poland in the first place.

Rising from the bed, she stormed across the room seething, ready to take on Tobias and whoever else got in her way. Pulling open the bedroom door, all her anger dissipated, replaced instead by instant confusion. With the exception of the orange leaf wallpaper and glass doorknobs, she had just stepped into her parents' living room. The chairs, long worn from years of use, were placed exactly where they had been in her parents' home. The couch, just as worn, took up the length of the far wall as it had on East Fort Street. Every detail was the same, including the quilt draped across the loveseat, also faded from years of use but much too good to throw away. It was the same quilt Helen, her new mother, had carefully tucked around her on the way home from the train station, jokingly referring to it as her birthing quilt, the one she used the day she brought her "baby" home. Alone in the room, she walked numbly to the couch. Pulling the quilt around her like a cloak, she wept.

The second time she woke, she heard muffled voices in the hall. Seconds later, the door opened, and Tobias came in carrying a box. The strain on his face told her the box was heavy. She hurried from the couch to help him. He waved her off, closing the door with his foot.

"You are awake. Are you hungry?" he asked as he placed the box on the counter.

"Quite," she answered in reply.

"Good. I brought cinnamon rolls from

the bakery."

She eyed the box on the counter. "They look heavy."

He caught the joke. "They are in a bag in the box."

She moved past him and opened the box. Lifting the bag exposed the rest of the contents. She gasped and placed the bag on the counter. Sifting through the box, she discovered many of her mother's favorite kitchen tools. The rolling pin, a cutting board, assorted bowls and dishes wrapped in linens from her mother's kitchen. Items she and her mother had used on numerous occasions. "Tobias, these are all things from my mother's kitchen."

He smiled. "They are."

"But why? You took …" She waved a hand toward the living room. "…everything."

The smile left his face. "We needed things for the apartment. I thought you would approve."

"I…I am not certain what to think. It feels wrong, taking from them."

"Mileta, Millie," he corrected, "I know this is hard on you, but if we don't take the things, others will. As soon as word gets out that they are dead, people will be crawling all over that house like roaches. Locks will not stop looters from stealing everything in the house."

Obviously not, she thought, looking around the room. "How did you get in the house? When did you do all of this? Did you not sleep?"

Tobias shrugged sheepishly. "I gathered a crew, and we picked everything up last night while you were sleeping."

A part of her wanted to thank him, but a larger part needed to lash out at someone. "So you did break in and steal these items."

His face turned solemn. "I broke in, yes, but I did not steal anything. Your parents are dead, Millie. Therefore, I merely brought these items to their rightful owner. I thought you would be happy to have them. I wanted to make you feel at home. I have money. I could have bought you new things. I was only trying to make you happy."

Tobias wrapped his arms around the box.

"What are you doing?"

"I'm taking everything back."

She placed a hand on his arm. "Please leave them."

"Are you sure?"

"Yes, I think so."

He released his grip on the box. "I will leave them here for now, but if you change your mind, say the word and I will take everything away. Agreed?"

"Agreed."

He started to speak then closed his mouth.

"What is it?"

"The boys are outside with the rest of the loot… your belongings." he corrected.

She walked to the window and let out a sigh. "Tell them to bring everything in."

Tobias' face brightened. He rushed to the window and whistled sharply. "Bring it all up, boys!"

The "boys" were, in fact, a group of three men, each looking to be close to or slightly older than Tobias' age. While they were all neatly dressed, there was something about the lot that made Mildred uncomfortable. It took them just over an hour to empty the truck and bring everything upstairs. When they finished, the once barren apartment had acquired a kitchen table with four matching chairs, two dressers, and several lamps, along with at least a dozen crates of belongings. From what she could tell, every item that once resided in Helen's kitchen was now in the modest apartment.

Tobias pulled out a thick wad of bills and peeled off several for each of them, before clapping each man on the back and telling them he would see them later.

"I do not even know where to begin," Millie said once they were alone.

"You will have plenty of time to figure it all out later."

Mildred swallowed her fear and went to search through the trunk she'd packed the previous evening. While she'd packed everything in her closet, not one garment seemed right to wear on her wedding day. Finally, out of desperation, she settled on the dress she'd planned to wear this weekend when she would have met the son of her father's friend. A light purple dress covered in lace that rested just below the knee. She pulled the dress out of the chest and made a futile attempt at smoothing the wrinkles. With trembling lips, she slid the wrinkled fabric over her head, suddenly grateful there were no full-length mirrors in the apartment. She fished out the matching shoes and slid her feet inside. She ran a comb through the length of her hair and opened the door, expecting to see Tobias. Instead, she was greeted with an empty room, devoid of people anyway. Piled high with boxes, the room was anything but empty. Her fingers lingered on a closed crate while Mildred wondered at the contents. Though her heart still grieved the loss of her parents, her tears never came. This was supposed to be a happy day, and to his credit, Tobias was trying to ease her pain. It was his special day too; she would do her best to remember that.

The door opened, and Tobias came in dressed in the grey suit that had been hanging in his closet the evening before. She wondered when he had retrieved it. He had a matching fedora tilted low on his head and held what appeared to be a garment bag. He looked her up and down and shook his head. "That dress will never do."

The tears she was trying to hide brimmed in her eyes. "This is the newest dress I own. I tried to get the wrinkles out…"

"It is not the dress, Millie. It is who the dress was intended for."

She felt a blush creep across her face.

"I told you I know everything about you." He moved across the floor and handed her the garment bag he was holding. "I would like you to wear this if you don't mind."

She pulled off the covering to find a delicately embroidered white on white chiffon dress. She pulled the fabric up to expose a thin layer of silk. While not a real wedding dress, the dress was stunning all the same. Hooked to the same hanger was a pair of white heeled shoes. "Oh, Tobias, the dress is beautiful. But how? Where?"

"I have my ways. Do you like it?"

She smiled. "Of course. As I said, it is very beautiful."

"It is but a dress. It is you that will make it look beautiful."

She had to hand it to him; the guy was a smooth talker. She started for the bedroom and then paused. "I will be quick."

He merely nodded in reply.

Moments later, she emerged from the bedroom to find him in the same spot as when she'd left. While Tobias had said it was she who would make the dress, she felt the opposite to be true. The coolness of the silk against her skin invigorated her. The laced chiffon fluttered against the silk like a butterfly trying to land on a flower but never actually taking hold. The fabric whispered as she moved, almost as if the dress was trying to tell the world her secrets. While the apartment did not have full-length mirrors, the look that swept over his face showed her she looked as pretty as the dress made her feel.

"You are stunning!" He said it as if seeing her for the first time.

"My mother would be horrified that you are seeing me before we are to be married."

"I'm afraid there is nothing that can be done about that."

Mildred shrugged. "I do not think it matters. She would not approve of the marriage; it is not as if we are getting married in a church."

He rolled his head as if to release tension, blew out a sigh, and held out his hand. "Come, Millie; it is time."

***

Mildred was shocked when they pulled up in front of Woodward Avenue Presbyterian Church. English Gothic in style, the church was rather imposing. "What are we doing here?"

"Why, getting married, of course."

"Here?"

"Unless you would prefer the courthouse."

A part of her wanted to say yes. "No."

Tobias opened the door for her and supported her elbow as they walked up the front sidewalk and in through one of the large double doors. Once inside, she could see the cavern of the enormous sanctuary. The ceiling was mostly stained glass, soft music from the huge pipe organ floated through the air, and the scent of flowers greeted them as they entered. A large crowd of people turned to stare at them as they approached.

Mildred froze. "Who are all of these people?"

"Friends who have come to see us wed. You look beautiful, and since your father cannot be here today, I will walk you all the way," he whispered. He pointed to the front pew. "See, you recognize the guys from earlier."

"I cannot…"

"You must, Millie. It is the only way I can keep you safe," he replied, urging her forward.

Her hands trembled as she held the bouquet. The preacher's words were lost in her confusion. She didn't know how Tobias had managed to pull off such an elaborate wedding in the time he'd had to plan. There were even flowers draped along the edges of the pews. Even if she hadn't been too busy to ask, she was sure she already knew his answer. *I have my ways.* It wasn't until the preacher asked for the rings and Tobias slipped her mother's wedding ring onto her hand that reality came back with a jolt. She tried to pull her hand away, but Tobias held firm, clasping his hand around hers. Unaware of her distress, the preacher asked her for Tobias' ring. A boy stepped up and handed her a single band. She relaxed slightly after seeing he did not intend to wear her father's ring. With strangers watching, she slipped the band onto his hand. The preacher pronounced them husband and wife and Tobias sealed the promise with a kiss that brought everyone to their feet and nearly made her topple off her heels.

"I love you, Mildred Lisowski," he said, using her new married name. "I fell in love with you long before we met, and I will love you until the day that I die."

She was about to ask him what he meant, when they were rushed by a throng of well-wishers.

It didn't matter much anyway; she was sure he had his ways.

***

"Don't tell me you are too tired to turn the page," Linda said when Cindy hesitated.

"Of course I'm tired, but that's not what's stopping me."

Linda laughed. "You are afraid your grandmother is going to describe her wedding night."

"And you're not?"

Linda laughed again, this one ending in a snort. "Come on; there is only one page left, she can't have gone into too much detail."

"Any amount of detail is too much," Cindy groaned. She couldn't believe her mother was so eager to find out. "I'm closing my eyes. You turn the page and tell me if it's safe."

"You're safe," her mother said with a sigh. "It is only a few sentences."

"You sound so disappointed."

Linda shrugged as they both read the final page.

I never did ask Tobias how he'd gotten the church or my mother's ring. While a part of me was still angry, a greater part of me was grateful to have the one item I knew my mother cherished above all others. True to his word, Tobias did not force himself on me; he waited until I was ready. He didn't have to wait long. I was sixteen and curious. The details of our intimacy are not anyone's business, but in case you are wondering, Dorthia was right.

"Well, that was disappointing," Linda said, closing the notebook.

Cindy turned and stared at her mother.

"What?"

Oh, why bother? It was the most spark she'd seen in her mother since her dad had passed. "I think it's time we call it a night."

"Bummer," Linda said with a yawn. "At least tell me there is more to the story."

"Yes, we still have more notebooks." Cindy refrained from telling her the extent of the reading yet to be done.

Linda's face brightened. "Good. We'll begin bright and early."

"Mom, it is after two, and this is still my summer break. I plan on sleeping in while I still can. Fine, I'll set my alarm for ten," Cindy said after seeing the look of disappointment that crossed Linda's face.

Linda lay her head on Cindy's shoulder. "I know it's silly, but I need to see how her story turns out. She lost her parents, married a boy she didn't know, and who has way too much money and clout for someone his age. I'm worried about her."

"It doesn't sound silly at all, Mom. I'm worried about her too." As the words came out of her mouth, Cindy was struck by the fact that she had more feelings for her grandmother in death than she ever did when the woman was alive. While that should make her sad, it actually made her feel better. For the first time, she was beginning to understand why her grandmother was so closed off.

Chapter Twenty-Two

Cindy was beyond surprised to find her mother gone when she awoke. The woman had not left the house on her own will since moving in with her two years ago. She was about to call Linda's cell phone when she heard the slam of a car door.

"Oh good, you're up," Linda said, bustling through the door as if it were nothing.

Cindy watched in amazement as her mother deposited several thin grocery bags onto the table and headed back out the door. The woman returned a second time with a large box whose packaging declared it to be a multipurpose printer. Linda sat the box onto the table and headed back outside without a word. Cindy knew she should offer to help, but in all honesty, Linda seemed to have everything under control. Curious, she walked to the table to peek inside the bags. Printer ink, printer paper, a new hairbrush, and a package of white powdered doughnuts. Cindy pulled out the doughnut box and opened it.

"Oh good, you found your breakfast," Linda said, returning with a watermelon and a pair of gardening gloves.

"You know you can't plant that, right?" Cindy said as she entered.

Linda's smile faded. "Just because I'm old don't mean I'm stupid. If I were going to plant it, I wouldn't have bought seedless."

Cindy stopped chewing and stared at her mother. *Crap, maybe I should start hiding the keys.*

"Haha, got you, of course I know I can't plant it. I needed new gloves and thought that since I was at Wally World, why not pick up a pair."

"Yeah, about that. And just why were you at Walmart again?" *Why were you anywhere*, Cindy thought but didn't ask.

"We needed a printer."

"We did?"

"Sure, you said yourself that we have more notebooks to read. I am not going to sit reading over your shoulder all day, and don't even think of asking me to wait until you are finished. I want to get to the bottom of things just as much as you do."

It made Cindy's heart happy to see her mother so full of life. Who would have known Grandma Mildred's notebooks would be the thing to pull her mother from her funk. She plopped another doughnut into her mouth then pulled the printer box closer.

***

It was after twelve before, working as a team, they had gotten the rest of Mildred's notebooks copied. Linda had excused herself long enough to run to the Arches to bring back lunch. Apparently, surviving her morning outing gave her courage. Fed, with bottles of water at their disposal, they were both snuggled on the couch, ready to dive into the rest of the journals.

"When you are ready for dinner, say the word. I have Pizza Hut on speed dial," Linda said, placing her cell phone on the side table.

"Sounds like a plan," Cindy replied. *I missed you, Mom.* She wanted to say it aloud but decided against it. The last thing she wanted to do was draw attention to the fact that Linda was acting normal, as if somehow in doing so would send her mother into a relapse. Instead, she sent her mom a mental hug and picked up her copy of the next journal. As she opened the cover, she realized there was a folded note pinned to the inside of the cover.

"Hmm, wonder how we missed this," she said, carefully peeling the tape away from the cover. Opening the note, she read it aloud. "My Dearest Cynthia, I struggled greatly whether or not I should destroy this section of the journal. In the end, I knew I had to leave it. Destroying this would have meant destroying the one before and then no one would have known of her existence. But alas, I am getting ahead of myself."

"I knew it!" Linda said, taking the note. "That boy done went and found him another woman."

Cindy's brow wrinkled. "I'm not so sure; Tobias seems to love her."

"What's love got to do with it?" Linda snorted.

"How about we read and find out? Whoever is wrong buys the pizza."

Cindy smiled at her mother. "Deal."

***

February 14, 1931

I woke to find a vase of red roses waiting for me on the kitchen counter. I wish Tobias would not be so reckless with his money, since it is in such short supply these days. He tells me not to worry, but how can I not when it seems as if each day brings another bank fail. I know we do not get our money the way most of Detroit gets it, but it appears even dishonest folks can be affected by this depression…

Mildred shifted in the chair to avoid the spring that was doing its best to poke through the fabric. She pulled at the quilt she was working on to center it once more. Just as she got comfortable, she heard shouting in the hallway; seconds later, the baby began to cry. She set her quilting aside and went to see to the infant, who'd only just fallen asleep. The baby held her arms against the side of her head, her tiny fingers clutched into tight fists as she screamed her displeasure. Mildred reached to untangle one of the fingers that had become tangled in one of the black curls. Mildred smiled as she freed the finger and watched as the strand of hair kinked and fell into place with the others. While she could not remember a great deal about her birth mother, she knew her daughter had inherited her grandmother's hair.

Mildred cradled her newborn to her breast and whispered, "Hush, Fannie, all the bad things are outside those doors. Your father will be home soon."

Fannie's screams continued until Mildred unbuttoned her blouse and placed the child to her breast. Mildred paced the floor, gently bouncing her daughter and smiling at the baby's greedy gulps. Fannie's eyes fluttered, then remained closed as the sucking lessened. Mildred waited until Fannie was fully asleep before returning her to the cradle in the bedroom. As she was leaving the room, she heard laughing and shouting in the hallway. Carefully shutting the bedroom door, she hurried to the main door. Unbolting the lock, she yanked the door open to confront the noisemakers. Mildred fumed as she opened the door and stepped out into the dim hallway.

Two men she did not recognize stood on the opposite side of the hallway laughing and joking, their voices echoing through the empty hall.

Mildred threw her hands up and addressed the men. "Must you make so much noise? My daughter is trying to sleep!"

Conversation forgotten, the men turned toward her, leering as they looked her up and down. Mildred looked to see what had caught the men's attention. To her horror, in her haste, she had forgotten to button her blouse. She pulled her shirt together and took a step backward. The door had shut behind her, and she found herself pressed against the sturdy wood.

"What's your hurry, pretty lady?" the smaller of the two men asked.

The larger man licked his lips. "Yeah, what's your hurry? You want us to be quiet. I'm sure we could find something else to do."

As the large man stepped forward, two small boys stepped out of the shadows. One of the boys ran between them, cut to the right, and raced down the stairs. The other, who looked to be around eleven, walked over and stood between Mildred and the two men.

With the men's attention averted, Mildred hurried to refasten her blouse.

"Beat it, squirt!" the larger of the two men yelled.

"Yeah, you know what's good for you, you'll follow your little chicken friend down the stairs."

The boy squared his shoulders. "I ain't going nowhere. I'm staying right here to protect the lady."

The first man laughed. "You hear that? This little stain is going to take us on. The lady don't need no protecting. She's got us to look out for her. Isn't that right, Lyle?"

"Oh yes, James and I, we're going to look after her real nice now."

Mildred swallowed hard and reached a hand behind her back to search for the doorknob. The knob twisted, and the door creaked open. Thankfully, the inside of the apartment was quiet.

James smiled. "Oh look, Lyle, the nice lady is inviting us inside."

She quickly twisted the lock and pulled the door closed behind her. Whatever they had planned, they would have to do in the hallway. They were not getting near her baby.

The men stepped closer; the boy doubled his fists, causing both men to hoot with laughter.

"Just what do you think you are going to do with those two little rocks?" James asked, pushing him out of the way.

The boy got up, leaned forward, and rammed into James' leg. As he did, he opened his mouth and bit through the man's pants.

James swore and kicked him off, sending the kid sliding across the floor. The boy landed in a heap against the wall. When he didn't get up, Mildred moved to check on him.

James caught her by the arm. "Boy's got guts, but I guarantee those guts will be splattered across the walls if he don't stay down. Now, what say we have ourselves a cozy little chat?"

"Yeah, I want to chat with her too." Lyle giggled, reaching for the door. Finding it locked, the giggling stopped. "Dame done gone and locked the door."

James pressed his fingers deeper into Mildred's arm. "Then the dame can unlock the door."

Mildred sucked in her breath against the pain. "I don't have the key with me."

The words had no sooner left her mouth than James' hand connected with her face, snapping her head back and reducing her to tears.

James yanked her in front of him. "We were going to play nice. But since you ain't giving us no choice, we gonna break down your door and take you right in front of that baby of yours. We might even take that baby when we leave."

The elevator dinged just as James finished his sentence. The doors opened, and seven boys raced out of the elevator. Mildred recognized them all but didn't know any of their names. One of the boys was the lad who had fled down the stairs. The boys were small, yet braced for battle, each child wielding a weapon of some sort. If Mildred hadn't been in pain, and afraid for her safety, she would have applauded the small group. As it was, she feared for their safety as much as she did her own.

"You think we're afraid of a few little street hoods?" James asked then spat at the group.

The boy who had run glared at him.

"It's not us you have to be scared of. You're new here, right?"

"What of it?" James snarled.

"Yeah, we're taking over Hastings Street," Lyle said, speaking up.

"Well, this lady has connections," the boy said with a nod to Mildred.

"What kind of connections?" James asked.

Yeah, what kind of connections? Mildred wondered.

The lead boy nodded toward Mildred. "She's not to be touched."

James laughed. "Says who?"

The boy grew a little taller and smiled. "Her old man's a Purple."

James' lips curved upwards as he increased his hold on her. "All the better. We've got a score to settle with the Purple Gang. Ain't that right, Lyle?"

Lyle nodded but appeared to be less enthusiastic than his friend. "I wasn't doing nothing but helping the lady. She locked herself out of her apartment, and I was trying to help her find the key. Ain't that right, ma'am? You can't go saying anything different; that Purple Gang is a tough lot. They'll have me killed."

"Shut up, Lyle," James growled. "This is the opportunity we've been waiting for."

Seeing their division, the boy addressed Lyle. "If you want to settle a score with the Purple Gang, you're in luck. They're on their way. A whole bunch of them right now."

Lyle's eyes darted from side to side. "We ain't ready for the whole gang."

For the first time, James' bravado faltered. "We're going for now, but we'll be back for you and that brat of yours."

Mildred glared at the man as he and Lyle took off down the hallway like scared rats. Once they were out of sight, her emotions took over, and she began to tremble. While the neighborhood had been pleasant enough when she'd first moved here, it had taken a turn over the last couple of years. Even with the change, she had always felt safe. Mostly that was because Tobias repeatedly told her she had nothing to fear.

He's a Purple. The words repeated in her head. Anyone that read the newspapers knew what that meant. The headlines were always filled with exploits of Detroit's notorious Purple Gang. They were ruthless. Ruthless enough to have saved her with the mere mention of the name. And Tobias was one of them. While she'd known he was into something, she hadn't dreamed it was this. She struggled with her feelings. Was it so bad in the changing city to have that kind of protection? And if he was so connected, why did he leave her safety to a bunch of street kids? *Because he knew you wouldn't feel threatened with children following you.* Each time she left the house, one or more of the boys followed her, tagging along like a bunch of stray puppies. While they kept their distance, one of them was always near, her private protection squad. She ran a hand under her nose and sniffed. She was still trembling, and her face and arm throbbed.

The scrawny, dirty-faced boy that had run to get help approached her. "You okay, Miss?"

"Just a little scared is all." She heard a moan and remembered the boy who'd hit the wall and hurried over to him.

"Are you all right?" Mildred asked, helping him up.

The boy rubbed his head. "I'm okay."

"Thank you for standing up for me like

you did. That was very brave of you."

"It's my job," the boy replied.

"Franky will be fine. He has a hard head," the taller boy interrupted.

Mildred turned toward him. "Good, and what is your name?"

"Hugh. Sometimes they call me Rabbit, 'cause I run really fast."

"Indeed you do. Thank you for bringing help," she said, glancing at the other boys. "You are all so brave."

The boys beamed under her compliment.

Mildred glanced at her door. "Hugh, you wouldn't know anything about locks, would you?"

Hugh looked to Franky, who nodded to one of the other boys. A small freckled-faced kid with holes in the toes of his shoes scampered to the door, and much to Mildred's relief, had it open within seconds. She walked through the open doorway and hurried to check on Fannie, who was blissfully oblivious to her mother's ordeal. As she walked back into the living room, she saw that the front door was closed. She thought about checking to see if the boys were still there but knew it would be wasting her time. Of course they were there; they had orders from a member of the Purple Gang, and no one crossed the Purple Gang and lived to tell about it. She thought about the men who had threatened to take Fannie and smiled.

Chapter Twenty-Three

Mildred checked on Fannie for what seemed like the hundredth time since her ordeal. She reached to adjust the small quilt and winced. Unbuttoning her blouse, she pulled her arm out of the sleeve to have a look. Sure enough, she had the imprint of James' fingers etched around her arm like a tattoo. She went to the dresser and picked up the mirror, holding it up to check out her face. The face that stared back at her looked frightened and bruised. She sighed, taking in the beginning of what was going to be a colorful black eye. The purple was already beginning to show.

Purple… she lifted her hand and traced the color with the tips of her fingers, cringing as she touched the tender skin. If her husband was a member of the Purple Gang, what did that make her? She placed the mirror on the dresser and returned to the living room. Glancing at the wall clock, she wondered what was keeping Tobias. If the boys were in charge of watching her, she had little doubt they had a way of contacting Tobias should something go wrong.

She heard excited voices in the hall and felt her heart rate increase. She looked around the room for something she could use as a weapon and settled on a long black umbrella. It wasn't much, but it was the first thing she found. She stood just in front of the door, heart pounding, tears welling in her eyes. The door lock clicked, and Mildred held her breath.

The door opened, and Tobias rushed inside, gathering her into his arms. She dropped the umbrella and wrapped her arms around him, sobbing into his shoulder.

"I'm here," he whispered as she'd often heard him do when trying to comfort Fannie. His embrace was strong, his words as comforting to her as they always seemed to be to their child. Only she was not a child. She was a grown woman, and if the stories in the paper were true, the arms offering her comfort were also able to cause great harm.

Mildred pulled back from his grip and

studied the man she'd grown to love. How could a man that was so tender with her, that held their newly born baby as if he was afraid she would break be capable of such atrocities? He held her gaze, then his eyes clouded as he took in her bruises, his face transforming before her eyes. She could see the anger take hold and instantly knew the stories were true. She took a step backward, and he grabbed her, wrapping his arms around her once more. Tears ran down her face as she struggled to free herself from the monster. She wanted to scream, to tell him to let her go, but she thought of their sleeping baby and struggled in silence. She wasn't sure how long they stood there struggling until the fight inside her grew weary. But when at last her fear subsided, and she stopped fighting him, he released her and looked at her with tears of his own. Having never seen him cry before, his tears tugged at her heart. A man afraid of losing everything had replaced the monster she'd seen moments earlier.

"I am scared." The words came out in a whisper.

"Those men will never hurt you again."

His words held promise she knew to be true.

Somehow, it didn't surprise her that he already knew the details. "That is not all I am afraid of. I know about you. About the Purple Gang. How could you be a part of something like that? According to the papers, the Purple Gang is the worst gang in the city. They even say those men are murderers. How can you be a part of that?"

"I was with them before we married. It was the only way I could survive on the streets."

"And now?"

"And now, I have you and Fannie. You do not realize how bad things have gotten since the recession started. Men who were once friends would slit each other's throat if it meant putting food on the table. I've seen it done. Proud men standing in line for hours just to get a cup of soup or slice of bread. People, and I'm not just talking about street kids, whole families living in crates, boxes, and alleyways. You haven't been hungry in years, Millie. You don't have to beg or steal. And you don't have to leave our child with strangers while you go off to whatever factory job you can find and work your fingers to the bone simply to bring a few coins home at the end of the day. I have never asked you to work, and I never will. But I will not have you judging me for doing what I have to do to put food on our table. Not when most of the country goes to bed hungry each night. I will do whatever it takes, and I mean whatever it takes to keep my family safe."

Tobias' nostrils flared as he glanced toward the door.

"Don't you hurt those boys!"

"They shouldn't have told you," he said more calmly.

"They did not tell me. They told the men who had just threatened to…" She waved him off as he moved to comfort her. "I think maybe this is all my fault. The men were in the hallway making such a racket, they woke Fannie. She has not been sleeping, and I am just so tired. I nursed her until she finally fell back to sleep. Then they started again, and I was afraid she would hear them, so I rushed out of the apartment to ask them to be quiet. I did not realize that in my haste, I had forgotten to close my blouse. The men thought I was—well, you are a man, you know what they must have thought. If their actions were my punishment, then so be it, but when they threatened to take Fannie, God help me, I wanted them punished. I was glad you are who you are because I knew you would punish them. Now I worry that my anger makes me no different than you."

He moved forward, and this time, she welcomed his embrace. "But you are different, Millie. That is what made me fall in love with you. You have been through so much in life, but you never let it beat you. You are good. You are kind. You are everything that I am not."

"But I hate those men and want to make sure I never have to worry about them harming our daughter."

"Did I forget to mention that as of five days ago, you are also a mother? It is a mother's job to protect her young. I once saw a woman shoot a guy who was trying to take her baby away. I've seen a mother rat attack a dog ten times her size to protect her young. It's what moms do. I hate to tell you this, Mildred, but you are normal."

She sighed. "What will become of those men?"

He kissed her lightly on the lips. "You

leave those two to me."

"You are going to kill them, then?"

"I'm going to make sure our daughter can sleep safely in her crib at night."

"By killing them."

He released his hold on her, walked to the window, and peered out. "I will not tell you what you wish to hear. I saw the way you looked at me when I first entered. I could not bear it if I saw that look every time I looked into your eyes. Just know that most of my life, I have lived with a single purpose: to do whatever is necessary to keep you safe. I would gladly go to my grave if I thought it was the only way to protect you. That is how much I love you, Mileta."

It had been so long since she'd heard her given name, it took a moment for it to register. "I will promise never to ask you about your life again if you make me a promise in return."

He turned to face her.

"I would like you to make a journal of your life for me. I am doing the same thing. I've been writing them for years. You may read it if you wish. Write it for me, so that one day I will truly know the man I married."

He pondered her request for so long, she wondered if he were going to answer.

"I will do as you ask under one condition."

"Which is?"

"You promise not to read my journals until after I die."

"And if I die before you?"

"Then you will go to your grave knowing only that I have loved you. It is a gamble, but then again, I am a gambling man."

Mildred smiled for the first time since Tobias had walked through the door. "I will agree to your terms."

He returned her smile.

"Wait, there is another matter I would like to discuss."

He paused. "I'm listening."

"About those boys."

"No harm will come to them. You have my word."

"I want more than that. The boys follow me. I have seen them before, but now I know it is not merely for their entertainment."

"They follow you to keep you safe. I will not order them to stop, and that is not up for debate.”

Good. “I am not asking you to. It is just if they are going to be my guardians, I want you to see to it they are properly dressed. It is the middle of winter, and one of the boys has his toes hanging out of his shoes. They do not have to look like dandies; their shoes don’t even have to be new. Come to think of it, would be best if they are not; something like that could get them killed in this neighborhood. I just want them to be warm. Oh, and one more thing,”

A smirk played at the corners of his mouth. “Oh, do tell.”

“I am going to make each of them a quilt to keep them warm. So I will need some fabric. Nothing too pretty, of course.”

“Of course,” he replied. “I’ll see it is delivered tomorrow. Is that soon enough?”

“It will do. The one little boy, Franky, got injured while trying to protect me.”

Tobias frowned. “The boy is tough. He stayed there when Rabbit ran?”

“He did. I think he would have taken a bullet if it had come to that. And, to be clear, Rabbit ran to get help.”

They were interrupted by a knock on the door.

Tobias crossed the room, opening the door without hesitation. Mildred could not see who was on the other side, or hear what was said, but from the depth of the voice knew it wasn't a child. Tobias closed the door and walked back to where Mildred was standing. When he looked at her, his face was hardened.

"I need to go out for a while. Will you be all right?"

She knew why he was leaving but said nothing to stop him. "I will."

He kissed her eye and laid his hand against the side of her face. "If anyone ever asks, the only thing you know about the Purple Gangs is what you've read in the papers. I am not nor will I ever be a member of the Purple Gang. It is important that you remember that, Mildred."

After he left, she realized she was shaking. More than that, the way he'd said her name had given her chills.

Chapter Twenty-Four

September 3rd, 1933

Mildred sobbed as she handed over the stack of quilts she'd spent years making. While she knew they needed the money, something told her she was making a big mistake. She narrowed her eyes as the merchant unfolded each of the ten quilts, carefully inspecting her workmanship.

"I assure you these quilts are of exceptional quality," she said, unable to hold her tongue any longer.

"Got to check them out all the same," the man said, unfolding the last one.

Mildred swallowed hard as the man stretched the double wedding ring quilt out for inspection. Tiny calico prints in hues of soft pink, purple, yellow, and white danced in midair as the man carefully examined the fabric. While the quilt had never been used, there was nothing new about it. It was the quilt she'd been working on the day her parents died, and it pained her to part with it. While the quilt was heavy with unfulfilled promises, it was also the last link she shared with her mother, who had gone with her to pick out and ultimately purchase the materials needed to construct the quilt.

"There is a bit of yellowing on this one," the man said, holding up the spot for Mildred to see.

She looked closer, and sure enough, there was a quarter-size spot on one of the corners. "I'm sure it will come out when it is washed." At least she hoped so. It was much too beautiful to be marred.

"Can't take that chance; my customers are the kind with real cash money. Those folks are hard to come by these days. You are lucky to find someone as generous as I. Most merchants can barely make ends meet, much less offer extras such as hand-pieced quilts. If my customers are going to lay down good money for a quilt, they are going to expect that quilt to be new."

Mildred knew he was right. She'd had to visit five stores before finding one agreeable to purchase her quilts. "But it is new. Maybe it brushed against something on the bus."

The man looked at her over his spectacles. "New doesn't have stains. I'll only pay you three dollars for this one."

"Three dollars? Why, I have more than that in the fabric."

"Horsefeathers!" the man yelled and slapped his hand on the counter. "You think I don't know what you women are doing? I see it all the time, women coming in here saying they purchased the fabric new so that they can get a better price. I'd know a feedsack quilt anywhere."

While she'd resorted to using flower and potato sacks in recent months, this particular quilt was made with new fabric straight from the department store. Mildred glared at the man and wiped the tears from her eyes. "I assure you that you are sorely mistaken. If you would care to inspect it closer, you will see that it is calico. You will not find a feedsack with those patterns if you scour the whole city. If you are not going to give me my full three dollars and fifty cents, I will sell it elsewhere."

The man engaged Mildred in a staring contest for several seconds before breaking eye contact. "Fine, I'll give you the extra fifty cents, but next time you come in, you had better make sure there are no stains."

Unfortunately, there wouldn't be a next time. The only quilt she had left was the birth-quilt, and it was so thin, it barely held the heat. The only fabric she had left was, in fact, the feedsacks the man accused her of peddling, and she would need those to make a quilt for her own bed before winter. She just prayed she had time to complete it before the weather turned. Detroit's winters could be extremely unforgiving. Mildred held out her hand and waited as the merchant counted out her cash, then wrapped her fingers around it as if it were all the money in the world. It might as well be. She had enough money to pay half the rent for the month, with enough left over to feed her, Tobias, and Franky for the next couple of weeks, as long as she used fillers like beans and rice to stretch the meals.

Mildred shoved the money into the hidden front pocket of her skirt, the one Tobias had insisted she add, explaining that it would prove much more difficult for a pickpocket to relieve her of her money if the money was in her front waistband. He'd gone as far as showing her several bump and pluck techniques so she could keep on guard and not be fooled by the seeming clumsiness of strangers. Catching the eye of Franky, who was her constant companion these days, she exited the store. A moment later, Franky followed.

"Did you get it?" Mildred asked once they were clear of the storefront.

The boy nodded his head and opened his jacket just enough to show her the blank journal stuffed down the front of his pants. "Storeowners don't pay no mind to kids like me when we are looking at writing supplies. They figure all of us are dumb and don't know what we are looking at. Now if I'd have been looking at the candy, that man would have been on me like a cockroach."

"I'm sorry to have asked you to take the chance." She was too. But writing in her journals was the only release she had. Unfortunately, spending a dime on a journal was a luxury she no longer had.

"Next time, give me a challenge." He reached into his jacket pocket, pulled out two gumballs, and handed her one.

Mildred rolled the pink ball in her hand

to remove the lint, then plopped it into her mouth. "I thought you said you couldn't get candy."

He shrugged. "I never said I couldn't do it, just that it was more difficult."

She stopped at the curb, eyeing the fresh flower stand on the other side of the street. "How are you at flowers?"

He smiled and followed as she stepped off the curb.

***

Mildred and Franky exited the bus on the corner of Elmwood Street. Mildred carried an impressively large bouquet of mums as they walked through the gates of Elmwood Cemetery. She easily led the way down and around the lane to the far side of the cemetery to where her parents lay buried. They'd had money then, and it showed by way of an impressive headstone that marked the family grave. Franky leaned against a nearby tree, allowing Mildred to speak to her parents in private. She walked to the side of the stone and allowed her fingers to trace the inscription that had been etched in the smooth marble long after her parents were buried. She did not have to see the writing to know what it said. Fannie Mileta Lisowski February 9th, 1931 – June 30th, 1931. The baby had died without warning. Mildred had awoken from the first peaceful night's sleep since she'd given birth. At first, she'd thought her daughter had slept through the night; however, when she went to check on her, she discovered she was not breathing. Tobias had come home a few hours later to find Mildred waiting on the couch holding their baby girl. While they'd had money for a stone, Mildred could not bear the thought of her precious daughter spending her eternity alone. Against Tobias' wishes, she had joined him under the light of a full moon and buried their daughter at the breast of her mother's grave. Each time Mildred thought of her baby girl, she pictured her safe within her grandmother's arms.

"I sold the quilts I made today." She thought about adding the special one she was making but figured they already knew. "While the money was less than I had hoped for, it will be enough. At least for now. Tobias is in some serious trouble, so if you have any extra pull up there, I would appreciate if you use it to help him. I know you probably do not approve of him, but I love him, and helping him would also help me. Give Fannie a kiss for me and tell her that her mother loves her. I need to be going now; it is not safe to ride the bus too late in the day."

Mildred kissed the palm of her hand then placed it on the ground centered over her daughter's grave.

***

Mildred had just finished with the dishes when she heard a rap at the door.

Franky rushed to look through the peephole before opening the door. "It's just Ducky."

Franky unbolted the deadbolt, pulled the door open, and greeted a boy Mildred hadn't seen before.

"The bulls just pulled up to the curb. They will be a minute; I pushed all the buttons on the elevator before I got off."

"Ha, good thinking. Roach still outside?"

"Yeah," the boy replied.

"Okay, hide in the shadows of the

hallway in case Mouse shows up so you can head him off."

Mildred hurried to get the stool and placed it in the center of the kitchen floor.

The elevator dinged. Ducky slid into the shadows, and Franky pushed the door without a sound, locking it as an added precaution. The boy raced across the room, clambered up the stool, and disappeared into the ceiling, replacing the tile behind him just as a second knock sounded at the door. Mildred placed the stool against the kitchen wall and slowly made her way across the room, giving Franky a chance to settle in. They both knew the bulls were not after the boy, but if he were seen inside the house, he would be forever associated with the Purple Gang. Being seen with her in town was something that could be explained away. She needed help carrying something. She wasn't sure of the neighborhood, and he was showing her the way. All lies, but no concrete evidence the boy was anything but a street hood. However, if Franky were to be caught inside the home of a suspected gang member, he'd be marked for life. She opened the door to two detectives whose faces had become all too familiar over the last few years, detectives Greene and Stim, each untouchables assigned to the special task force assembled to break up the city's increasing gang population.

Greene greeted her as she opened the door. He'd put on a couple of pounds since she'd last seen him. Obviously, not everyone in the city was going hungry at night. "Mrs. Lisowski, is your husband home?"

"He is not," Mildred said, moving aside. There was no reason to block them; they would insist on coming in, and she would eventually allow them inside. Since Tobias wasn't at home, there was no need to delay their entry. "Go ahead and have a look. I've told you before we have nothing to hide."

Both men entered. Greene moved through the apartment while Stim stayed to keep her occupied. "Looks like the weather is starting to turn," Stim said casually.

Mildred thought about the quilts she'd sold earlier in the day, and a chill raced down her arms. "Now, Stim, surely you did not drive all the way over here to discuss the weather."

She had to give him credit; the man actually had the decency to blush. "Just doing my job, Mrs. Lisowski."

"Hassling my husband hardly seems worthy of the wages they are paying you these days." Mildred didn't have a clue of the man's income, but it seemed the thing to say at the moment. "You should be out there busting real criminals, not an innocent man trying to put food on the table."

Greene had made his way to the kitchen and was lifting the lid off the soup pot as she spoke. He inhaled, pulled a spoon from the drawer, and took a taste. Opening the cabinet, he reached for the bowl she had only recently put away. "Seems like Mouse is doing a mighty good job of keeping you fed."

Mildred glared at him. It had not escaped her the man had used Tobias' street name. "It doesn't look as if you have been missing any meals, detective. Surely you wouldn't think of helping yourself to my leftovers. It is hard enough to stretch the meals to last more than a few days."

Greene sighed and returned the bowl

to the cabinet. He made a show of washing the spoon and returning it to the drawer. He returned to the living room and nodded for his partner to follow. "When your husband returns, tell him we were here, and if he has any questions, he knows where to find us."

The second the men left the apartment, Mildred locked the door and hurried to the window. Only after she watched the men get into their sedan and drive away did she retrieve the stool and give Franky the okay to come down.

"Boy, you sure told them," Franky said, dropping from the ceiling. "Mouse is going to be really proud of you. You sounded like a regular gangster's wife."

Mildred thought of Helen, her adopted mother, and a wave of sadness washed over her. Maybe it was a good thing her mother hadn't lived to see what she had become. "Why Ducky?"

Franky replaced the ceiling tile and turned toward her. "Huh?"

"The kid in the hall. How did he get the name Ducky?"

Franky hopped off the stool and carried it back to where it belonged. "Me and some of the boys were spying on one of the other gangs over in Hamtramck. Anyhow, he was the new guy, and too small to be much good in a fight, so we placed him as a lookout. We told him to do a bird call if he saw anyone coming. Everything was going as planned until, all of a sudden, we all heard this loud quacking ruckus. It sounded like a duck invasion. Apparently, the kid heard a noise, got nervous, and a duck was the only bird he could think of."

Mildred smiled. At the end of the day, even street kids could show their innocence.

Chapter Twenty-Five

December 6th, 1933 2 am.

The quilt lifted and Mildred was instantly awake. Even in the darkness, she knew it was Tobias. She could feel him trembling as he pressed his body against hers. "You are burning up!"

"And you are freezing," he replied through chattering teeth.

"The landlord turned off the heat," she said, pulling the quilt closer. "He said if I do not pay the rent we owe by the end of the week, he will turn off the electricity as well."

"I will grab another quilt."

Mildred stopped him before he could get up. "There are no other quilts. Except for my birth quilt, which I gave to Franky to use. It is so threadbare, I am not sure how much good it is doing him."

As if in testament, Franky coughed and moaned in his sleep.

"Where are you going?" she asked when Tobias left the bed. A question that was answered seconds later when he deposited Franky in the bed on the other side of her. Franky sighed, then rooted out the warmth of her body as he slept. She felt a slight breeze as Tobias draped the second quilt over them both and climbed back into bed. While not perfect, the added body heat along with the quilt did make the room more tolerable.

"How much do you owe?"

"Two and a half months. I sold my quilts in October but didn't get enough to cover the full month."

His voice hardened. "You sold all your quilts and could not pay a month's rent? Who did you sell them to?"

"Mr. Simpson on the corner. Do not go down there. You are in enough trouble." Things had not been the same since the Collingwood Manor Massacre two years ago when several heads of the Purple Gang were arrested. The cops were able to turn Solly Levine, and since that time, Purples were more apt to shoot each other than to trust one another. "Were you able to find protection?"

He didn't answer.

"It is all my fault; I should not have

gone into the hallway."

Tobias sighed. "Millie, we have been over this too many times. You did nothing wrong. Louie, Sammy, and I are the ones who took care of those guys. How could we know they were connected with Chicago? It was just poor dumb luck they picked our building…"

Mildred turned to face him in the dark. "It was not poor dumb luck. I've heard the rumors, Tobias. I know Chicago suspects the Purples of being in on the St. Valentine's Day Massacre. Those men were here looking for you."

"Then why run when they could have taken off with you?"

She had to admit she hadn't figured that part out just yet. "Maybe they went to get help, or maybe they were afraid of the kids."

The boy moaned in his sleep, and they both snickered.

"Why are you home?" Mildred asked after several moments of silence.

"What? A man cannot return to his home?"

It was Mildred's turn to stay silent.

"It's over," Tobias said with a sigh.

"Prohibition? Yes, I heard. Someone shouted it down the hallway. Another lady used colorful language telling him to shut up and that was that. I guess it does not matter in a city where liquor can be found even during the dry season."

He kissed her on the forehead. "Yes, but now they will not need to go elsewhere. Everything has changed. Not just Prohibition, everything."

The warmth of his kiss lingered long after he pulled away. "I don't understand."

"The city, the life we had, the friends I had when I first got here; we've had a great run, but it is over."

He was starting to scare her, and her voice quivered when she spoke. "I…I don't understand what you are saying."

"I've tried my best to keep you safe. But I am afraid I won't be here to protect you. No matter; I'm poison to you."

Though he was rambling, she got the gist of his words. She pulled up on her elbow. "I will not allow you to leave me. Look what I've become in the three months since you've been in hiding."

Franky mumbled in his sleep, and Mildred realized she'd been yelling.

She lowered her voice. "I send a child out to steal so that we can have food. Do you know what they would do to him if they caught him?"

"Franky just turned twelve. He is not a child. And you are not making him do anything he wouldn't be doing anyway. At least now you are giving him a purpose."

"You make it sound as if stealing for me is a good thing."

"Mildred, if not for you, the boy would be sleeping on the streets, or worse."

"What could be worse than sleeping on the streets?"

"Things have changed, affiliations have changed. I have seen things…done things that I never thought I would do."

Tobias grew quiet. Moments later, his breathing told her he was sleeping. Lying there in the darkness listening to both him and Franky breathing, she felt safe for the first time in months. He was tired. She knew he really didn't want to leave. It was the fatigue talking. He would be easier to reason with after he rested. Mildred closed her eyes and snuggled closer to her husband. In the morning, she would find a way to make him stay.

***

She woke to an empty bed. Scrambling out from under the covers, she realized that for the first time in days, her teeth were not chattering. She hurried to dress, only this time, it wasn't because she was freezing. She opened the bedroom door, and her suspicions were confirmed; the heat was back on in the apartment. While the room was still cool, she could hear a ticking noise coming from the radiator. Tobias must have paid the rent.

Franky was on the couch glancing at the morning paper when she entered the living room. She swept a glance to the kitchen area. Several eggs and a small bundle wrapped in brown paper sat on the counter.

"Bacon," Franky said, watching her. "There is fresh bread in the breadbox as well."

She wanted to admonish him, to tell him it was too much, but she hadn't had fresh bread in weeks. "Thank you, Franky."

"Boy, if I could only find a way to slip this into my pocket." He turned the paper for her to see. In a small square at the bottom of the page was an advert for a used 1931 Buick Sedan, the ad telling the reader it was a steal at $395.

"Those would have to be some mighty big pockets."

His face took on a determined look. "Maybe I could ask Mouse to show me how to steal a car."

The thought of either of them being caught stealing a car terrified her. "Franklyn, you will do no such thing. It is bad enough you steal what you do."

Franky's eye grew wide. "Jeepers, you sounded just like my mother."

"Good. I am sure she would not be pleased if you stole a car."

The boy folded the paper and placed it on the couch beside him. "The only thing that would make her mad is if I were not stealing it for her."

"Where are your parents, Franky?" She had asked him before, but he had always avoided the question.

"Around."

"Around where?"

The question was met with a shrug.

"Don't you miss your family?"

Franky opened his mouth, but before he could answer, the door opened, and Tobias entered. His face ashen, and his hands clung to a small crate. He walked the short distance to the counter, where he deposited the crate with a thud. Turning to face her, he opened his mouth to speak, yet no words escaped. His glazed eyes met hers as if pleading with her to understand. Seconds later, the eyes went blank as he collapsed to the floor.

"He's zozzled," Franky said, shaking his head.

Mildred rushed to his side. Rolling him onto his back, she could feel the heat emanating from his body. She remembered how warm he'd felt last night and the lingering heat from his kiss. Why hadn't she realized he was ill? She tried to think. What did her mother do when she was sick? Her first thought was to sweat out the fever, but that would be difficult to do with only two quilts. Especially when one of those quilts was nearly see-through. If she couldn't sweat it out, they would need to find another way to bring the fever down.

"He is not drunk. He is burning with fever. Help me get him into the bathtub."

As they removed his jacket, Tobias moaned. It was then Mildred saw the bandage on his arm. It took some doing, but they were able to get the rest of his clothes off and into the tub. She filled it with cold water in an attempt to cool the fire inside his body. "We need ice, Franky. Do you think you can get some?"

The boy nodded and was off without a word.

Mildred lifted Tobias' arm, gently unrolling the wet bandage. She smelled the rot even before she had the arm fully unwrapped. Her stomach lurched at the pungent odor, making her grateful she had not yet eaten her morning meal. She laid the bandage aside and realized her hands were trembling. It had been a long time, but she recognized the odor. It was the unmistakable smell that accompanied death. She'd smelled more than her fair share of the odor on the long, arduous journey to America. The land of promise, as her father had called it. Tears spilled from her eyes as she traced the red lines that traveled up Tobias' arm. So far, the only promise the journey had produced had been heartache.

She heard the front door open and excited voices followed. Seconds later, Franky and Ducky raced into the room, carrying two large chunks of ice wrapped in burlap. Seeing Tobias' arm, both faces went pale. Mildred took the ice from them and placed the chunks into the already cool water, knowing the act to be fruitless.

"We'll give him a few more moments and then we'll get him into bed," she said, wiping the back of her hand across her eyes.

"Those marks are death streaks," Franky whispered.

"Mouse can't die." Ducky's voice sounded incredulous.

"Don't be daft; everyone can die," Franky countered.

The boys remained silent as Mildred dipped a washcloth into the cool water and placed it upon Tobias' forehead. She kept waiting for him to regain consciousness as she tried to cool him, but he merely groaned.

"Help me get him out of the tub," Mildred said a few moments later.

It took some doing, but the three of them managed to get him out of the tub and into the bed. Mildred tore off several strips from an old sheet and carefully rewrapped the infected arm. The ice bath had done nothing to lower Tobias' fever. She packed the two quilts around him and then climbed into bed next to him.

"Do you want me to go find a doctor?" Franky asked.

"We have no money with which to pay him," Mildred replied softly. She refrained from telling the boy what he already knew. It was too late.

Franky set his jaw. "I will try my best to persuade him."

"And I will help," Ducky said, copying Franky's stance.

Mildred figured the task would keep the boys from giving in to their fears. "Okay, boys."

The boys ran out of the room. Seconds later, she heard the front door slam. Tobias' heart rate increased, and his head thrashed from side to side as he mumbled something she could not understand. She moved closer, whispering his name, telling him she was here. His heart rate slowed, the thrashing quelled, and moments later, his breathing ceased.

She was still holding him when she heard the click of the front door and the whisper of voices in the living room. She was just about to call out to tell the boys that the doctor was no longer needed when she recognized one of the voices.

"You are too late," she said as detectives Stim and Greene breached the bedroom door. "My husband is dead."

Greene gave a nod to Stim, who walked over and placed his ear to Tobias' nose, then stood and nodded his agreement.

"Guess we won't be needing the bracelets," Greene said, putting his handcuffs away. "No matter, the sergeant will be happy to have another Purple crossed off the list. You got a blower?"

"No, there is a telephone on the first floor," Mildred said numbly.

"We will call for the meat wagon. Got anyone else you need us to call?"

Mildred shook her head. With the exception of Franky, she was once again alone. She walked to the window, wondering what was keeping the kid and was startled to see him sitting in the back of the police car. "Franky!"

"You know that kid?"

She took a moment to choose her words. "He lives in the building. I saw him outside, called out to him, and asked if he could fetch me a doctor."

Greene let out a sigh. "We were in the drug store when he and another lad ran in looking for a doctor. The other boy got away."

Mildred turned from the window. "Surely you will let the boy go free. He should not be punished for trying to be helpful. He is just a boy after all."

"You see a boy. I see a future problem."

"Please, detective. My heart is hurting enough at losing my husband. Don't add to my grief by punishing that innocent boy."

Greene shrugged. "No skin off my nose."

Mildred bit a trembling lip.

"Oh, and Mrs. Lisowski?" Greene said, opening the door. "You tell Franky next time I put him in my patrol car, I will take him downtown. That goes for Ducky too."

As he pulled the door closed behind him, Mildred collapsed in a heap upon the floor.

***

Cindy closed the journal and looked to her mother, who had finished only moments prior. "Good God, Mom, no wonder the woman never smiled."

Linda's mouth quivered. "Losing a husband takes a lot out of a person. But to lose her baby as well, I cannot fathom the pain that blackened her heart."

"Are you okay? I can read the rest and tell you how things turn out," Cindy offered.

"I'm good. It helps to know Mildred survives. So I guess you've figured it out."

Cindy looked at her mom in question. "Figured what out?"

"That Uncle Frank is not really your uncle."

"Wow, you are right. I was so caught up in the story that I did not connect the two. Do you think we should pay him a visit?"

Linda gave the next stack of writings an eager glance. "The man is ninety-eight years old, with rarely a lucid moment. He hasn't said anything about the trains in all the years I've known him. What makes you think he is going to start now?"

Linda was right. Like it or not, they might never get the answers they wanted.

"I say we pick up where we left off. We can pay Uncle Frank a visit when we are finished," Cindy said, handing her a copy.

Chapter Twenty- Six

December 10^{th,} 1933

Four days had passed since Tobias died. Mildred had used the neighbor's phone to call the Detroit Police, but no one seemed to know where they had taken her husband's body. Except for rising to make the phone calls, she had spent her days curled up in the bed where Tobias had drawn his last breath. It wasn't until Franky had physically pulled her from the bed that she'd finally taken a shower and put on clean clothes. The boy had left shortly afterward, promising to find out where they had taken him.

After staring at the crate for several moments, Mildred finally gave in to her curiosity and now sat going through the sturdy wooden box, most of it filled with the journals she had asked him to write. She set those aside to read later, after the pain from his passing lessened. At least she hoped it would someday ease. She pulled out a stack of envelopes tied with a thin string, each addressed to Tobias at an address she did not recognize. She lifted one to check the return address. A. Taylor, 1743 West 43rd Street, New York. Opening the envelope, she pulled out a single sheet of paper.

My Dearest Tobias,

I hope this letter finds you well. Between the banks closing and so many people out of work, things in the city are becoming increasingly worse. The soup lines are growing longer, and I find myself grateful I can earn enough money that I do not have to beg for my supper.

I've developed a cough. Nothing much, just a little nag that started off as a tickle.

Little Paulie is growing bigger by the day. He reminds me a great deal of you. His hair is starting to come in. I believe it may end up being red. I'm not sure where he gets that from. I think I may remember Mother saying her grandmother had hair that was flaming red. Then again, maybe not, that was all so long ago. Sometimes I long to speak with Mother to tell her of Paulie and also that I have found you. I had a visitor from the Almshouse today. They said they were checking on Paulie and me, but something about the way they looked at me frightened me. I told them it was time to put Paulie down for his nap and bid them farewell. Something tells me they will return. If they do, I think I will pretend not to be home.

Please let me hear from you, as your letters keep me from feeling alone.

With all my love,

A.

Mildred hurried to read the other letters, hoping to find out who this mysterious A person was. She'd nearly given up hope of learning more until she began reading the final letter.

My Dearest Tobias,

I hope this letter finds you well. I hate to hear you have fallen on hard times. The city continues to change here as well. I will not waste energy telling you of my woes, as from your letter, I see that yours are much the same.

I have a cough these days. It started simple but seems to be taking hold. It keeps me awake at night. A pity, since wee Paulie is now sleeping all the way through until morning. Oh well, I am sure this too will pass.

Paulie is growing so quickly, and it makes my heart swell that each day he looks more and more like you. I fear it will be no time before he is crawling and worry that I simply will not have the strength needed to chase him down. He is a bright and handsome boy, and I cannot wait for you to meet him. I am sure you will love him as much as I do. I pray that meeting is sooner than later as I have had two further visits from those who think I am not fit to care for my sweet boy.

Please do continue to write as I always love hearing from you.

With all my love,

Anastasia.

Mildred sat staring at the letter, as if waiting for words to appear to fill in the gaps and frightened of where her thoughts were taking her. Could this be the same Anastasia she knew from the asylum? The address was not the same, so probably not. Right? If it were, in fact, the Anastasia from the asylum, then how could she possibly know Tobias? He had not lived at the asylum. He had joined the group on the train. According to what little he had told her of his life, he had spent it living on the street. What troubled her most was this woman, this Anastasia, claiming that her child looked like Tobias. *That would mean…* She stopped, unable to finish the thought. Her hands trembled as she reached for the stack of envelopes. She pulled out the first letter, noting that each one began and ended the same way. *My dearest Tobias*, followed by *with all my love, Anastasia*. She read all seven again. For the most part, the contents of each were in keeping with the letter prior. It wasn't until the third read-through did she begin to notice subtle differences. Almost as if each subsequent letter appeared to sound a touch more desperate. It was delicate, but if one were looking, they could be seen. The increased cough that was merely a passing comment in the first letter. And that sentence in the final letter where she mentioned being visited by "those who thought her to be unfit to care for her son." The only thing that kept Mildred from ripping the letters into shreds was the fact that Anastasia had referred to the child as hers and not theirs.

Setting the letters aside, she continued going through the contents of the crate, pulling out a newspaper clipping. Unfolding the paper, she read the advert.

WE RODE THE TRAIN. I AM LOOKING FOR MY BROTHERS AND SISTERS. PLEASE CONTACT PADDY JONES BOX 132 SANDUSKY MICHIGAN 48471.

Paddy… The last time she'd seen him, he'd been worried she didn't have a coat. She had, in fact, had one, but refused to wear it since it was covered in travel grime. She smiled, remembering his face. The image broadened until each of her friends were standing there smiling back at her. For a moment, she wished it was true that she and her friends were back at the asylum, hurrying to eat their food so that it could not be taken from them. As fast as the image appeared, it vanished, and she found herself staring at the newspaper clipping once more.

The important part was that Paddy had placed the advert just as he promised. She always could count on Paddy. If he said he would do something, he did it. He'd once promised her a new pencil, which he'd produced. It wasn't until she noticed him walking gingerly so his pants wouldn't rub against the welts on his backside that she'd learned he had stolen it from the headmistress' office when she was out making her rounds. Once again, she wondered what had become of him before returning to the task at hand.

She turned the clipping over, but it provided no clue as to which paper it had been placed in or when. It had to be local, since Tobias saved the clipping. But why go to the trouble of saving it and not showing it to her? He had to have known she would be interested in reconnecting with those she held dear. He must have had his reasons for keeping things from her. She sighed, realizing she might never know the answer. Guilt washed over her as she realized she was angry with him. Women were not supposed to question their husband's actions; it just wasn't done. Pushing her emotions aside, she folded the paper and placed it within the fabric of her bra for safekeeping.

Reaching into the crate, she pulled out a small Bible. She wasn't sure what surprised her most, that Tobias had a Bible or that the book appeared to be well read. She opened the book to find an inscription written inside the front cover.

A lad who is willing to accept that he needs help will grow into a man who can achieve greatness. I give you this book so that you too may someday find your way.

Charles Loring Brace.

Mildred ran her index finger over the inscription. *Had she heard this name before?* It wasn't a relative, as Tobias had never spoken about his family. *Why would a man who never went to church possess a Bible, which appeared so worn in, it looked as if it could be memorized?* Just another mystery to add to the ever-growing list. She placed a hand on the stack of journals, wondering if the answers to her questions were waiting for her inside. Just as she decided to read them, the door to the apartment opened, and Franky raced in.

The boy glanced at the crate and scattered contents before waving a long brown envelope in front of her.

"What is it?" Mildred slid the journal back onto the stack, feeling somewhat grateful for the interruption.

"It is for you." His breathless response made it clear he had raced up the stairs.

"Yes, but what is it?"

"The man told me I should not look inside. He said to give it to…" A blush crossed his face. "To the tomato in 307."

Mildred took the envelope. A simple note accompanied an enormous stack of twenty-dollar bills. ***We've taken care of things. Your husband is keeping your folks company. This dough will help you fade. Be out of the city by noon tomorrow. Unless you wish to join the rest of your family, keep that pretty little yap of yours shut.***

P.S. I hear Florida is nice.

Mildred's hands trembled as she returned the note to the envelope without counting the money. "Franky, who gave this to you?"

The smile left his face. "I was just returning, and a man stopped in front of the building and motioned me to his motor car."

She narrowed her eyes at the child. "Who was the man, Franky?"

He shook his head. "I don't know his name."

She increased her stare.

Franky glanced at the contents on the table before answering. "I've seen him with Mouse, but I do not know his name."

"Did you look inside?"

"He told me not to."

"That is not what I asked you."

"I hear Florida is nice too," Franky said and looked at his feet.

Mildred walked to the window. Peering out, she studied each motorcar, wondering which one was watching her building, waiting for her to leave so that they could follow her. Would they actually allow her to go? Or was this just a ploy to get her to leave the safety of her building? So they could follow her and make sure she never spoke of the things they thought she knew. They would be surprised at how little she actually knew, as Tobias never told her of the things he did or the people he dealt with. She had asked him once why he did not trust her enough to tell her about his life. In answer, he merely kissed her on the forehead and walked away. The headlines in the morning paper the next day spoke of increased gang activities and mentioned some of the Purple Gang by name. When

Tobias returned two days later, he had a black eye and two broken ribs. He did not explain and she decided at that moment she would never question him again. She knew he was connected with the Purple Gang, but beyond that, she knew nothing. Apparently, the Gang, or what was left of it with most members being either dead or in jail, wanted to ensure her silence. She stared at the envelope, torn between throwing it out the window and shoving it into her pocket. If she sent it back, she would not only be putting herself in danger but Franky as well. Without Tobias alive to provide for her, that left Franky, and it was only a matter of time before he got caught or became further indebted to the gang that ultimately killed her husband. While they would never allow her to prove it, she felt certain it was gang activities that contributed to his death. Reluctantly, she slid the beefy envelope into the pocket of her dress and retrieved her coat.

A bright smile crossed Franky's face. "Does this mean we are going to Florida?"

"We are going to check on my husband."

Franky opened his mouth, but no

words escaped. Not a fan of cemeteries, the boy always kept his distance whenever she visited her parents and infant daughter.

"It's December, Franky. It hasn't been so cold that the ground should be completely frozen, but I need to see for myself that Tobias is where they say he is. Understand?"

She could tell by his face that he didn't. To his credit, he nodded his head anyway and followed her out the door.

They took the elevator to the first floor. As the door opened, Franky took hold of Mildred's arm. He placed a finger to his mouth and motioned for her to wait. She did as she was told, figuring he had more experience with evading people than she. He stepped out of the elevator and was back within seconds, waving her forward.

Franky held out his hand. "Give me the envelope."

She raised her eyebrows.

"Keep the dough; I just want the envelope."

She pulled the envelope from her pocket, removed the cash along with the note, and handed him the envelope. He was a smart kid. If not, Tobias would never have trusted him to watch out for her. "What do you have planned?"

"I'm going to go out first. If anyone is watching, I'll make sure they see me with the envelope. They will follow me to see why I didn't give it to you. Wait until they are well down the street before you leave. And make sure to stay close to the building so they cannot see you.

"Don't worry," he said when Mildred started to protest. "I've done this before with Mouse. There is a small alley two streets down, which is too small for a motorcar to follow. I'll ditch the tail and be waiting for you when you get to the graveyard."

Since she couldn't think of anything better, she nodded in agreement, then stayed out of sight as Franky ran out the door, envelope clearly in view. He let the wind swoop it from his hand, then raced to retrieve it before heading off down the street. Sure enough, a few seconds later, a black coupe pulled from the curb and followed in the same direction.

She waited until the car was out of sight then exited the building, making sure to stay in the shadows as she headed to the trolley stop. She heard a motorcar approaching from behind and froze. She considered running but knew she would not be able to outrun whoever was inside. Closing her eyes, she waited for the impact of a bullet and nearly jumped out of her skin when instead she heard the blare of a horn. Turning, she saw it was not in fact a gang member trying to silence her, but the driver of a yellow cab trying to get her attention.

"Yo, lady, need a ride? It's too cold for a stroll, and the skies look like they could open at any moment," the man said, leaning out the window.

Mildred wanted to tell him she was okay with taking the trolley, but she wasn't. She was terrified the driver of the coupe would come looking for her once they realized Franky had given them the slip. She smiled and waited for the driver to pull to the curb.

"Elmwood Cemetery," she said once inside. While clean, the inside of the cab smelled of a woodsy cigar and reminded her entirely too much of the smell that lingered on Tobias, even though she'd never actually seen him smoke.

"You got money to pay?" the cabbie

asked, looking in the mirror.

"Maybe you should have asked me that before you let me inside," she replied curtly.

Dark hooded eyes peeked out from the brim of his flat wool hat. "It's a slow day. I mean, you've got some nice gams. I kind of figured we could work something out."

Mildred pulled her coat tight and buttoned the top button. "I have money for the fare."

The man laughed and pulled from the curb. "You want the direct route or the scenic route?"

"Unless you believe us to be followed, I prefer you to take the direct route."

The driver checked his side mirror. "Listen, lady, I don't want any trouble. Maybe I should just drop you at the trolley stop."

"There won't be any trouble as long as you put your foot on the pedal and drive before someone sees me inside your cab," Mildred said with a glance over her shoulder.

"Who is after you?" the man asked, increasing his speed.

"Do you really want to know?"

"No, I'm just used to making conversation."

"How about this time we just agree to stay within our own thoughts?"

"Works for me, lady. Oh, and I was just kidding about working things out. I knew you were a lady with means. I mean, there is no reason to tell anyone what I said. I mean, I wouldn't want your husband or whoever is after you to be sore at me for something I said."

Mildred looked at the name tag hooked to the dashboard and attempted to sound reassuring. "Don't worry, Nickolas; my husband is the least of your troubles."

Chapter Twenty-Seven

True to the words written on the paper, there was a fresh grave just to the right of her parents' headstone. There was no stone to announce the occupant, no inscription to document his passing. He'd been buried as quietly as he had lived. She supposed it fitting for a man with the moniker of Mouse.

Mildred stooped to remove the wet leaves that lay plastered against the headstone and thought of the first time she had stepped inside her adopted parents' home, eyes full of wonder at how they had managed to bring the beautiful colors from the trees and place them against the wall. It felt like a lifetime ago that she'd rode the train with her friends. For the first time, she realized she and the other children were not much different from the leaves that fell from the trees, each one taken from the place they called home, riding the wind to some unfamiliar location. As she removed the last leaf, she stared in childlike wonder at the nearly perfect image it left behind. Not of the leaf that she had removed, but one of a tiny mitten wet against the stone. If not for the small hole in the middle of the mitten's thumb, it would be perfect. She instantly thought of her baby daughter buried within her adopted mother's arms.

Tears, the first of the day, fell as she traced the outline. "Don't worry, Fannie; your grandmother can mend your mitten."

Mildred stood and turned her attention to the freshly disturbed earth. "My husband, I'm sorry you didn't have a proper burial. I doubt the people who placed you here thought to say words over your grave. I am sure you have met my parents by now. I hope you all like each other. I found the letters, and though I do not know what they mean, their words frighten me. My mind has questioned your loyalty. My heart has not."

A horn sounded nearby, startling her. Turning, she saw it was an elderly couple sounding their horn to scatter a flock of snow geese that blocked their way.

Mildred wiped at her tears and continued. "I think the men who put you here mean to harm me. They gave me money to get out of town, but I suspect they will never allow me to leave. You know it is thought that women cannot be trusted to stay silent. If I can get away, I will take Franky with me. If I leave him here, I fear he will wind up in the ground like you. I will collect what we can carry and be gone before morning. They gave me until noon tomorrow; maybe if we leave under cover of darkness, we will have a chance to get away. If there is any way for you to watch over us, I pray you will continue to do so. I only wish I could hear from you once more, to seek your advice on where we are supposed to go. I am frightened, my husband. My only consolation is knowing that you are now on the other side with our daughter. Now when I think of my Fannie, I will picture her smiling as she sleeps in her father's arms."

Mildred heard the crunch of leaves and spun around, expecting the worst.

"I didn't mean to disturb you," Franky said, stepping up beside her.

Mildred placed her arm around the boy and wiped tears with her free hand. "I am glad you are here. Would you like to say anything?"

The boy became rigid. "You mean talk to the dead?"

"I mean talk to Mouse."

"How do you know he can hear me?"

"How do you know he can't?" she countered.

He seemed to consider that. "What should I say?"

"I cannot tell you that. Just tell him whatever is in your heart."

Franky stood there so long, she actually wondered if he would speak. Just as she was about to ask him if he'd rather leave, he removed his cap and began talking.

"I've never talked to the dead before, so don't you laugh."

Mildred was about to respond when she realized he was not speaking to her.

"My mom always said one should not speak ill of the dead, but I can't help it. I'm pretty sore at you for dying. I know you weren't my dad or nothin', but I kind of thought you would make a pretty good one. You treated me swell and taught me how to dip pockets real good. I never knew my dad, but if you see him where you are, and he tries to pick a fight, you just tell him that you are my real dad and I said he should leave you alone." Franky sniffed and placed his cap back on his head. "Do you think he could hear me?"

Mildred swiped at fresh tears. "I think he heard you just fine, Franky."

"Good, can we go? I don't want anyone to see me talking to the dirt."

Mildred released him and glanced at the spot where the mitten had been. Much to her disappointment, it was gone. *I guess your grandmother fixed your mitten,* she said silently.

"Yes, it is time for us to go. Did you have any trouble getting here?"

Franky sniffed and wiped his nose on his coat sleeve. "Na, Mouse taught me real good."

If only he had taught you how to speak properly. "Just the same, I would feel better if we slip out the back way. Oh, and Franky, do you know where we can find ourselves a map?"

"So we can find our way to Florida?" Franky asked, starting out.

Mildred shook her head. "No, we are not going to Florida."

Franky stopped. "But I thought the note said…"

She cut him off. "I know what the note said, but we are not going where they want us to go. If they know where to look for us, they could maybe find us."

Franky blew into his hands. "Yeah, well, I hear Florida is warm."

"I'm sure there are other warm places, which is precisely why we need a map."

"I miss Mouse," Franky said softly.

"So do I," Mildred said and followed the boy through a hole in the fence.

***

It took some doing, but they finally found a gas station that carried more than a local map. To avoid questions, they'd purchased a map of Michigan along with one that showed the entire country. The latter was now splayed out in front of them on the counter. Franky was the epitome of innocence, pointing out states and proclaiming that was where they should go. For all accounts, he looked more like a child trying to decide what candy he should spend his penny on than what location they should call home. Mildred, on the other hand, was trying to be more practical, wanting to get far enough away to make a difference but not so far it would be too costly. While she had money to relocate, she had no idea how she would be able to get any more once they got there. Best to be frugal.

"How about California?" Franky said, pointing to the far side of the map.

"How about something a little closer?" Mildred countered. She folded the map multiple times until they could only see Michigan and the close surrounding states. She was concentrating on the states that neighbored Michigan when she saw it. She blinked several times to be certain, then trailed a finger around the image. "Franky, look at this and tell me what you see."

The boy leaned closer. "I see Michigan."

"Yes, but this shape; what does it look like?" She traced the lower part of Michigan once again.

"A glove?"

Mildred smiled. "A mitten, to be exact. Hand me the other map."

Franky handed over the map of the

state and Mildred unfolded it. Closing her eyes, she pictured the image she'd seen on the headstone, remembering precisely where she'd seen the hole. Opening her eyes, she scanned the map mentally, placing the hole on the exact spot on the map. She gasped out loud when she read the name of the town.

"What is it?" Franky asked, peering at the spot where her finger now lay.

The boy's cheeks turned crimson as Mildred lifted her finger, tucked her hand inside her blouse, and pulled the newspaper clipping from its hiding place. Unfolding the paper, she re-read the advert that Paddy had placed in the paper. *Contact Paddy Jones, Sandusky Michigan.* Just as she thought, both cities were the same. She checked the map once more and knew it wasn't a mere coincidence. It just couldn't be. With the decision made, Mildred instantly felt the weight lift from her shoulders.

Closing the map, she turned to Franky. "Time to get packing. We will leave when it is dark."

His face brightened. "Are we going to Florida?"

"No, we are going to visit my family."

***

Packing this time was easier than the night she had left her parents' home. With a few exceptions, she had sold anything of value. It is amazing what a person can part with when they are desperate for food and warmth. She kneeled on the floor and opened the bottom drawer to her dresser. She lifted the small silk sack that had once housed her mother's jewelry and sighed. Except for her wedding ring, she had sold every piece of jewelry that once belonged to Helen. Pulling at the strings to open the sack, she took a breath to steady herself. She had shed enough tears when deciding to sell the baubles and currently did not have the mental strength to travel that road again. She lifted the dress she'd worn when she first went home with her new parents and placed it into a pillowcase. She picked up the bottle of cologne that had belonged to her adopted father and resisted uncapping the lid. Again, there was no time at present for emotions. Since her father's pocket watch did not work, she had never attempted to sell it. She held it for the briefest of moments before shoving it into the sack. Next, she pulled out the long silver spoon that Tobias had lifted from the Book Cadillac Hotel the day he'd surprised her with her first kiss. A simple gesture proclaiming his love, it was the only thing of value he had ever given her. She held it to her cheek before placing it into the pillowcase. Looking in the drawer, Mildred stared at the remaining item for several moments before finally removing the doll and holding it to where her heart now drummed beneath her chest. As she held the doll Helen had bought for her, she trailed her fingers over the gown it now wore. And for a brief moment, the doll was the child who once wore that same gown. As memories of holding Fannie flooded her senses, Mildred collapsed into a heap on the floor. She cried until she had relinquished all her tears, then continued to shed away her remaining emotions in bursts of silent sobs.

Chapter Twenty-Eight

Mildred sat alone in the dark apartment waiting for Franky to return. The items they'd selected to take with them were stacked neatly by the door. In addition to the contents of the pillowcase, she had packed her clothing, sewing basket and a few pieces of feedsack fabric, the photo of her with her parents, and two quilts, one being the threadbare birth quilt Helen had made. She had considered taking the traveling trunk but decided against it. She was not taking enough to fill it, and besides, it was too heavy for her and Franky to carry by themselves.

Franky's pile was even smaller than hers. It included a change of clothes and a cigar box, the contents of which remained a mystery to her. The crate Tobias carried in the day he died proved to be the only thing of his they would be taking.

Franky had left in the guise of a casual stroll, when in reality, he was checking to see if anyone was watching the building. Mildred felt guilty allowing the boy to take such risks, but this was the life he lived, and she knew he would not have listened had she objected. She took solace in the fact that it was Tobias who trained him. Even still, he had been gone over an hour, and she was beginning to worry. Since she had no clue of his destination, she wouldn't begin to know where to look for him. Therefore, her only choice was to wait.

She pulled the threadbare quilt from the pile and took it to the couch. As she waited, she let her mind drift back to the events of the last few days. She thought about Tobias shivering in the bathtub. Then she thought about the quilts she'd sold. If only she would have had more quilts, she could have sweated the fever out instead. Would that have made a difference? It was a question for which she would never know the answer.

She heard footsteps in the hall and held her breath as someone jiggled the door handle. The door opened and that someone stepped inside.

"Mrs. Millie?"

Mildred let out the breath she was

holding. "I'm here, Franky."

She heard the door click shut. "Do not turn on the light. There are two men watching the building."

Mildred's heart sank. "So we cannot leave?"

"Sure we can. I worked it out with a few of the boys. They are going to make trouble and get the men to follow."

"Those men do not play nice, Franky."

"The boys have dealt with their sort before. Do you have everything ready?"

"I do, but how are we going to get it to the train station?"

"We don't need to. We have Mouse's motorcar."

"How? I thought the police took it away. And who shall drive it?" Mildred knew she should be grateful they had a way to escape, but fear pushed her into panic mode.

Franky moved to the window, careful to stay in the shadows. "That's the difference between guys and dames. Dames sure ask a lot of questions. If I told the boys what I just told you, they'd know things would work out. You need to trust me, okay?"

For a moment there, he sounded just like Tobias. While too dark to see his face, she knew there had been some type of transformation in the boy. While he always had an edge, this was a side of him she hadn't seen, a no-nonsense miniature carbon of Tobias.

She closed her eyes to steady her nerves. "Okay, Franky, I'll leave our getaway up to you."

"Good. It's time to go." He opened the door, walked across the hall, and pushed the button for the elevator. The doors opened immediately. Franky stepped inside and stopped the elevator long enough to transfer everything they were taking from the apartment. When they finished, he patiently waited for Mildred to say a silent goodbye.

Mildred thought about doing one last search to make sure she wasn't forgetting anything. However, that would involve turning on the lights, so she decided against it. She did not need light to picture the contents within the apartment; she knew every item within the space and exactly where each item was located. She stood looking into the darkness for several moments before pulling the door shut and hurrying to the waiting elevator. She managed to keep her tears in check until the elevator began its descent, only then giving in to the pain of once again losing everything she held dear.

"We must hurry," Franky said, softly touching her shoulder.

Maybe it was the gentleness of his touch. Maybe it was the way he looked at her as if to say *I'm hurting too*. Whatever the reason, Mildred was able to pull herself together before the elevator reached the lobby and once again opened its doors. She didn't apologize for her tears; she simply brushed them away with the sleeves of her coat before nodding her readiness.

Franky stepped out into the dark hallway. Only then did it occur to her that the third-floor hallway was also dark. Franky was right; Tobias had taught him well. The boy made a low whistle, and two boys joined them, each hurrying into the elevator to help carry their belongings. Mildred picked up the pillowcase and a sack full of clothes and followed silently behind. They moved to the doorway, each making sure to stay out of view. A few moments passed before a third boy pulled the front door open, letting in an icy rush of air.

The boy was older than the rest and unlike the other two boys; his clothes appeared to be new and stylish for the time. "The chumps bought it, but it won't be long before they figure out the ruse. If you hurry, you should be good for a clean sneak."

Mildred looked to Franky for translation.

"We need to go," he said, leading the way to the Ford, which was idling at the curb.

Mildred put the items she was carrying in the back and climbed into the passenger seat. Even though she was much older than Franky, she had never learned how to drive. She only hoped that Tobias' lessons included learning how to drive the machine. Franky jumped in and maneuvered himself behind the wheel, and for the first time in days, Mildred found herself laughing.

"You can't even see over the wheel!" She snickered.

He narrowed his eyes. "I can see plenty fine."

"Can you even reach those?" she

asked, pointing to the three pedals on the floor.

"How do you think I got the car home?" He maneuvered the pedals, pulled the gearshift down, and the car lurched forward.

To Mildred's surprise, the boy could not only drive, he did so rather well. He drove for several moments without turning on the headlamps. At first, she worried that he didn't know how, then watching him check the mirror before turning the switch to illuminate the road, she realized he was simply being cautious.

"Do you know where we are going?"

"You said you wanted to go to Sandusky," he answered without taking his eyes from the road.

"I mean, do you know how to get there?"

"I studied the map."

"It didn't look very far."

It was his turn to laugh. "It's a map; nothing ever looks very far. Go to sleep, Mrs. Millie; it's going to be a long night."

As Mildred closed her eyes, the image of the well-dressed boy flashed in her mind. Opening them once more, she turned to

Franky. "Who was that guy?"

"Which one?"

"The one who looked to be around my age."

"His name's Hoffa. He goes by Jimmy. He's nobody," Franky answered without taking his eyes off the road.

***

It was well into the following morning before they arrived in Sandusky. Mildred was not sure what surprised her more, that she'd slept the entire way or that the town was so small. There was a smattering of businesses in town. Thankfully, one of them was a hotel. Franky angled the Ford to the front of the building and killed the motor. Only after he'd pried his fingers from the steering wheel did Mildred realize how white the boy's knuckles were. As he smiled at her through droopy eyelids, it was clear he was exhausted. It was also clear that the bravado he'd shown during their escape was gone. In its wake was a scared boy who now looked to her for direction.

"You did good, Franky. I'll go in and get us a room." Mildred went into the hotel and stood at the front desk.

A thin man sat behind the desk reading the morning paper. He stood, folded the paper, and sat it on the counter as he appraised them. "Be needing a room?"

"Yes, sir," Mildred said, nodding.

The man pushed up his spectacles. "Just you and your son?"

Mildred looked over her shoulder. She hadn't even heard Franky come in. Yes, Tobias had taught him well.

Franky moved up beside her. When he spoke, the bravado had returned. "The lady would have had to be mighty promiscuous at rather a young age to have a son my age, don't you think? I believe you owe my sister an apology."

Mildred struggled to keep from laughing as the desk clerk's face turned crimson.

"I…um…I assure you I meant no ill regard. I just assumed…" The clerk glanced at Mildred's wedding ring. "I mean, I knew he was too young to be your husband. Will he…your husband, be joining you later?"

Mildred felt her eyes grow misty.

Franky drummed a finger on the counter. "My brother-in-law grew ill and died a few days ago."

The man's blush deepened. "My condolences, ma'am. Influenza has taken a great many folks ill."

Mildred worried that Franky was growing impatient with the man. "A room, if you please, two beds."

"You don't sound like you are from these parts. What brings you to our town?" the man asked, reaching for a key.

Franky balled his hands into fists. Mildred placed a hand on his shoulder to calm him. "I am here to see a family friend. My brother and I have had such a long drive and would like to rest up a bit before we visit."

"Oh, yes. Yes indeed. A local, then? What's the name? I know most everyone in town."

"His name is Paddy."

The man's brow creased. "Don't recall anyone with that name. Sounds like one of those nicknames. What be his given name?"

Mildred felt her heartbeat increase. She couldn't remember ever hearing him called any other name. He'd always been Paddy. Even if she knew his given name, there was nothing to say it hadn't been changed. Her new parents had changed hers the day she arrived. What if she couldn't find him? They would have traveled all this way for nothing. "We, my family and I, have always called him Paddy."

The man adjusted his spectacles once more. "What about the last name? You know that?"

Mildred reached into her pocket and pulled out the newspaper clipping. "Jones, it says his name is Paddy Jones."

The man leaned forward to see the clipping, but Mildred folded it closed before he could read what it said. "We have several Joneses in the area, but I don't recall any of them going by that. You two go on up to your room. I'll do some asking around and let you know when you come down."

"Thank you," Mildred said, taking the key.

"Boy, that man gave me the heebie-jeebies," Franky said once they were in the room. "I know bulls that don't grill people like that."

Mildred looked around. The room was simple, but it was clean with brightly colored quilts draped over the end of each bed. The space was delightfully warm, and for the first time since Tobias brought him home, the boy would have an actual bed to sleep on. "He did seem a bit hinky. Maybe that is just his way."

"You said we were coming to see family. What was that paper?" Franky asked on a yawn.

Mildred pulled out the clipping and handed it to him.

"So this guy we are here to see, this Paddy, he's not family?" Franky asked when he finished reading.

Mildred took the clipping and returned it to her pocket. "He is as much family as you are."

Franky yawned. "What train?"

Mildred had been told many times never to tell anyone about the trains, warned that people would think ill of her. She remembered the look she'd received in the mercantile when Mrs. Shively told them of her plight, and wondered at how much to tell him. Still, this was Franky, and he was after all the only family she had at the moment. She nodded toward the beds. "Pick one."

Franky's face lit up. He jumped onto the bed nearest the wall and bounced up and down.

Mildred laughed. "They are for sleeping."

"I know, but I've always wanted to do this."

"I did it too, the first time I was alone in my new room after my parents picked me."

Franky stretched his legs out and landed on his bottom with a thud. "The people in the graveyard picked you?"

"They did. Right after we came over on the trains."

"Were they good to you?"

Good, he wasn't focused on the trains. She smiled. "They were very good to me."

Anger flashed across his face. "I wish the people who picked me were kind. If Mouse hadn't come for me, I would have killed them with my bare hands."

Dumbfounded, Mildred sank on the bed opposite him. "What are you saying, Franky?"

"I'm saying that I rode the trains too. Mouse came to find me to see if I was okay. When he saw how bad things were, he took me with him. He told me not to tell you about the trains. He said you wouldn't understand."

Mildred felt a pain in her temples. It seemed the more she learned about her husband, the less she knew him. "Did you know Tobias before he came to see you?"

"No, he just showed up one day. Said someone had sent him to check on me. When I told him how bad things were, he made me leave with him. He said he had a job for me."

"What was the job, Franky?"

Franky yawned. "Why, to take care of you, of course. In return, he promised to teach me a trade. He showed me how to fade when I followed you, just in case your parents or someone else would see me. Then he taught me how to dip the pockets. When I got good at that, he taught me other stuff."

Mildred was confused. She hadn't met the boy until after her parents had died. "Wait, how long have you been following me?"

He shrugged. "A long time."

"How long, Franky?"

Another shrug, followed by a yawn. "Maybe two or three years before your parents died."

"But why?"

"Because Mouse said I was family, and that is what family does. We look out after one another."

Mildred stood and paced the small room.

"You look mad. Mouse was right; I shouldn't have told you."

"I am not angry with you, Franky. I am just so confused, and I wish Tobias were here to answer my questions."

Franky lay down, resting his head on the small pillow, and closed his eyes. "I miss Mouse."

She missed the man too, but currently, the only emotion she had was one of utter confusion. Why did Tobias think she needed watching? Did he think her to be in danger? If so, why send a boy to watch over her? Franky couldn't have been very old when he first started following her. She turned to confirm his age and saw that he was sleeping. She walked over to his bed and pulled the quilt over him. She sat beside him, looking at the boy who'd been left to look after her. Yesterday, she'd questioned his abilities to keep her safe. Now, as she sat watching him sleep, she realized he'd been performing that task for many years. She would never laugh at him again. Nor would she question his devotion.

Chapter Twenty-Nine

December 13th, 1933

It was nearly dusk, and Franky had yet to wake. She wasn't sure if it was because the drive had taken so much out of him or the fact that he was sleeping in an actual bed. After a short nap of her own, Mildred used the water closet to freshen up. The window in their room faced the road. She sat there for hours watching as people passed by using various modes of transportation. Motorcars seem most prevalent, but she saw her share of horse and buggy, riders on horseback, and a fair amount of foot traffic as well. She wondered about the people of the town, mostly wondering if they were the sort of folk who would welcome strangers. Multiple times, people lifted their hands in greeting as someone passed by. Despite the cold, men and women stopped along the sidewalk, gesturing and talking. One man pointed to the sky, and she realized he was probably complaining about the weather. Still, instead of appearing angry, he seemed to shrug it off. No use getting upset at things you could not change.

She thought of Paddy and wondered if he still sported his brilliant red hair. Surely so, as she doubted that shade of red would simply fade away. Soon, soft snowy flakes began to float from the sky. Watching them, she made a mental note to buy Franky and herself a warmer coat and some rubbers to slip over their shoes.

Her stomach rumbled. She looked at the bed and wondered if she should wake Franky so they could find something to eat. He made a noise and snuggled deeper into the pillow. Franky moaned, his lips curling upwards, and he mumbled something in his sleep. The boy's face relaxed and he quieted. She didn't have the heart to wake him. Somehow she doubted he'd ever had the opportunity to sleep so soundly. Was it the bed or the mere fact that they were far away from the troubles that besieged them? She suspected it to be both.

She walked to the desk, pulled out the chair, and sat staring at the blank sheet of paper. Lifting the pen, she contemplated her words.

What did one say to a harlot anyhow?

Wasn't that what one called a woman who slept with another woman's husband? As much as the thought pained her, it was the only reason she could fathom for the woman's son to look so much like Tobias. She thought of her daughter, Fannie, and wondered if the boy looked anything like her. Her jaw clenched. She closed her eyes, picturing Tobias as she had seen him dozens of times, joyfully cradling Fannie in his arms. Even in death, it was Tobias who came out ahead, and she who was left alone to bear the burden of questions that would probably never receive answers. While a part of her wanted to know the details, a larger part of her preferred to bury the past. The only way she knew to be free was to give the unknown its freedom. It took everything she had to place pen to paper without sounding too threatening.

Anastasia,

I am writing to you as I found your letters in my late husband's belongings. I do not know what ties you have to my Tobias, but whatever they were, they are no more. My husband is dead and buried and his good name buried along with him.

Best,

Mrs. Mildred Lisowski

Mildred re-read the letter, decided it too cold, and then rewrote the entire thing, adding this line. *I trust your health has improved and your son is safe within your care.* Best to take the high road when dealing with such delicate matters.

She had no sooner finished when she heard a knock at the door. She hurried to answer and was greeted by the same desk clerk that had checked them in. He held a brown covered crock in one hand and a woven picnic basket in the other. Mildred moved aside, and the man stepped into the room.

"Don't mean to interrupt but thought as you might be wanting some supper. I told my wife we had some out-of-towners and she fixed you up some chicken and dumplings. Also got two pieces of pumpkin pie in the basket along with some eating utensils and plates. Got two jars of lemonade in there as well," he said, keeping his voice low.

Franky moaned in his sleep and turned toward the wall.

A deep frown crossed the man's face. "The boy ill?"

"No, my brother is just tired," Mildred replied.

"You sure? The boy said your husband had been ill. We don't be needing any more of that influenza around here."

"The roads coming down from the city were plain awful. My brother is just tired from the driving is all." She regretted the comment as soon as it left her mouth.

"Yes. I can see where those conditions would wear a body out. The boy's a bit young to be driving," he said, glancing at Franky.

Mildred worked to make her lip tremble. "He is, but I was just so distraught at losing my dear husband and had to get away. We had my husband's motorcar, but I have never learned to drive it. He was a good man and so doting on my brother after our parents died. He taught him to drive to keep his mind off his sorrows. I guess we could have waited and found another way to travel, but I was afraid. Detroit just isn't what it used to be, you know. My brother and I lost our parents a few years ago and now my dear husband…I was just so worried at how my brother would turn out if we stayed in the city. Him not having a proper father figure to look up to and all." At least some of it was the truth.

The man's face softened. "Yes, I would say it is better to raise a boy like that in the country. Plan on staying then, do you?"

His question caught her off guard. "Why do you want to know?"

The man saw her expression and put up a hand to apologize. "Oh, excuse my manners. I don't mean to be so inquisitive. It's just we are a small town, and we don't get a lot of visitors these days. Our town seems to have fared better than some in this here economic decline. People don't seem to get out much anymore. FDR is going to change all of that. I voted for him, you know. Roosevelt, that is."

Mildred nodded. "Yes, I know who President Roosevelt is."

"Good. Good. I wasn't sure, you being a woman and all. And a pretty young one at that."

Mildred felt her face turn red. "Thank you, and thank you for bringing up the food.

I didn't realize how hungry I was until I smelled it."

The man walked over and placed his load onto the desk. He picked up the folded paper and turned to Mildred. "This a letter?"

Did the man's curiosity have no limits? She reached over and snatched the paper from him. "It is."

"Oh, well, I have some stamps at the desk. Cost you three cents each. And another penny if you'll be wanting an envelope."

Mildred realized the man was only trying to help and relaxed. "That would be much appreciated. Thank you."

The man turned to leave and stopped. "I guess if you are staying, I should properly introduce myself. Bill Winters."

"Mildred Lisowski," Mildred said and reached out her hand, which he took and gave a hearty shake, letting his fingers linger a tad too long.

"Got any money?" Bill asked, releasing her hand.

"For the stamps? Yes, I have money to pay."

"No, I mean to pay for a room for the month. That is mostly what we do. As I said, we don't get too many visitors these days."

She wondered how much to tell him; then again, he seemed trustworthy. "I have some money set aside. Though I'm not too sure about staying in the hotel, not that it isn't a nice one. I think my brother and I would be much happier in a more permanent home. A fresh start, without so many sad memories."

"I hear ya; a boy that age needs room to run and play. He'll need a role model too. Not that a woman can't care for a boy properly. But it helps to have a man he can look up to. I'll bring up the stamp and envelope when I come to collect the dishes," he said and left the room without waiting for a reply.

Mildred stood by the door staring at Franky and wondered if there were ever a time when the boy actually got to act like a child. If what he'd said were true, he had been living on the street for years. She only had to remember Tobias to know how much the streets could age a child. Franky already emulated the man in many ways.

Her thoughts went to her own childhood and how her life changed the moment she and her birth parents stepped foot onto the ship bound for America. Mildred thought of her life while at the asylum and how she and her friends stood by the fence waiting for strangers to bring them something extra to eat. She glanced at the food sitting on the desk and realized, for all that had changed in her world, much had stayed the same. She was still just as lost, and still just as dependent on strangers to bring her food.

Taking a deep breath, Mildred pulled herself taller. It was not the same, and she was not alone. She still had Franky, and he needed her guidance to keep from getting in deeper with the street gangs he ran with. He was a good kid and deserved to be able to act like one. They were in what seemed to be a safe town. It was small and quiet, where people could walk down the street and not fear for their lives. She wondered about Paddy and why, if he lived in such a small town, the man who asked so many questions didn't know his name. She had no clue how old the newspaper clipping was; maybe he'd already moved along. Was she ready to stay in this small town without him? She thought of her birth father, remembered him telling her of the land they were heading to, and smiled. He would not have approved of the big city. Not of New York with all of its people and not of Detroit with its gangs and crime. No, she was certain her birth father would have insisted they keep moving until they found a town just like this one. While she had mulled it over, it was right then she made a firm decision to stay and make a life for her and Franky. She hurried over to the bed to wake him for supper, to tell him of her decision to stay and ask him to stay with her. While she didn't have any hold on the boy, she knew in her heart that he needed her as much as she needed him.

Chapter Thirty

Bill was sitting at the front desk when they descended the steps. As they approached, he stood. "You two are up bright and early this fine morning. Got plenty of rest, did ya, boy?"

Franky nodded then walked away.

Mildred looked over her shoulder at the boy who stood gazing out the front window, then turned her attention to Bill. "We've decided to stay and make Sandusky our home."

Bill laughed. "Mighty big decision since you've barely seen anything of the town. Must have been the wife's fine cooking that helped you make up your mind. It sure as heck wasn't our weather."

Mildred cast another look out at the freshly fallen snow. "We are used to snow. We have had our share of blizzards in Detroit."

"You say Detroit, but I detect a bit of an accent," Bill said in reply.

"This is America; everyone has an accent," Mildred replied.

Bill nodded and turned his gaze to Franky. "Yes, but some have more than others."

She followed the man's gaze and saw Franky stiffen. The clerk's inquisitiveness was one of the objections Franky posed when she told him she planned to stay and make a home here. She watched Franky clench his fist and knew he was about to lose control. Just as he turned around, Mildred rushed to ask a question of her own. "Mr. Winters, do you happen to have that paper I saw you reading yesterday?"

Bill returned his gaze to Mildred. "Would that have been the *Sandusky Republican Tribune*, or the Port Huron paper?"

"I think I would like the *Tribune*, since it is the local paper."

He reached under the counter and pulled out the paper. "Looking for anything in particular?"

"Why, yes, we are looking for a place to live." She skimmed the small classified selection, which listed two rentals and one property within the city limits of the town.

"Do you know of any properties for sale in the area? We would like to get settled before the weather worsens."

"Not a lot of people move during the winter months," he said when she sighed.

"It is not that; I was hoping to find something with a bit of land. My brother has only known city life, and I was so hoping to get him a horse." They hadn't discussed it, but she was fairly sure Franky would be open to the idea, providing he liked animals.

"There are two properties in town that aren't listed in the paper. Both are a bit on the small side with no land to speak of. I did hear of one just yesterday while at the barber shop if you are looking for a really sweet deal." Bill leaned in and lowered his voice, even though they were the only three within earshot. "Seems Howard Moore is in danger of losing his farm. Belonged to his parents, who for some reason neglected to pay their taxes for several years. The way I hear it, Howard sold most of the land to pay off the house, but there wasn't enough left to pay the back taxes. Word I get is if he doesn't pay off the tax debt by the end of the year, the Bureau is going to seize the remaining property. Hate seeing that, as the land has been in the family for years. If you ask me, the kid got dealt a bad hand. He didn't know the property was in arrears until it was too late to do anything. Even with much of the land sold, the house still sits on a nice plot of farmland, all of which can be had for the low price of paying a few years' worth of taxes."

Franky, who'd obviously been listening, stepped up beside Mildred and posed a question of his own. "So, let me ask you this: if it is such a grand deal, why hasn't anyone jumped on it?"

"We are a farming community, son. As I told you yesterday, we don't get a lot of strangers in town these days. The land got scarfed up fairly quick, but the people here already have homes."

Mildred folded the paper and handed it back to Bill. "Maybe we should pay this Howard person a visit. Can you give us directions?"

Bill leaned over the desk and pointed toward the left. "Go back the way you drove in. About two miles out of town, you are going to take a right onto Henderson Road. Follow it nearly all the way down, and it will be the last house on the right just before you get to the woods. Two-story white house. Got a couple of barns and outbuildings if I recall right. One of them is made out of creek rock; you can't miss it. Howard's got a couple of big dogs, so you might want to blast the horn before you get out of your automobile."

"What do you know about farms?" Franky asked as soon as they reached the Ford.

"I know as much as you do," Mildred replied.

"Just like a dame." Franky laughed. "You've done gone all soft from that story he told. How do you know that guy in there ain't trying to flimflam you?"

"What do you mean?"

Franky backed out of the parking space, grinding the gears, and headed out of town. "Come on, think about it. That guy has done nothing but ask questions since we pulled into town. He knows you are a widow and you told him you have money. Now, out of the blue, he just happens to know a guy who will sell you his farm on the cheap. You're such a chump, you are walking straight into their trap. Why couldn't the house be in town? Naw, he is sending us down some back road. You heard him; the house is next to the woods. How hinky is that? Probably where they will bury our bodies after they rob and bump us off."

They passed the cemetery as he made the comment and Mildred shivered. "You have been living in the city too long. This is the country. People in the country don't kill people for their money. Besides, the house has to be out of town; it's a farm. They don't have farms in town. Where would you keep your horse?"

Franky stole a glance at her. "You were serious about that?"

"I was…if you want one. Do you even like animals?"

He shrugged. "Guess I have never given them a thought. A horse might be all right. Or a dog, as long as we don't have to eat it."

Mildred thought he might be joshing, but the look on his face told her otherwise. She almost asked if he had ever eaten dog, then decided she'd rather not know the answer to that question.

Franky slowed and turned the car onto Henderson Road. "All the same, you had better let me do the talking. And don't stand too close to me. Anything goes down, you run and hide in those woods. If I can get away, I'll come find you after I put a knife in the guy's gut."

Mildred stared at Franky in disbelief. *What had happened to the kid to make him so distrusting?* "Franky, I know you have seen things that you don't want to talk about, but I am pretty sure we are safe here."

The snow was deeper on the less traveled backroad. Franky remained quiet as he concentrated on staying within the tire ruts of a previous driver. The house in question looked to be a similar style of the house she'd lived in with her family in Detroit, only the front door faced the side of the house instead of the front. Two large south-facing picture windows made up the front of the house; the one on the right had narrower side windows that opened. Both, of course, remained closed this blustery winter's day. Mildred could almost imagine herself inside the house standing in front of the window bathed in warm sunlight as the summer breeze pushed its way through the side windows. Inside, she would be looking out at fields of crops, not a house to be seen for miles. A stark difference from either of the cities she had once called home. A welcome difference all the same. She could see herself living here, scrubbing clothes on the washboard and hanging them on the line to dry. The large barn would have no trouble housing a horse or two, still leaving room for the cows. She pictured Franky sitting on a low stool with a scowl on his face as he tried to figure out how to drain milk from a cow. The image changed to him standing there knife in hand, telling the cow to go milk itself. For a moment, she questioned the impulsiveness of her decision and thought about telling him to turn around.

Too late, Franky pulled the Ford to a halt and pushed the horn to announce their arrival. At the sound of the horn, two large black dogs raced out of the barn, furiously barking their arrival. A moment later, a man followed them out of the barn. It was hard to gauge the man's age, as he was dressed for the weather. Wearing a heavy brown coat, knit hat, and black rubber boots, he had a black scarf wrapped around his face, allowing only his eyes to show.

Franky placed his hand on the door handle. "I'd feel much better if you stay inside the car."

She started to object then reconsidered. Franky was only doing the job Tobias trained him to do. "Only if you stay where I can see you and keep your knife inside your pocket."

"Dames," he muttered then opened the door.

As the man approached, he kept his head hunkered down. It was the posture of someone bracing against the wind, not one preparing to do battle. She hoped Franky was good at reading body language.

The man stretched out a gloved hand toward Franky. The boy accepted the greeting but kept the other hand tucked into his coat pocket. She had no doubt Franky's fingers were tightly wrapped around the knife. The man released Franky's hand and gestured toward the house, hospitably inviting him inside. Franky took a step, then looked at the car as if debating. The dogs continued to bark until the man lowered the scarf covering, whistling for them to cease.

The snow was sticking to the windshield. Mildred leaned over and turned the wipers on. As the blades pushed the white slush from the window, she saw the brilliant red beard that covered the young man's face. She was out of the car before realizing what she was doing. It didn't dawn on her that she could be mistaken. She slipped, caught herself, and slipped yet again. Gathering herself up, she all but jumped into the bewildered man's arms. It took him a minute to recognize her, but when he did, his arms clung to her as if he was afraid she would disappear. It was freezing out, and tears she didn't realize were being shed lay frozen on her cheek. People might know him as Howard, but to her, he would always be Paddy.

***

Cindy stared at the open journal in disbelief.

"That bit caught me off guard as well," Linda said when she'd finished the page.

"Mildred I get, but Howard? He always seemed so open and straightforward. Why he never told us about him riding the trains, I don't get," Cindy agreed.

"Well, it does answer two questions,"

Linda mused.

"Which is?"

"We now know what happened to one of the other kids and that Paddy was not missing teeth because he was malnourished."

Cindy closed her eyes briefly. "What?"

"When Mildred—I believe she was Mileta then—when she was describing the kids, she made the comment he had a near toothless grin. I thought it might be because the boy had a vitamin deficiency that made him lose his teeth. I happen to know your grandfather had most of his teeth when he died."

Cindy bit her bottom lip to keep from laughing. Her mother had always been one to guess the ending to movies and television shows well in advance. "You should have been a detective, Mother."

Linda beamed with delight. "That's what your father used to say."

"How about we see what other surprises she'd left for us?" Cindy replied and turned the page in the journal.

Chapter Thirty-One

At Paddy's insistence, Franky had pulled the Ford into the barn. The three of them now sat at the dining room table drinking sweetened coffee to break the chill. Franky sat petting a small black and white cat, which had climbed onto his lap the second he sat down, quietly listening as Mildred told of her life since leaving the train. She told of finding the newspaper clipping, however, refrained from mentioning the letters. She told of the stack of money, how they'd managed to escape without being followed, and smiled at the boy as she told how he'd driven all the way to Sandusky under such terrible driving conditions.

Paddy reached across the table and placed his hand upon hers. "I'm sorry you have had such a difficult life."

Franky cleared his throat, and Paddy removed his hand. Mildred bit her lip to keep from smiling. Friend or not, Franky was still intent on protecting her.

Paddy leaned back in his chair and spoke directly to Franky. "Thank you for getting the both of you here safe."

"It was nothing." Franky shrugged and continued to stroke the cat.

Paddy turned his attention to Mildred. "I understand how you came to be in this town, but how did you find me?"

Mildred took a sip of her coffee. "We didn't know we had found you. Bill from the hotel told us some guy named Howard was about to lose his farm. He said if I would agree to pay the back taxes, that he would sell the farm to me."

Paddy's face turned crimson. "The taxes are not my fault. My parents were good people, but lousy at finances."

"Yes, Bill made that clear. He said they left you with a huge debt that no boy your age would be able to recover from."

"Boy, I've seen more crap than half the people in this town, and they still treat me like a kid. If they knew where I came from and what I did before I got here." He shook his head.

"They…the people of this town, don't know you rode the trains?" Mildred asked then realized she'd nearly whispered the question.

Paddy looked at Franky before answering. "They told us not to tell. That is why I didn't use my real name when I placed the advert. I put that in the paper five years ago."

Five years... "Tobias had it all that time and yet never told me. Did you hear from any of the others?"

Paddy waved his hand. "Most of them. I've been corresponding with a few. I'll let you read the letters later."

Mildred was surprised he didn't sound more excited about being in contact with the others. So many times she had wished to speak to them, to hear their voices one last time.

"I would go into town every Friday to check that box, hoping to hear from you. And each time, it felt as if a knife jabbed me right in the heart," Paddy said, pointing at his chest. He leaned forward in his chair. "It doesn't surprise me much that Mouse found you. He had his sights set on you for years. It didn't matter that he knew I was in love with you. He was going to have you, and that was that."

Now Mildred was even more confused. She knew Paddy had a schoolboy crush on her, but to say he was in love with her, and how could he have known that Tobias followed her? *Wait, had he just called him Mouse?* Maybe she mentioned his street name when she was telling of her life. "You came straight here from the trains, did you not?"

Paddy nodded. "I did."

"Then how could you know about Tobias' keeping an eye on me?" She looked to Franky, who was silently taking in every word. She'd purposely left out the fact that Tobias had made Franky spy on her as well.

"I knew because Mouse came from the same streets I did. Our paths had crossed even before I was locked up in that asylum. When me and the boys went out for instruction, he would stop us and drill us about how you were doing, and make sure none of us kids were messing with you. One day, Slick made the mistake of telling Mouse I had my sights on you, and he about beat me to a pulp."

Mildred stared at him in shock. She remembered that day. Paddy had come to dinner with a busted lip and two black eyes; he'd told everyone he'd got jumped by a kid looking to steal his coat. "Tobias did that to you? But why?"

Paddy drained his cup before answering. "Because he wanted you for himself."

"What was there to want? I was a kid," Mildred said heatedly.

"None of us were kids, Mileta. We weren't allowed to be. We were small adults living in an ugly city. If not for the trains, we would have all died in that city as well."

Mildred stood and moved to the window, watching as the snow blew across the unprotected field across the road. "You've heard my story and about everyone I have lost. Are you saying I am better off than if I'd have been left behind?"

"On some accounts, yes. Think about it. Even as bad as things were, at least you have lived. You have known love. Isn't that better than being institutionalized and rushing to eat your mush before someone bigger stole it from you? They would have turned you out when you were eighteen. You have to have read a newspaper or two.

What would have happened to someone as pretty as you on the streets of New York when the banks collapsed? How many quilts did you make before the trains? How many times could you simply sit and play the piano just for the sheer joy of doing so?"

"I haven't played the piano since I left New York," she said without turning around.

Paddy leaned forward in his chair. "Why in heaven's name not?"

"Just like you said. They told us to forget our past. I never even told my parents that I played."

"And your husband did not see to it that you played?" His voice was incredulous. "What kind of a man was he?"

She heard a chair scrape against the hardwood floor and turned to see Franky on his feet, knife in hand. Mildred walked toward him, keeping her voice calm. "Franky, put the knife down."

"I will not have this guy speaking ill of Mouse." Franky's voice was shaking.

Paddy held his hands out. "I did not mean to put your friend down. It just surprised me he did not do everything in his power to make Mileta happy."

"Quit calling her that! Her name is Millie or Mildred," Franky spat.

Mildred had moved to Franky's side. "Franky, Paddy didn't mean to disrespect Tobias. Please give me the knife."

"I'm sorry," Paddy repeated. "I think we are all letting our emotions get the best of us."

"Franky, Paddy is family. Just like you, remember? We are all family," Mildred soothed.

The boy's arm relaxed. He lowered the knife, but instead of handing it to Mildred, he folded it and stuffed it into his pocket. He narrowed his eyes at Paddy. "Don't speak ill of the dead."

Paddy's shoulders relaxed. "Never again."

Mildred sighed. "I guess Franky and I should be on our way."

The muscles in Paddy's jaw twitched. "I thought you were interested in buying a small farm."

"And throw you out on the street? Never," Mildred replied.

"I could stay." His words were merely a whisper.

Mildred laughed. "And what would the

town's people say about me living in sin with you?"

"It wouldn't be living in sin if we were married." His voice held a mixture of hope and fear.

Mildred felt the shock of his words. "I am a widow but a handful of days. The people of the town would think me a harlot."

"The people of this town would think you a woman being taken advantage of, not the other way around. It is I who would yield the bad reputation, taking advantage of a young widow in the throes of her grief."

Mildred lifted her chin. "And how do I know that is not the case? Obviously, you know me to have money, or I would not have come."

"Yes, your money is a great consideration. We can think of it as a dowry. But I assure you money is not the reason I asked you to marry me."

"And just what is that reason?" Mildred couldn't believe she was actually considering his proposal. She looked to Franky, who was watching the exchange. He met her gaze, but his expression held no emotion.

"Mileta, Mildred," he corrected. "I have

loved you for so long. My heart has ached for you from the moment we left the train. I have dreamed of finding you, yet had no idea where you had gone or who had taken you. I thought you were in Detroit, but for all I knew, you could have been a million miles away. Still, I dreamed one day I would find you and promised myself I would do anything in my power to keep you safe and love away the hurts in your life. Marry me. I will transfer the farm into your name, and if I ever prove to be a bad husband, say the word, and I will leave. It is my promise to you in front of the boy."

Mildred tilted her head toward Franky. "Ask my brother."

"Excuse me?"

"Bill at the hotel thinks Franky is my brother. Since I do not have a father, I must insist that you ask my brother for my hand in marriage." *What was she doing? Of course Franky would object to the marriage.* Maybe that was her plan. Franky would object, and she could use the boy's objection as an excuse.

To her surprise, Paddy stood and asked Franky to follow him. The two of them walked past the stairway and stopped at a closed door off the living room. Paddy opened the door, and Franky looked inside. Paddy whispered something to Franky, who nodded his head and closed the door.

"You have my permission to marry him," the boy said when he returned.

Mildred's mind filled with mixed emotions. Could she marry another man she barely knew? Then again, in some strange way, she felt she knew Paddy better than she ever knew Tobias. And, truthfully, this would be a marriage of convenience. Wasn't that the reason she'd agreed to marry Tobias in the first place? To keep her from being sent back to the asylum? Sure, she grew to love him, but she never did truly know the man. She was twenty years old and already a widow. What if she never had this chance again? If she had to be truthful, she was afraid of being alone. Then there was Franky to think of; even Bill had told her the boy needed a man to look up to. Paddy was a kind and gentle man. Franky could do with a man like that in his life. She studied Franky's face to see if it held any doubts. When she did not see any, she turned to Paddy. "Will you allow Franky to stay with us for as long as he sees fit?"

Paddy grinned. "Of course your brother can stay. He is family."

"And will you stay?" she asked, turning to Franky.

Franky looked at Paddy. "Will I have my own bed?"

"Yes, and a room all to yourself to put it in," Paddy replied.

"Will you buy me a horse?"

Paddy chuckled. "Better ask your sister; she's the one with all the money."

Mildred laughed and nodded her agreement. "So I guess that means no wedding present?"

"What did your last husband get you?" Paddy looked at Franky to make sure he had not said anything that would change the boy's mind.

Mildred laughed once more. "I'm afraid Tobias set some pretty high standards. He gifted me with a spoon he'd stolen from me when I was thirteen."

A slight smile played at the corners of Paddy's mouth. He crooked a finger and motioned her to follow. He walked to the same room he had just visited with Franky and turned the doorknob. As the door swung open, Mildred's eyes filled with tears. There in the center of the room was the very piano she'd played when biding her time in the asylum. While fully restored, she had no doubt it was the same one. As she stood there sobbing, she knew the person who had restored the rugged old piano was the same person who had just promised to help put her back together.

"How? Why?" she asked, her voice filled with emotion.

"Because, even though I thought you a million miles away, I always felt you right here," Paddy said and tapped the left side of his chest once more.

Chapter Thirty-Two

December 16th, 1933

Mildred stood at the sink swirling the dishcloth over the last of the breakfast dishes. When she finished, she handed the glass to Paddy, who rinsed it in the basin and placed it on the towel to dry. At Paddy's insistence, she and Franky had spent the night, and already, the house felt like home.

Mildred looked out the window just in time to see Franky race across the yard followed by the two large black dogs. "It makes my heart happy to see the boy run for the sheer joy of it. To be honest, I didn't know if he even knew how."

"Kids usually figure things out if you give them enough time," Paddy replied.

"Franky isn't like most kids. He has a hard edge." Mildred dried her hands on the towel and moved to the living room while Paddy followed.

"And we didn't at that age?" he said, sitting opposite her.

Chilled, Mildred pulled the threadbare quilt from the back of the chair and draped it over her lap.

Paddy nodded toward the quilt. "I guess once you get settled, you should make yourself a new quilt so you can throw that one away."

Mildred flattened the wrinkles across her lap and sighed. Each time she looked at the quilt, she saw the pride in Helen's eyes as her new mother lovingly tucked it around her to keep her warm on their first drive to her new home. "My mother, Helen, made this for me. I could never bear to part with it. I have thought about mending it many times over the years, but then I would look at it and see her. If I were to be truthful, I guess I am afraid if I alter it, I will stop seeing her face. I seldom see my birth mother's face anymore. Do you ever see your family? I mean, the ones you had before the asylum?"

Paddy shook his head. "I dream about them sometimes, but no, not really. It is more as if I know who they are and they are there in my dreams, but I do not recall their faces. Your adopted family, they were good to you?"

Mildred's face lit up. "Oh yes, they were most kind. Yours?"

"Yes, I have had a good life here. They worked me hard, but then they worked hard themselves. It is a lot of work keeping up with a dairy farm."

"Do you like it? Farming?"

"It is all I have known."

"That is not what I asked. I asked if you enjoy it."

"I like having my own land." He laughed. "Well, until I place it in your name, that is. I cannot say it is what I would do if I had another choice. You look surprised."

She smiled. "You always knew what I was thinking, even when we were young."

"You are not that old now, Mileta, Mil…you agreed to marry me, and I do not even know what to call you. Which name do you prefer?"

"Mileta doesn't feel right anymore. My mother called me Mildred; she liked things proper. My father called me Millie. I liked that, but that is the name Tobias called me." She thought about it a minute. "I think I would like you to call me Mildred. And you, what shall I call you?"

He pondered her question briefly

before answering. "You can call me Howard."

"Because your new parents gave it to you?"

He shook his head. "No, if you are going to be proper, then I think it fitting for me to be formal as well."

She giggled. "Okay, but you cannot get mad if I forget and call you Paddy."

He held her gaze. "I could never be mad at you. I love you."

Mildred lowered her eyes and played at the wrinkles on the quilt once more. "You have said that, yet you barely know me. I am not the same scared little girl I once was."

Howard smacked his knee and laughed. "You, scared? Never! You are like one of those tigresses in the *National Geographic* magazine."

His comment took her by surprise. "I was terrified at the asylum. I have been scared so many times in my life. I am absolutely petrified right now."

"Exactly! But you do not show it. It was that way the first day you arrived at the asylum. Most new kids walked around the first day crying because they missed their family. Or whining because they had their hair chopped off. Not you. When Anastasia stole your bread, it lit a fire in you, even though she was several heads taller. If Mary had not have stopped you, I think you would have marched over and punched her right in the nose."

Mildred felt the blush creep up her cheeks. "Gosh, I guess I have not thought about that in years. Do you remember her face when I licked the mush?"

"Ha! I remember everyone's faces. It was a brilliant move. I think that is the precise moment I fell in love with you." His eyes met hers once more. "I know you are scared, but yet here you are, sitting here facing your fears. You will always be my tigress, Mileta."

Mildred studied the man sitting across from her. As he spoke, he used words that showed someone raised him well. He sat straight in his chair and kept his gaze trained above her chest. Even the way he waited for her to finish speaking before adding a comment showed Howard to be a perfect gentleman. He was the total reverse of Tobias. "You said that you and Tobias came from the same streets, yet on all accounts, you seem to be the exact opposite. How can that be?"

Howard remained quiet for a moment. "I guess it is the same way you face your fears; you either let it eat you up or you overcome it and push forward."

It was several moments before either of them spoke.

"When do you want to get married?" Mildred even surprised herself by her boldness.

He smiled. "That a girl. Face your fears. Well, let's see. We have to plan the wedding, get you a dress, and I have to save up enough money to purchase you a wedding ring. I can't let you go around wearing the same ring your previous husband bought for you, now can I?"

Mildred's right hand instantly covered her ring. Howard's shoulders dropped. He made a move to rise.

Mildred put a hand up to stop him. "Wait, it is not what you think. Tobias did not purchase the ring for me. It is my mother's, Helen's wedding ring. I …I would prefer to keep wearing it if you have no objections."

Howard's face relaxed. "If it brings you

comfort wearing it, then please, by all means, keep wearing it."

She closed her eyes for a moment and then continued. "Do we have to have a large wedding? Can we not just say we are married and be done with it?"

He stared at her wide-eyed. "Why, Mildred, I thought all women wanted big weddings."

She told him some of the details from her wedding to Tobias. How she had stood in front of strangers and of being surprised when Tobias presented her with her deceased mother's ring without asking. To her surprise, his face remained impassive.

"The courthouse works for me if it works for you," he replied when she finished.

Mildred raised an eyebrow. "I'm surprised you do not have more to say."

They both looked up as Franky entered the small vestibule, stomping the snow from the rubber foot coverings Howard had loaned him. Franky saw them looking and smiled.

Howard nodded in Franky's direction and lowered his voice. "I promised the boy I would not speak ill of the dead. At this particular moment, I cannot think of anything nice to say."

Mildred smiled her understanding.

"You look frozen," Mildred said when Franky joined them in the living room. "Did you have fun?"

Franky shrugged. "I liked it well enough. The dogs are pretty swell, but I think they are cold. They wanted to come inside with me."

Howard shook his head. "Dogs do not belong in the house. They have a barn full of hay to keep them warm."

Franky's brow furrowed. "So why is it okay to have a cat in the house?"

Howard looked at the cat sunning herself on the windowsill before commenting. "Cats eat mice; dogs eat shoes. You should take a soak in the tub. It takes a few minutes for the water to get hot, but it will get there."

Franky started toward the stairs. "I've got my own room and a bed to boot. Now I am to take a soak in a tub. I think I could get used to this."

Franky stopped on the middle landing and called down, "Mrs. Millie? Do you think maybe you could make me a quilt for my bed?"

"Did you get cold last night? I am sure Howard has some more blankets if you did."

"No, I was warm enough. I was thinking that since I have my own room, it would be nice to have a quilt I can call my own. You know, kind of like that one you use all the time. But nicer," he said with a chuckle.

"When we go into town tomorrow, you can pick the colors you would like. Oh, and Franky, so we don't have trouble remembering the ruse, you need to stop calling me Mrs. Millie. Howard, as he prefers to be called, is going to call me Mildred. I think it would be best if you do so as well. That or you can call me 'sister' or 'sis' if you prefer."

"Woohoo, I have a sister!" Franky retorted and raced up the stairs.

"You are going into town tomorrow?" Howard asked when he was gone.

"*We* are going into town," Mildred corrected. "I cannot get married without you."

Howard cleared his throat. "We are getting married tomorrow?"

"Unless you have changed your mind."

"No, no, not at all."

"Do you have other plans?"

"I thought we should maybe pay off the taxes and get the farm changed over to you first."

"Yes, and since we will be at the courthouse anyway, we may as well save ourselves another trip into town," Mildred said, being practical.

"There, see, that is my tigress," Howard said affectionately.

"I think it is my lot in life to have short engagements," Mildred answered in return.

Howard leaned back in the chair and folded his hands on top of his chest. "And now it is my lot in life to see that you have no further engagements."

Chapter Thirty-Three

December 17th, 1933

The day's agenda read like a shopping list: go to town, pay off the back taxes, transfer the farm into Mildred's name – something Howard still insisted on – pick up fabric for Franky's quilt, and get hitched. Franky had written the note. He had also added "buy a horse," but both Howard and Mildred objected, insisting he wait until after the spring thaw so they would not have to feed the animal over the winter. While the boy looked disappointed, he did not push the issue.

Mildred pressed the pen to the paper, hesitated, then signed her new name. "Well, that is much easier."

Howard looked over her shoulder. "Mildred Moore. I hope you do not think it too boring."

She turned to him and smiled. "I like it just fine."

The court clerk slid the document over

so that Franky could sign as a witness. He wasn't of age, so the clerk added her name as well. The woman handed the paper to Howard for inspection. When Howard lowered the paper, his face appeared white.

"What is it?" Mildred asked.

"Oh, nothing…I guess I just realized that I am an old married man now." Howard's color started to return. However, his brow remained furrowed.

Mildred knew there was something he wasn't telling her. Instead of pressing for the truth, she decided to wait until they were alone to ask. She had another matter much more pressing at the moment. She moved to the far side of the room and crooked a finger. "Franky, can I talk to you for a moment?"

Franky walked toward her and spoke loud enough to be heard by the others. "What is it, Sister?"

Mildred exhaled and kept her voice low. "We agreed to stay in the town and begin a new life did we not?"

"We did," Franky agreed.

"Then you must return the woman's coin purse before she notices it is gone,"

Mildred whispered.

His eyes flew open. "You saw me take it? I was careful."

Mildred narrowed her eyes. "You were not the only one who took instruction from Mouse."

A knowing grin spread across the boy's face. He couldn't have looked more proud if he had trained her himself. "The lady did not see me. Why do I have to give it back?"

"Because we are going to stay here. If things start missing, people will talk. They will realize it started after we moved here and will throw you in jail. Maybe they will toss me in there with you," she added for good measure.

The grin turned into a frown. "Then how shall I take care of you if I am unable to do my job?"

"Franky, that is the best part with our staying here; you do not have to take care of me. We have plenty of money left, and now it is Howard and I who shall take care of you. You can even go to school."

The boy bristled at that. "What do I need to go to school for?"

"Because someday you might want a

real job," Mildred replied.

Franky snorted.

"We will talk about that later. For now…" She tilted her head in the direction of the lady clerk, who was at the desk speaking with Howard.

Franky shrugged and rejoined Howard, and as smoothly as he had taken it, returned the coin purse to the lady's sweater pocket. When he'd finished, he told Howard he would meet them outside and left empty-handed.

"Is everything okay with the boy?" Howard asked once they'd left the clerk's office.

Mildred turned toward the stairs and stiffened as Howard slipped his arm through hers and pressed a firm hand against her elbow to safely guide her down the stairs. Howard glanced at her but did not remove his hand. "Yes, Franky just needs to adjust to life in a small town."

"Agreed. While the townsfolk do not hang people these days, they do not take too well to stealing." Mildred stopped mid-step, and Howard laughed. "The two of you are not the only two who knew Mouse."

Franky raced up the stairs with two dime novels the second they'd returned from town. Mildred had helped him with selections of fabric for the quilt she'd promised to make him and had picked out fabric to make another quilt that she would use on her and Howard's bed. While she had a perfectly good quilt packed away in the room she'd been using, it was the quilt that had covered Tobias the day he died. While it was new, she did not think it proper to bring that quilt to her marriage bed. It was early in the day, so she decided to cut some of the fabric so she could get started. She pulled out her sewing basket and removed the scissors and several cardboard squares to begin cutting the pieces.

"What pattern are you doing?" Howard asked. To her surprise, he pressed the cardboard to the fabric and began cutting squares.

"I think Franky would prefer a simple quilt. I am going to make him a basic nine patch. Where did you learn to do that?" Mildred asked, watching him.

"My mom taught me, Mrs. Moore," he said to clarify. "Dad was always in the barn or the fields. When he didn't need my help, Mom did."

"You told me yesterday that you did not like farm work."

"I said it is not what I would prefer to do," he corrected.

"Then what would you like to do?"

"I like to work with my hands."

Mildred placed the end of the thread into her mouth then pulled it through her pressed lips to stiffen it. "Like quilting?"

"Quilting is woman's work."

"I did not ask for your help," she said, reaching for the scissors.

"That is not what I meant, and you know it. I enjoy helping you."

"Then what?" she repeated.

"I like working with wood. I like the way it feels in my hands and the way it smells when it is freshly cut. I like taking a slab of wood and making it into something totally different. And I like taking old stuff and making it look new again."

She thought about the piano and smiled. "Like the piano?"

"You have yet to play it."

"If you do not mind, I think I would just like to look at it for a while." While she loved the gift more than she could put into words, she was afraid it would bring back too many unwanted memories if she played it. For now, simply having it in the house was enough.

"It is there when you are ready."

"Thank you, Howard."

"For what?"

"For not pushing me to do things." Their eyes met, and Mildred knew he realized she was speaking of more than just the piano.

"I will also be here when you are ready."

Mildred sighed. "Your new family, they used you a lot?"

"They kept me busy. Something about idle hands," he said, placing another square on the table. "When I got older, they paid me some. So I cannot complain. Some of the others did not have it as good."

"That is right; you have been in touch with some of the others," Mildred said, pulling a string of thread through two squares. "I would love to read the letters."

"I'll pull them out a bit later."

"I was surprised when I saw the boy's last name. I did not know that was who he was. Then again, I guess it makes sense. I am just surprised you did not tell me," he said, keeping his voice low.

Mildred remembered the shocked look on Howard's face when he'd held the marriage document. "I have no clue what you are talking about."

Howard set his work aside and leaned forward. "Franky's last name is Castiglione, right?"

Where had she heard that name before? Mildred swallowed back her fear. "I guess; what of it?"

Howard's eyes searched her face. "You really do not know?"

"Know what? Paddy, you are frightening me."

"Franky is Anastasia's son. And if he is Anastasia's son, that means Tobias is…"

"Franky's father," Mildred blurted out.

Howard looked as if she'd slapped him. "What? No! Where did you come up with that?"

Mildred's heart beat as if it would jump out of her chest. "Because Anastasia has another baby and Tobias is the father."

Howard ran his hands through his hair and stared at her as if she were speaking another language. "I think you need to start from the beginning."

Mildred told him of the crate Tobias had carried in and of finding the letters from the mysterious woman named A, who kept writing and telling that her child looked like him. She told how the last letter finally spelled out the woman's entire first name. "I have not figured out all the details yet."

The expression on Howard's face was a mix of bemusement and hysterics. "So because this woman's child looked like your husband, you automatically assumed that she and your husband had relations?"

"Yes, how else would you explain it?"

"And she was in New York, and you and your husband lived in Detroit?"

"Yes." When he said it like that, she felt less certain.

Howard ran his hands through his hair once more. "Did you not stop to think there could be another explanation?"

"No." The word came out on a whisper.

"Dames," Howard said and laughed. "Do me a favor."

"What?"

"If you ever suspect me of wronging you, let me tell my side of the story before you put a bullet in my heart."

Mildred stood and narrowed her eyes at him. "I do not appreciate being made fun of. Especially when I do not know what the joke is."

Howard stood and caught her arm as she was leaving the room. He pulled her to him and wrapped his arms around her. "Tobias was a lot of things, but I do not believe he would have ever done anything that would have dishonored you. Not what you are thinking anyway. For all his faults, he loved you. Anastasia was not Tobias' lover; she is his sister! Franky is Tobias' nephew."

Nephew? Suddenly, all the pieces came together. Why Tobias had gone after Franky and why, on more than one occasion, the boy had moved a certain way or said a certain thing that made her take a second look. What she had summed up to emulation was, in reality, a family trait. She thought of the letters Anastasia had written and the baby she was now raising and wondered how they were faring. She thought of the letter she herself had written and so far had neglected to mail. She would write another letter; only this one would be one of congratulations, not contempt.

Mildred's thoughts went to Tobias and how she'd failed to save him. She glanced at the fabric on the table, and at that moment made herself a promise she would never part with another quilt. Instantly, all the guilt she'd been holding toward herself and anger she'd felt for Tobias melted away. In its wake came a deluge of tears. She'd been so angry at him for leaving that she needed to find a reason to hate him to help absorb the pain. With that reason gone, she was left defenseless. As her body released its sorrow, Mildred melted into Howard's embrace. When at last she'd finished sobbing, Howard kissed away her tears.

Chapter Thirty-Four

Wednesday, July 12ᵗʰ, 1939

Mildred wrung her hands as she looked out the living room window for what had to have been the hundredth time. She could see halfway up the road, and yet no cars were in sight. She walked into the dining room and checked that window as well. A fruitless effort, as both windows allotted the same view.

"Mildred, you are going to wear a hole in the floor if you don't stop all that pacing," Franky quipped.

"I don't know how you can remain so calm," Mildred said, retracing her path. "Howard called from the gas station; he and Paulie should be here any minute."

Franky laughed. "It's just some orphan, Mildred. Don't let a six-year-old get you all worked up. He'll be scared, but he will also be grateful to have a home. You must remember how that felt. Besides, this kid has had it good. He's never had to live on the streets."

Not for the first time, Mildred questioned their decision not to tell Franky that he and Paulie were brothers. Doing so would have opened up old wounds for each of them, something she and Howard felt best left closed. Franky had a tough enough time adjusting to living in the small town once boredom set in as it was. After a few years of struggling to leave his questionable past behind, he'd grown into a promising young man. If he'd ever noticed his uncanny resemblance to Tobias, he had never mentioned it. Mildred feared if he knew the truth, he would take it as a sign to revert to his past to pay homage to the man he held in such high esteem.

"Franky, I hope you will refrain from making those types of comments once the boy gets here. You have had your share of trouble in your life. You best remember that and make sure Paulie feels welcome in our house."

Franky shrugged. "Don't worry; I'll go easy on the kid. I'll show him the ropes."

Mildred cast a glance over her shoulder. "So long as you don't show him any of the tricks Tobias taught you."

Franky narrowed his eyes. "If it wasn't for the tricks Mouse taught me, we both would have died of hunger when the Depression hit."

Mildred sighed. They'd had this conversation more times than she could count. "You know I am grateful to both you and Tobias, but that part of our life is over. I know we do not lead the most exciting life, but we have a good life, Franky. Better than most, and whether you wish to admit it or not, Sandusky is a great place for a boy to grow up. You are a man now; look how well you turned out."

Franky's jaw relaxed as the corners of his mouth turned upwards. "Yes, and one day soon, I will join the army and see the world."

It was Mildred's turn to tense up. Franky had been talking about joining the army for years, and so far, she'd been able to talk him out of it. Lord knows she could not bear to lose another person she loved. Before she could remind him of that, the sounds of dogs barking had her rushing back to the window. Pressing into the glass, she turned her head and peered down the dirt road. Sure enough, she could see a trail of dust announcing their arrival.

"They are coming!" she said, hurrying to the small vestibule and slipping on her shoes. She stepped out onto the side porch and waved as the car turned into the driveway.

Howard blared the horn and stuck his arm out the window in greeting.

Mildred craned her neck to get her first real glimpse of the boy. She'd seen one photo of the child, taken by a photographer at the almshouse where he and his mother were living. The photographer had grouped Paulie into a photo with several other children. Two boys near the same age stood in the back row while two smiling little girls, each a head shorter, stood in front of them. Anyone looking at the photograph would assume it to be a happy family photo, not a staged catalog photograph for child adoption, sent to them at Anastasia's insistence.

The photograph arrived a few weeks earlier, along with a note telling of Anastasia's declining health, further urging them to agree to adopt the boy before they sent him to the asylum with the others.

Unfortunately, in the sender's haste to post the letter, the woman had neglected to say which of the two boys was, in fact, Anastasia's son. Not that it mattered; neither she nor Howard was about to allow the boy to fall into the same perils as they once lived, even if they did each have their own reasons for the adoption. Howard was so desperate for a child that it did not matter that he had not actually fathered the boy.

Mildred had multiple reasons. The first being, even though the child was not related to her by blood, he was family. The second, the look on Howard's face after receiving the letter from Anastasia asking them to give her son a home. How could she possibly tell him no when he'd never asked for anything else. Nor had he ever complained she had yet to give him a child of his own. She had spoken to both Howard and Franky on separate occasions, telling each of her fear of opening herself up to more pain. While she was not sure either had fully understood, both men had agreed to help her through the adjustment period.

"How was the trip?" Mildred asked as soon as Howard opened the door.

Howard stood stretching his arms in

the air to rid himself of kinks. "Long, but good. It sure was different riding the train as a paying customer. They had a separate train car to take a meal in, called it a dining car. It had tablecloths and real linens. And did you know they have bunk cars? It cost a few dollars extra, but I slept halfway across Canada."

Mildred felt her mouth drop open and closed it. "Well, what will they think of next?"

Howard laughed. "They probably had those same things when we came across, but us being kids and poor and all, we did not rate that kind of service."

It had been years since Mildred thought of her journey over on the trains. She thought about the couple that wanted to take her home and felt a chill race up her arms. She wondered at how different her life would have been and if Tobias would have come for her as he did for Franky. The chill left, and she smiled. Something told her the answer was yes.

Howard rounded the automobile and opened the side door and disappeared from sight. A few seconds later, he stood and hoisted up a little blonde-haired boy high enough for her to see.

The boy giggled and pointed at the dogs jumping and sniffing at his feet.

"Look there, son, that is your pretty new mama I have been telling you about the whole way home. You run over and give her a big hug." Howard sat the boy down, and he ran up the small set of stairs and greeted Mildred with outstretched arms.

Mildred smiled but resisted embracing the child. Instead, she reached down and rubbed the boy's mop of hair. "You are a fine-looking fellow. Are you hungry?"

Paulie lowered his arms and nodded his head solemnly.

"Good. Mother made some cookies. Come inside, and we will get you one." As she turned to follow the boy inside, she saw the frown of disappointment pulling at Howard's face. She wanted to turn to him and tell him it was the only way she knew to keep the boy safe. Instead, she went into the house without further comment.

Franky was standing just inside the door when they entered, his expression unreadable. He held out his arms and Paulie all but jumped into them, making it apparent the child was starving for attention. Mildred swallowed hard. Seeing the two boys side by side left no question of their heritage.

"Hey, kid, I'm your uncle, Frank. Come with me, and I will give you the grand tour. We will start our tour in the kitchen, of course. Your mother Mildred makes some fine-tasting oatmeal cookies," he said, winking at Mildred.

Howard came into the vestibule carrying his suitcase and a smaller bag that she assumed belonged to the boy. Mildred put up a hand to stop him. "Leave that bag outside. I want to wash the boy's belongings before we bring them into the house."

Howard nodded and placed the smaller bag on the porch. Once inside, he set his suitcase in the dining room before turning his attention to Mildred. "He is a good kid, Mileta."

She took in a breath. It had been ages since Howard called her that. "I can see that."

"He could use a mother's love."

She pulled her chin up. "I know."

Mildred fought tears as he pulled her

into an embrace. Then, kissing the side of her head, he whispered into her ear, "It is okay, my dear; I can love him enough for both of us."

***

Tears trickled down Cindy's face as she read the last line. She'd known her grandmother to be distant with her, but she hadn't realized the extent of her disconnect with her son. Nor had her father ever told her that he too had been adopted. Was there any truth in her life? She went to the wooden box, and for the first time, knew the meaning of the carving on the front. A tigress, not tiger as she once had thought. She lifted the lid, expecting to find a journal to continue her grandmother's journey. Sifting through the notebooks within the box, she realized she had read them all.

"Mom! Did you take one of the journals?" Cindy called down the hall.

"No, just the copies you gave me," came Linda's reply.

Panic set in as Cindy pulled each journal out, verifying it had been read. She was just about to give up when she noticed a large white envelope lying beneath the tissue paper. She opened the envelope and pulled out several papers. Dropping to the floor, she began to read.

My Dearest Cynthia,

At last you come to the end of my journals. I hope you do not feel slighted that I stopped writing them shortly after I married your grandfather. Life was simpler then, so there was not much to write about, lest I bore you with my daily chores. Howard, as I came to call him, was good to me. After a time, I grew to love him in my own way. He was a kind and loving man. I could not have asked for a better person with which to spend my years. I am not sure he could say the same for me.

Sadly, by the time I married Howard, I was afraid to open my heart. It seemed that each time I did, the universe saw fit to rip them from my life. So instead, I just shut down. I often regretted marrying Howard. Not because I didn't love him, but because I did. I felt he deserved more than I was able to give him. I could not give him children. Not because I was physically unable, but I couldn't bear the loss of another child.

I robbed your father of much of the same happiness. But in my mind, by not showing the universe that I loved him, I was keeping him safe. I tried to get him to tell you he was adopted, but he never would. I think that was our fault. Howard's and mine. How could the boy not feel ashamed of his past when both Howard and I refused to share ours? I did keep a small journal of things regarding your father, but I put those in with his mother's journal. It seemed the fitting thing to do.

I will never forget the Christmas of 1941, as the day before came the news my brother, Frank, as he came to be known, received his draft notice. Oh, to be assured, Frank was tickled beyond belief. He'd been chomping at the bit to join but had promised to wait until after spring before doing so. We maybe could have fought it, him being a dairy farmer and all. Then again, our dairy operation was so small, I do not think it would have done much good.

Besides, it was right after Pearl Harbor, and like most of the country, Frank was raring to go. I was not as excited. I feared what would become of him. The universe knew I loved that boy as if he were my own son. And that scared me. You couldn't turn on the radio without hearing of boys dying. The papers were full of names of those who died. I think maybe that was why Frank returned to us. There were so many deaths; the universe just lost track of him. He saw a great deal in his life, but then, that is his story to tell.

I could see in Howard's eyes that he wanted to join Franky in fighting the war, and that scared me something fierce, as I had lost so many people in my life already. Thankfully, Howard had begun doing woodwork and had lost a finger to a lathe machine two years before. I wondered at the time why Howard had lost that finger. But after the war began, it was clear; he had lost it because of me. You see, the army did not deem him fit to serve. So he stayed home with Paulie and me and lived vicariously through Franky's letters.

One day, I decided to read the journals Tobias left for me. I didn't get far into his writings before I stopped. If I would have kept on, I might have found the answers to some of the questions I have, but something told me not to continue. It is enough for me to remember the time I had with him and be happy that he cared enough to see me safe. Tobias was a child of the streets and did what he had to do to survive. Please remember that whilst reading his story.

If you have made it this far, you now know of all the secrets I kept from you. You know of my loves, and of my losses, and you know why I felt it best to keep things from you.

What you do not know is of my biggest regret. You. I regret not letting you in. I thought that by holding you at a distance, I was keeping you safe. However, the reality is I built a wall so as not to allow myself to get hurt anymore. The truth of the matter is the only infant I ever held was my baby daughter. To this very day, I can still remember how she felt in my arms. With the exception of that doll in that faded baby gown, the memories of holding Fannie in my arms are all that I have left of her. I was terrified that if I held you, or any other infant, I would not be able to remember my little Fannie. Many times I cried over you, as my arms ached so much to hold you. Then I would think myself selfish, as I knew the instant I did, I would be once again holding her and not you.

I know your mother did not care for me much. I cannot say I blame her. The truth is I did not give her reason to because she had something I did not possess. She had the ability to love. I am grateful to her for being there for both Paul and you and showering you both with the love you both longed for. She is a good woman, even though she will swear it was not I who wrote this.

I have been in contact with the others over the years. While none of us knew it at the time, there were many others. Some of us had good lives; some had fair. Others, well, sometimes people are so broken, they simply cannot be fixed. For some reason, I seem to have inherited all of their journals. Maybe it is because it was I who asked that they be written. I was surprised at how eager the others were to write about their pasts and lives. I pondered that one day and think I have discovered the answer. Maybe when enough people tell you not to talk about things, you are more inclined to have your story told. Then again, my mind is old, so what do I know?

If you are interested in the others' stories, they too are hidden in the attic. Your grandfather was a very gifted carpenter and began work on the attic as soon as we sold the farm and moved into town. The stories of us orphan train riders are all around you. Do not let their memories fade away.

All my love,
Grandma Mildred

Chapter Thirty-Five

Current Day

Cindy sat pondering everything she had just read. Key points stuck out, but her thoughts kept drifting back to the piano and what it must have taken for Howard to get his hands on it. That kind of love and devotion was hard to wrap her head around. Especially since Howard had no clue if he would ever see the woman again. She was still sitting there thinking this when Linda joined her in the room.

"You look a million miles away," Linda said, placing her stack of papers on the coffee table.

Cindy smiled. "Funny I was just thinking of Grandpa Howard's devotion to Grandma. I remember he used that same term."

Linda returned her smile. "People talk about the great loves; if they knew about Howard and Mildred, they would be included in the mix."

Cindy looked at her mother. "Do you think so?"

"You don't?"

"I'm not sure. It is obvious that Grandpa Howard was head over heels for Grandma Mildred, but I am not sure she felt the same way."

"Sure she did. She was just afraid to show it."

"Maybe. I used to think you and Dad had that kind of love, but now I am not so sure." She regretted the words the instant she said them.

"What do you mean?" Linda didn't try to hide the hurt in her voice.

Cindy blew out a sigh. "You were married to the man for forty-five years and not once in all those years he thought to say, oh by the way, I just wanted to let you know I'm adopted."

Linda sniffed back a tear. "You read the letters; he was too ashamed to say anything."

Cindy tried to conceal her anger. "If it wasn't for Grandma Mildred and Grandpa Howard adopting Dad, I might not even be here. Adoption is a beautiful thing. Heck, I might even give it a go someday."

A smile played across Linda's lips. "I was wondering if I would ever get to be a grandmother."

Cindy laughed. "I'm not an old maid yet, Mom. You didn't get married until you were thirty. Dad was what? Forty?"

"That is correct. Even though we didn't talk about this doesn't mean our relationship was flawed. Your father had his secrets and I had mine. It worked for us."

Cindy hesitated. "God, Mom, please don't tell me I was adopted."

Linda chuckled. "You've seen the scar."

Her mother was right. She had seen the scar. After two miscarriages, Cindy was born healthy and plump enough for Linda to have had to have a C-section. "Haha, enough with the guilt trip over ruining your bikini line. I was fat and comfortable. As a matter of fact, I should be blaming you. Seems like that has been my lot in life from the beginning. Fat and comfortable."

"You aren't fat. You are…fluffy." Linda's gaze drifted to the attic. "So… do you want to go on a treasure hunt?"

"Not just yet."

"Seriously? I thought you would be as eager as I to find those journals."

"Trust me, I am just as eager. I also know that once we get them, we will not be able to refrain from reading them. I need to take care of a few things first."

Linda sighed. "What could be more important than finding out what happened to the rest of the kids?"

"I need to finish going through Grandma Mildred's storage unit."

Linda released a second sigh that ended in a full-mouth pout. "Party pooper."

"I can't believe you are not as eager as I am to go on a treasure hunt."

Linda's face crinkled. "Treasure hunt?"

Cindy tapped a finger against her head. "Think about it, Mom. Grandma Mildred made it a point to tell me she had kept the spoon from the Book Cadillac Hotel, the pocket watch, and several other things. I don't think she would have done that if she weren't hoping I would go look for them."

Linda's face brightened. "Ohhh, I think you are right. Give me a minute to put on some clothes; I'm going with you."

***

Cindy lifted the gate to the storage unit and nearly burst into tears when she saw the pile she had labeled as trash. Hurrying to the pile, she began sifting through the contents.

"What on earth are you looking for?" Linda inquired.

"Give me a second," Cindy said, digging through the pile of items she'd set aside and praying the mouse had not returned to the storage while she'd been away. She moved several items before finding what she was looking for.

Linda's eyes grew wide. "Is that what I think it is?"

"It has to be," she said, inspecting the well-worn quilt. "Grandma Mildred's birth quilt. I cannot believe I nearly threw it away. I didn't know the significance and thought it was trash. I see holes, but I think they are from age, not mice."

Linda reached out and touched it, and Cindy felt shivers run through her. To think she'd considered taking the pile home to the trash can the first day she'd come. The only thing that had stopped her was the garbage didn't run until the end of the week. By then, she was so into the journals, she hadn't returned. "I came so close to throwing it away, and after everything it has been through."

Linda took the quilt from her, folded it with care, and placed it in the back seat of the car. "It is safe now. Let's see what else we can find."

Cindy searched through the piles she had made for a second time, only this time, all the quilts were carefully added to the backseat of the car with the first. While she would have preferred her grandmother to have given them to her directly, she now understood why the woman was unable to part with them while she was alive. Through the woman's journals, Cindy now knew her grandmother had gifted them to her the only way she believed possible.

"I think I found something," Linda said, holding up a small, covered pink and white porcelain dish.

"I don't recall anything about the dish in the journals," Cindy said as she approached.

"No, there wasn't, but this box had an

x on it, and the dish has a folded envelope stuffed inside." Linda opened the lid and handed Cindy the envelope. "This stuff was meant for you, so you should be the one to open it."

Cindy opened the envelope and swallowed her excitement. "Oh, Mom. Look at this," she said, holding up a ticket to Houdini's last performance. She handed the ticket to her mother to see and unfolded the paper that accompanied it and reading it aloud. *"Little was I to know this would be Houdini's final performance, as he died just a few short days later. The newspapers told how he had missed his mark and that his performance was off, but I never saw it. Maybe it was because I was so young. Maybe it was because it was my first theater experience and I was caught up in all the hoopla. Or, maybe I was still reeling from the effects of both the liquor and my first kiss. Whatever the reason, I had a marvelous time. A time I chose not to speak of because if I did, I would have had to admit I was in love with a boy who would have cut the fingers off a piano player if only I'd given the word."*

"That must have been some kiss,"

Linda said, handing her the ticket.

Cindy placed everything back in the dish and waited as her mother brought another item out of the box. Both squealed with delight when Linda unwrapped a long silver teaspoon. It was tarnished, but neither had doubts that, when polished, they would be able to see the words Book Cadillac on the back.

Cindy took the spoon and looked at it with wonder. "It is hard to believe this spoon is what convinced Grandma Mildred to agree to marry that boy."

"I wish I would have known her better," Linda said, reaching into the box.

Cindy felt the shock of her words as if Linda had slapped her in the face with them.

Linda looked up, saw her face, and laughed. "Think about it, that woman had two men who were willing to both die and kill for her. She must have been one heck of a woman."

Cindy considered her mother's words. "I guess it is a good thing she got out of Detroit when she did."

"Why do you say that?" Linda asked, unwrapping yet another item.

Cindy couldn't believe she had caught something her mother had overlooked. "Think about who she met the day she was leaving."

Linda stopped what she was doing and slapped her leg with a snort. "Ha, can you imagine if your grandmother would have married Jimmy Hoffa instead of your grandfather! Boy, wouldn't she have had stories to tell."

Cindy took the tissue paper from her mother and finished unwrapping the contents.

"I think her stories are plenty fascinating the way they are," she said, holding up a long-empty bottle of cologne and a pocket watch for her mother to see. Cindy gave the small knob a turn. "Hey, look, someone fixed the pocket watch."

"Think it was Howard?" Linda asked, taking the watch.

"I wouldn't put it past him," Cindy said, twisting the cap off the cologne. She sniffed the empty jar, nothing left to give away the scent. *Too bad.* She frowned her disappointment and recapped the bottle.

Linda handed Cindy the watch and unwrapped the next item, holding it out for

Cindy to see. "It's the photo of Mildred with her Detroit parents."

Cindy took the photo and ran a finger across the glass. "I am so glad they were kind to her."

"She would have had a totally different life if the man hadn't had a drinking problem," Linda agreed.

"Wait, what?" Cindy asked, staring at her mom in disbelief.

"Think about it. It was the middle of Prohibition, and the man knew how to get liquor. Then he ignored the signs that warned of a strong current, causing both him and his wife to drown. I say the man had a drinking problem."

Cindy's heart sank. "And you call me a party pooper."

"Just calling them as I see them," Linda said with a shrug. "This box is empty."

"That's okay; I think we found most of what we were looking for."

"Except for the doll."

"What doll?"

"The one Mildred took that was wearing Fannie's dress."

Cindy felt a moment of panic. She

remembered the doll, what had she done with it. "No, it is here. I remember seeing it."

Cindy found the box marked "dolls" and ripped the tape from the box. The doll in question was on top of the rest staring up at her as if happy to be found.

"I remember that doll. Mildred kept it in the middle of the bed in the guest room," Linda said the second Cindy lifted it from the box.

Cindy felt a knot forming in the pit of her stomach. Just a few days ago, she was more than willing to sell everything just to recoup some of the money she'd spent paying for the storage unit. This doll included. What if her mother hadn't called that day asking her to stop what she was doing and bring her an onion? Would she have continued breezing through the boxes, tossing her grandmother's memories away as if they were no more than a bothersome way to spend the day? Sadly, she knew the answer to be yes.

"That thing would probably bring a small fortune on eBay," Linda said, pointing toward the doll.

Cindy gaped at her mom and held the doll closer. She pictured her grandmother not much older than the children she taught in school each year and wondered if any of those children could endure everything her grandmother did and survive. Over the last few days, she had grown to know the woman whose love she yearned for and discovered the reasons, real or imagined, her grandmother withheld that love from her. The thought of getting rid of those memories and losing that love again filled her with remorse. "You know, Mom; I think I am going to hang on to this stuff."

Cindy carried the doll over to the piano and lifted the cover, exposing the keys. As her fingers drifted across the ivory keys, she smiled. "Who knows, I may even learn to play this thing."

Author's Note

In 1840, the population of New York City was just over 300 thousand. By 1920, the population of the city had grown to over 5½ million, and yet the size of the city itself remained the same. With the great influx of people, the infrastructure of the city proved inadequate. Families were crammed into tenement buildings. In many cases, multiple families shared units designed to house a single family.

The sewer and trash systems proved inadequate, and because child labor laws were nonexistent, men and boys were competing for the same jobs.

With too many mouths to feed, children were often pushed from the family home and wound up living on the streets.

By the mid-1850s, New York City had over thirty thousand children living on the streets, many of them as young as four and five years old. With so many children living on the streets, people soon became desensitized to them, walking over them much the way one would walk over a sleeping dog. Instead of being sympathetic, people would turn up their noses at the way children looked and smelled. Children would sleep in doorways, in boxes and crates. In the wintertime, children would sleep on the vents in the city streets just to stay warm.

The children were in desperate need for an advocate, and that advocate came by way of Charles Loring Brace. Brace came from a well-to-do family with high social status. Arriving in New York in 1848, Brace was appalled not only by the number of children living on the street but with the way society treated them. Brace made it his mission to help the city's homeless children. He reached out to his high-society friends, and using monies donated, founded the Children's Aid Society in 1853. The Children's Aid Society offered the children religious guidance and helped to teach the boys trades, which they could use to help support themselves in an attempt to help the children become self-sufficient. While the Children's Aid Society's efforts helped, it could not keep up with the number of children who were abandoned on a daily basis. Looking for a more permanent solution, Brace thought to send the children out to stable farms, where he envisioned families with good morals and food in abundance.

The Children's Aid Society started the "family placement" or "outplacement" program in 1854, sending out its first group of children via two boats and two trains to Dowagiac, Michigan. The placements proved a success and the program took off. The Orphan Trains (as they were later called) ran from 1854 to 1929. During the seventy-five-year period, it is estimated that over 250,000 children from New York and Boston rode the trains.

Agents from the Children's Aid Society went forward in advance of the trains help the towns select committees to help see to the children's placement. Prospective parents did not have to adopt the child. However, they were made to sign a contract stating they would feed and clothe the child and see to religious training. The child was also expected to receive some education. The families were told that if for any reason the placement did not work out, the children could be returned at the agency's expense.

It was the mission of all agencies to find good homes with people with strong morals. That is not to say that every home was a good home. As we all know, while a home can have a Norman Rockwell feel, no one knows what really goes on behind closed doors. Some children ended up with great homes with loving families, and others ended up being used as labor. While some children were worse off than before they rode the orphan trains, most of the children were much better off than if they would have stayed in the city. It is estimated that 87 percent of the placements turned out well.

Continue the journey with

Shameless,

Book Two in The Orphan Train Saga

https://www.amazon.com/gp/product/B07S G51XN5?

Credits

To my editor, Beth thank you for allowing me to keep my voice.

To Laura Prevost, thank you for being my graphics guru; the cover art is amazing, and your talents never cease to amaze me.

To my beta readers, Becky, Tina, Lisa, Laura P, Laura W., Brandy, Trish, Marie, Monica, Deb, and Katy, thank you for your help in bringing the book to life.

To my fans, thank you for following along on my journey.

And I must thank my mom, who tells everyone she meets about her daughter, the author.

And lastly, to the most important person in my life, my Prince Charming. Thank you for being a constant source of love, and laughter. Your inner strength never ceases to amaze me. I pray the universe will allow the happily ever after to continue.

About the Author

Sherry A. Burton writes in multiple genres and has won numerous awards for her books. Sherry's awards include the coveted Charles Loring Brace Award, for historical accuracy within her historical fiction series, The Orphan Train Saga. Sherry is a member of the National Orphan Train Society, presents lectures on the history of the orphan trains, and is listed on the NOTC Speaker's Bureau as an approved speaker.

Originally from Kentucky, Sherry and her Retired Navy Husband now call Michigan home. Sherry enjoys traveling and spending time with her husband of more than forty years.

www.ingramcontent.com/pod-product-compliance
Lightning Source LLC
Chambersburg PA
CBHW070813190726
48292CB00006B/1989